He drew in a deep breath, then said on the exhale, "I'm not Zahir."

Miah's ears buzzed. Had she heard him right? She frowned so hard her face ached. "What did you say?"

"I am Prince *Javid* Haji Haleem of Anbar. Zahir is my twin brother."

"Bull." Miah laughed at the absurdity and glared at him. "Zahir hasn't got a twin."

"Yes, he does. Me." His voice was so impassioned, his expression so earnest, her fury faltered.

Her skin burned. She'd met Zahir last January, had dated him, spent time with him during these past six months, but she'd never noticed when one twin took the other's place? No way. If that were true... No. *That* was too humiliating to contemplate.

Dear Reader,

We have a fabulous fall lineup for you this month and throughout the season, starting with a new Navajo miniseries by Aimée Thurlo called SIGN OF THE GRAY WOLF. Two loners are called to action in the Four Corners area of New Mexico to take care of two women in jeopardy. Look for Daniel "Lightning" Eagle's story in *When Lightning Strikes* and Burke Silentman's next month in *Navajo Justice*.

The explosive CHICAGO CONFIDENTIAL continuity series concludes with Adrianne Lee's *Prince Under Cover*. We just know you are going to love this international story of intrigue and the drama of a royal marriage—to a familiar stranger.... Don't forget: a new Confidential branch will be added to the network next year!

Also this month—another compelling book from newcomer Delores Fossen. In *A Man Worth Remembering*, she reunites an estranged couple after amnesia strikes. Together, can they find the strength to face their enduring love—and find their kidnapped secret child? And can a woman on the edge recover the life and child she lost when she was framed for murder, in Harper Allen's *The Night in Quesiton*? She can if she has the help of the man who put her away.

Pulse pounding, mind-blowing and always breathtaking— that's Harlequin Intrigue.

Enjoy,

Denise O'Sullivan
Associate Senior Editor
Harlequin Intrigue

PRINCE UNDER COVER

ADRIANNE LEE

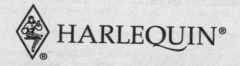

TORONTO • NEW YORK • LONDON
AMSTERDAM • PARIS • SYDNEY • HAMBURG
STOCKHOLM • ATHENS • TOKYO • MILAN • MADRID
PRAGUE • WARSAW • BUDAPEST • AUCKLAND

Special thanks and acknowledgment are given to Adrianne Lee for her contribution to the CHICAGO CONFIDENTIAL series.

ISBN 0-373-22678-0

PRINCE UNDER COVER

ABOUT THE AUTHOR

When asked why she wanted to write romance fiction, Adrianne Lee replied, "I wanted to be Doris Day when I grew up. You know, singing my way through one wonderful romance after another. And I did. I fell in love with and married my high school sweetheart and became the mother of three beautiful daughters. Family and love are very important to me and I hope you enjoy the way I weave them through my stories." Adrianne also states, "I love hearing from my readers and am happy to write back. You can reach me at Adrianne Lee, P.O. Box 3835, Sequim, WA 98382. Please enclose a SASE if you'd like a response."

Books by Adrianne Lee

HARLEQUIN INTRIGUE

Don't miss any of our special offers. Write to us at the following address for information on our newest releases.

Harlequin Reader Service
U.S.: 3010 Walden Ave., P.O. Box 1325, Buffalo, NY 14269
Canadian: P.O. Box 609, Fort Erie, Ont. L2A 5X3

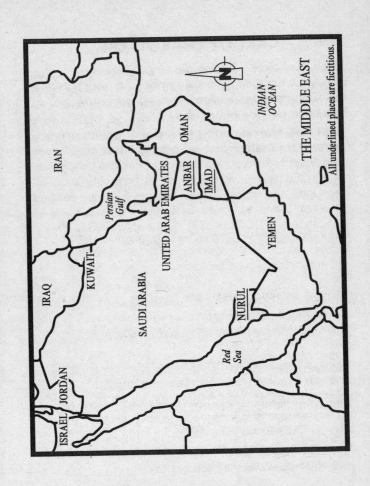

THE MIDDLE EAST

All underlined places are fictitious.

CAST OF CHARACTERS

Miah Mohairbi—Finding out she's a real live princess betrothed to a real Prince Charming puts this Chicago-raised all-American woman on the roller-coaster ride of her life.

Javid Haji Haleem—The Prince of Anbar is keeping secrets that could get not only himself killed, but Miah, too.

Zahir Haji Haleem—Javid's twin brother wants to rule the world, and will stop at nothing to gain this end.

Sheik Khalaf Al-Sayed—Miah's newly discovered father is like a fairy godfather, lavishing her with riches and adoration. Could he be anything but what he seems?

Big Tony De Luca—This former wrestling champion now publishes a tabloid that thrives on lies and innuendo and seems to be waging a vendetta against Javid.

Bobby "The Buzzard" Redwing—Is this paparazzo as much of a vulture as his nickname implies?

Cailin Finnigan—Does Miah's best friend have pre-knowledge of events because she's fey, or because she's behind the danger?

Rory Finnigan—Cailin's brother is suddenly spending money he hasn't earned tending bar.

I dedicate this book to those we lost on Sept 11, 2001,
for not only were they lost to their families,
friends and co-workers, they were lost to us all.
We will never forget.

SPECIAL THANKS to all the men and women
in our armed forces. God bless you and keep you safe,
and thank you for risking everything to keep
our wonderful country free.

Prologue

"Hurry, Javid," Zahir Haji Haleem urged his twin as they raced up the stairs to the second level of their American grandparents' Victorian summer house, their movements as quick and furtive as the warm, sea-scented breeze stealing in through the open windows.

Their destination: the attic, that forbidden refuge of irresistible treasures—Grandfather Hayward's stash of antique war relics, daggers, swords, helmets and rifles. All were tinged with a musty scent of bygone days, of mysterious lands, of adventurous times, their lure irresistible. Especially after Nana Hayward, ever fussing at Grandfather about the dangers of weapons and "boys being boys," insisted he store "that junk" away under lock and key. Grandfather had informed Nana that what she called "junk" belonged in a museum. She'd suggested he put them in one, but he refused to part with even one item. In the end, he'd stored them in the attic not only under lock and key, but with an alarm system for protection against theft.

The rattle of the keys Zahir had taken from Grandfather's desk brought Javid up short. He hesitated as Zahir worked the right key, disarmed the alarm, shoved the door wide and quickly ducked inside.

Torn between the pull of temptation and the push of wrongdoing, Javid held back, weighing the pros and cons of disobeying Father. He could no more help his prudent nature than Zahir seemed able to help his reckless one. His brother was forever rushing into mischief as though he didn't understand right from wrong, as though he hadn't been taught the same virtues as Javid, as though his DNA makeup was the polar opposite to Javid's.

But that was impossible.

They were identical, their fourteen-year-old faces mirror images, down to their pitch-black hair and date-brown eyes, down to their love of competition, their need to win.

But there were differences.

The boys—sons of Anna Hayward, American playwright; and Salim Rizk Haleem, Emir of Anbar, a small oil-rich nation on the Arabian Gulf—had inherited traits, good and bad, from both parents' diverse gene pools.

While Javid hated incurring Father's disapproval, Zahir, who would one day succeed to the throne of Anbar, seemed to relish it, as though his manhood relied on his asserting his will, on defying authority. Javid, younger by five minutes but quicker both mentally and physically, worried that this streak in his brother was more than defiance. There had always been in his twin something ruthless—something dark and indefinable.

"I've found the case, Javid. Come." There followed a *click* of a latch being opened. "Ahh."

Zahir's sigh held pleasure as thick as the velvet protecting the specially lined case that cradled the matching

daggers, and despite Javid's struggle with right and
wrong, he was seduced into the attic by the thrill swirling in his belly. He hurried to Zahir's side, shoved back
a hank of unruly raven hair and eyed the weapons, the
prize of Grandfather's treasures. Father had given them
to Grandfather on the day of the twins' birth. One had
been forged in Anbar, the hilt shaped like the head of a
king cobra, the other forged in America, the hilt shaped
like a bald eagle. The daggers represented the equal
halves of the twins' heritage. More than once, the boys
had been warned not to touch the dangerous weapons—
which made touching them ever more tantalizing.

Zahir fingered the solid gold hilt shaped like the head
of a king cobra. Full-carat rubies served as eyes. The
twenty-two-inch blades were curved at the tip and honed
to razor-keen edges.

"Careful," Javid cautioned as his brother lifted the
bald eagle-headed dagger and presented it to him, hilt
first.

Javid gathered the handle in both hands, surprised at
the heft, at the surge of something almost electric that
undulated from his grip into his flesh, heating his veins
as though the weapon possessed the potency of lightning, as though it had imbued him with the power and
strength of the eagle. A grin tugged at his mouth, and
he lifted his gaze to meet his brother's.

Zahir's handsome face was alight with wicked pleasure, and Javid's guilt at touching the forbidden object
dissolved in a soft chuckle. He hoisted the blade chest
level and took an offensive stance learned in fencing
classes. "I am Khalaf, Sheik of Imad, come to slay the
Emir of Anbar and claim his country as my own."

"I will see your blood ground into the sands, hyena,"
Zahir spat, accepting the challenge with a fierce arch of

one ebony eyebrow. He raised his dagger, the curved blade glinting in the lamplight as it connected with Javid's. The ensuing metallic *clink* echoed in the vast attic, but neither boy feared discovery. The adults had walked into town and would be gone for at least an hour.

The swordplay ensued with exuberance, the boys thrusting and parrying, leaping and sidestepping, kicking up dust as they ducked between antique dressers and tables, their excitement raising their voices.

Javid laughed, danced, light on his feet. Sweat popped across his forehead, beneath his arms, at his groin—and he grew bolder. Confident in his ability to best Zahir as he always bested him in fencing class.

They leaped and dodged and darted dangerously close several times more. But the heavy dagger was not an epee and soon its heft made Javid's arms ache from the weight. But he would not give up. Or in. Not with victory in sight. For Zahir was also tiring. He could see it on his face. Tasting triumph, he swung at Zahir as Zahir dipped toward him. Too late, he wrenched the blade back. Zahir yelped, dropping his dagger and grabbing his ear. Curses spewed from him.

Javid stood horror-stricken at the injury he'd inflicted on his brother, at the blood seeping between Zahir's fingers. All the guilt he'd abandoned earlier rushed at him now and the dagger slipped from his hand, clattering to the dusty floor near his feet. "Zahir, I'm sorry. I didn't mean—"

Zahir's furious growl cut off the apology. He lunged. His head rammed into Javid's gut, punching the wind from him, knocking him off his feet. Javid's spine smacked the floor. Zahir landed on him, pinning him down.

Blood from Zahir's wound—not to the ear, but behind

it, he realized—dripped onto Javid's dusty, sweat-smudged T-shirt. He started to apologize again, but the fierce hatred emitting from his brother stilled his tongue.

"You did this on purpose. Your jealousy offends me, Javid. You must always best me. Humiliate me. As though you, and not I, deserve to be the next Emir of Anbar."

"No—" Javid choked. "Accident." Stunned at the accusation, he tried bucking Zahir off, but Zahir, in his fury, possessed inhuman strength.

"Well, that will never happen, brother." Zahir grabbed something off the floor and scooted higher on Javid's chest, cutting off his intake of air.

Then Javid saw it, the eagle-headed dagger that moments before had been his confederate. Fear shot through him. He wrenched against his twin's hold. But for once, Zahir was faster. He sliced a small *X* into Javid's chest, right over his heart.

Javid's breath hissed as the pain and his shock gave way to fury. "Let me up, Zahir!" Blood sprang from the wound, wetting the front of his shirt. "We're even now, brother."

"Even?" Zahir's laugh chilled Javid. "I don't want to be even. Not with you. Not with anyone."

Pure hatred shone in Zahir's eyes, a light so clear it was as if a window had opened on his soul. Javid shuddered at what he saw there. "Get off me, Zahir."

"*X* marks the spot." Zahir lifted the eagle-headed dagger high, the ruby eyes as bright as fresh blood. He meant to thrust the blade into Javid's chest, right through the *X* he'd sliced there.

"No!" Javid bucked. Twisted. Squirmed. He couldn't get free. He was going to die.

"Zahir!" Their father's voice resounded in the murky attic. "What is this madness?"

Zahir scrambled off Javid. "Nothing, Father. We were playing war. Javid lost." Zahir gathered control of his expression, his manner and voice now contrite, humble—as though he hadn't meant to kill his brother.

But Javid knew. He shoved up on his elbows, struggling to drag in a deep breath. His ribs felt bruised. The cut on his chest burned. But it was a deeper pain that immobilized him, a wrenching sadness, a sense of great loss, a disjoining of some vital part of himself, as though the dagger *had* plunged into him and severed the blood cord between himself and his twin.

No apology could heal the wounds inflicted this day.

He and Zahir were no longer allies, but enemies. From here on out, Javid must watch his back.

Chapter One

Chicago—present day
July

"I won't lie to you, Ms. Mohairbi." Dr. Elias Forbes's long face seemed even longer this afternoon, his slanted eyes grayer, as solemn as his tone. He tapped his pen on an open file folder. "Your mother's condition is deteriorating. The sooner she gets that heart transplant, the better."

Miah clutched her hands in her lap, reminding herself to breathe. Her mom's name had been on the national registry for ten months now, but so far no donor had turned up with Lina Mohairbi's rare blood type. All they could do was wait and pray as precious time, time she might not have to spare, slipped away.

"Should I be preparing for the worst?"

"Well, now, I can't—"

"Darling, don't put Dr. Forbes on the spot," her mom said, interrupting the doctor.

The door to the examining room had opened so silently, Miah blinked seeing her mother standing there. Lina Mohairbi crossed the elaborately appointed office in this exclusive section of Chicago on Lake Shore Drive, touched Miah's shoulder with affection and settled her tiny frame on the neighboring chair.

As the doctor repeated for Lina what he'd told Miah, Miah considered the pair, thinking it odd that though this man held her well-being in his hands, her mom could not bring herself to call him by his first name, as though she believed keeping their relationship formal somehow preserved or increased his surgical skills.

But Miah knew Elias Forbes was just a doctor. A better doctor in every way than that cold-blooded jerk at the neighborhood clinic who had treated her mother like one of the mannequins she used to dress in Macy's windows—before becoming too ill—instead of a living, breathing woman who deserved compassion along with a diagnosis.

Thank God, Fate had stepped in and given them the means to afford this doctor whose credentials were impeccable, who kept his patient load small these days in order to pursue other interests, professionally and privately, in his spare time. She'd been assured he was the best surgeon for the job. Lina's best chance of surviving. Worth every cent he was costing. But she liked what she'd seen with her own eyes, in particular his concern for her mother and his attention to detail.

Miah shoved a thick lock of long ebony hair from her cheek. "I was trying to get the doctor to give us an idea of how much longer we should expect before a donor comes available."

"Well, now—" The doctor started once again, tapping the pen with renewed vigor as though punctuating the point he hoped to make. "That's just it. We could have one tomorrow. Or next week. Or—"

"Next month," Lina added. "Or the month after that."

The doctor winced, and Miah's stomach dipped. His dour expression confirmed her worse fears. Her mom was rapidly running out of time. Miah wanted to scream. Instead, she gave herself a mental slap. Panic would serve nothing. Only depress her mother. Frighten her. Stress her out. Weaken her ailing heart more. Miah had to stay positive. Upbeat. No matter what.

"Miah, Dr. Forbes is giving you his best guess. That's all he can do. We knew from the start that my rare blood type was a factor. But on the upside, it also puts me on a much shorter waiting list. So, we're going to live for today. Enjoy every moment we have together and leave the donor up to God."

"That's the attitude, Lina," the doctor said. "At all costs, continue to avoid stress."

Avoid stress, Miah thought with bitter irony. Six months ago, the clinic doctor had prescribed that very medicine. And as though he'd been predicting disaster on the horizon, stress arrived on their doorstep within days of the warning—striking like a tornado. But with the tornado had come the wherewithal to secure this doctor, and his care had managed to keep her mom stable through all of the heartache and all of the joy; even too much good news could bring stress.

No more extremes, Miah determined. She would see that stress stayed far from her mom in the days ahead.

"Oh, one thing more, Doctor." Lina scooted to the edge of her chair. "Will I be able to travel overseas at the end of the month?"

"No, no, no." He glanced up from her chart, shaking his head. "It's out of the question. Not only should you avoid flying, you need to be near the hospital should a donor become available.''

"Oh, of course." Her mom looked chagrined, as though just remembering the doctor had already told her this a while ago.

Miah wondered if the heart problem was cutting off or short-circuiting some of the blood circulation in her mother's brain, affecting her memory a bit.

"Don't frown, Me-Oh-Miah," her mom said, teasingly calling her by the pet name she'd used since as far back as Miah could remember. "I'm not happy about missing your coronation and the royal wedding in Nurul either, but that's okay. It has been an incredible and lucky time for both of us, darling. It's no good to be selfish. To want more."

But Miah did want more. So much more. She wanted her mother's heart healed, healthy. But if her mom wasn't going to survive, wasn't going to be lucky enough to find that special donor, Miah didn't want whatever time they had left shadowed by negativity. She covered her mother's tiny hand with her own much larger one, feeling these days as though *she* were the protector, the parent, and forced a grin.

"All right. I'm smiling. See?"

"That's better, darling."

As the doctor wrote something more in her mother's chart, Miah and Lina sat in silence, holding hands. Miah wrestled with the inner struggle that consumed most of her days lately. Last winter, she and her mom had been getting by paycheck to paycheck. Then the tornado had swept in, picking up their lives and spinning everything around and around, then counterclockwise, so that when the dust settled, nothing looked the same.

The unpredictable winds of change had dumped on them a golden rainbow, a key to utopia. Wealth beyond their wildest imaginings. Of course, there were conditions attached, but experience had taught her early on that most things in this world came with conditions.

Miah could still taste the desperation she'd felt just before then, and recall the desperate bargaining with God. She'd have sold her soul to save her mom. Fortunately, the required conditions asked considerably less of her.

She touched her engagement ring—a white-gold band with a three-carat diamond surrounded by emeralds on one side and blue sapphires on the other. Her betrothed said the ring was an heirloom, passed from his grandmother to his mother to him. No, Miah didn't regret the bargain she'd made. It had given her options she'd never dreamed possible.

Her first priority had been *this doctor*.

Lina smiled. ''At least I'll be able to give my daughter away at her wedding tomorrow.''

Miah squeezed her mom's hand. The arranged marriage—the main condition attached to the golden rainbow—would bring her a royal title, her own wealth, the incredible and new sensation of everyone treating her as if she were special, making her feel special. On the other hand, she barely knew her groom-to-be, and that scared her. She had, however, kept this secret worry to herself.

She glanced lovingly at her mom. Lina seemed even smaller than usual, frail. Her lips a bit blue beneath her pink lipstick. Even her hair, which had always been thick and black like Miah's own, was thinning, graying. Her mom didn't need to know about Miah's misgivings. Couldn't deal with even one extra burden. She needed to smile as she was smiling now, a Mona Lisa glow in her brown eyes.

Lina stood. "I've been afraid, Dr. Forbes, that I'd finally be joining my darling Grant, leaving our daughter without either of her parents to see her married. Or that I'd be bedridden, in which case Miah would insist on the ceremony taking place in my hospital room."

"I would do it, too." Miah gathered her purse and rose.

"Yes, I know. But I'll be grateful if a donor doesn't show up tomorrow to spoil your wedding." Lina's smile widened as she joked. "Day after tomorrow would be fine, though, Dr. Forbes. See if you can arrange it."

Laughing, she winked at Miah, and Miah allowed herself to embrace the joy she saw in her mother's eyes, that she felt trickling through her worry. Life had held so little happiness in the past, she still struggled with accepting the good things that had befallen them these past six months. She'd wake up some nights in a cold sweat, certain it had all disappeared because she'd believed in it too much, enjoyed it too much.

"Go and enjoy yourself." The doctor held the door open. "You're a fighter, Lina. Just keep fighting."

Miah ushered her mother out of the doctor's office, down the hall and onto a crowded elevator. All the while, she mulled over the doctor's last words. As far back as she could recall, her mom had had to fight for everything. She'd been widowed when Miah was twelve. Grant Mohairbi had been a freedom fighter in his youth, and a firefighter later on. He'd died a hero's death, rescuing three small children and their mother from their blazing apartment building, before being overcome with smoke inhalation.

Grant and Lina had shared the kind of love everyone strives for and few find. He had been a wonderful father to Miah. His loss had devastated them both.

But instead of falling apart, as she had had every right to do, Lina had wanted to honor Grant's memory, make him as proud of her as she had always been—and remained still—of him. She had picked up her five-foot frame, gathered her ninety pounds and assessed their situation, then threw herself into doing whatever it took to keep a roof over their heads.

The survivors' pension had only stretched so far. Lina had worked two minimum-wage jobs, coming home worn-out, but always finding time for Miah—helping her with homework, listening eagerly to her talk about her day, keeping their connection strong and intact—before falling exhausted into bed.

So tight was their bond, Miah had never had an inkling she was adopted. It had come as quite a shock, one she still battled to believe, even with daily, hourly proof staring her in the face.

Like the chauffeured limousine awaiting them at the curb, provided by her birth father—her real-life fairy godfather—Sheik Khalaf Al-Sayed, a multimillionaire oil mogul. It amazed Miah how quickly a person could come to accept luxuries as the norm.

The chauffeur helped Lina into the back seat, then turned to Miah. "Ms. Mohairbi, I found this on the floorboard. I thought perhaps it had fallen out of your pocketbook."

Miah frowned, accepting the envelope. The moment she recognized the block lettering, she froze. This hadn't come from her purse. Someone had placed it in the car.

When? How? "Did you leave the limousine unattended at any time, Mehemet?"

His black eyes became evasive. "Only one moment…to answer nature. But I lock first."

"Okay." It was a silly thing to lie about, but she knew he couldn't have locked the car. Otherwise, the note would not have been in it. And it was unlikely he'd seen whomever had put the envelope inside it. She quickly read the enclosed note, feeling the heat drain from her cheeks.

"Avoid stress," the doctor had said. *But this…this…* Miah squished the blackmail note in her fist and shoved it into her pocket. *This would bring her mother's ailing heart to a dead stop.*

Miah squelched the urge to curse and got into the car, letting the soft leather embrace her. She'd thought the first payment to the vile extortionist would be the end of it. But there had been a second demand. And now another. God, how naive she'd been. He wanted ten thousand more or he'd ruin her wedding. Destroy her mother. Start a scandal that could strip her of her future. She stared out the window as the limo merged with traffic. She hated the shivering in her stomach that felt as if she'd swallowed a full glass of ice shavings.

Fear.

Truth didn't scare Miah. Lies did.

Perhaps that was because she'd discovered last January that her whole life had been a lie. Had Grant Mohairbi's life also been a lie? Had the father she'd grown up loving, adoring, honoring been who her mother and she had thought he was? Had he been a freedom fighter? A hero? Or had he been a mercenary? An assassin?

"Darling, is something wrong?" Lina touched her

clasped hands. "You're very pale. For a moment there, you looked absolutely...terrified."

"Terrified? Don't be silly. No, no," she managed to say in a tone that sounded normal. "I was thinking about the wedding. Nothing for you to fret about, honest."

But her mom's brow knit, a sign she wasn't going to let this go so easily. "Are you having second thoughts about marrying someone you've been betrothed to since you were a baby?"

She doubted anyone would blame her if she were having second thoughts, but she couldn't afford them. She had agreed to the marriage without coercion from anyone, agreed to it for all that it would give her—including her own money, an enormous inheritance that would allow her to pay off the extortionist once and for all. She said, "No second thoughts."

None she would admit to out loud, anyway. Not to her mother. Not to herself. Outside, stifling damp heat prevailed; inside, air-conditioning froze the sweat on Miah's brow.

"You're going to be a beautiful bride, darling." Lina touched her hand as the car inched along in heavy morning traffic. "I'm so excited about tomorrow."

Miah's internal alarm went off, shredding all thoughts of the blackmailer's note. "Well, you don't want to get too excited, Mom. Perhaps you should take a nap this afternoon."

"That sounds like a great idea, but not if you're going to pace the floors, bored while I rest."

"I'm not going to pace. Fact is, there are a few minor details, a couple of items for my trousseau I want to pick up. So, I'll be plenty busy."

The limousine pulled up to their building farther along

Lake Shore Drive. They occupied a penthouse with a magnificent view of Lake Michigan. It was a far cry from the tenement apartment they'd called home for most of her life.

Miah walked Lina through the lobby to their private elevator. "I'm just going to change into something a little more comfortable."

"MORE COMFORTABLE" was impossible for Miah to achieve. The ice chips in her stomach still had her shivery half an hour later. She had to get the money and drop it off before one today, and it was nearly that now. She caught a glimpse of her reflection in the glass doors as she exited the apartment complex. Her long, lean legs flashed from beneath the scrap of hot pink skirt that hugged her slim hips, while her slender upper body sported a neon green, sheer top over a creamy camisole. Her thick, blunt-cut raven hair swung across her midback and shoulders with every step, and framed her face...which looked shades too pale at the moment.

Her outfit drew a look of disapproval from the chauffeur as she met him at the curb. She climbed into the back seat of the limo and waited until he closed the door, then tugged on the hem of her short skirt. Her mother had tried to steer her toward the conservative styles *she* favored, but Miah needed variety. Color. Flash.

Making her clothing allowance stretch had meant shopping in consignment stores and thrift shops. Even though she could now afford to buy her favorite designers new, or spend thousands on a single blouse, she still shopped in the same stores she'd always frequented.

She liked *her* style. But no one else seemed to. Not her mother, not her newly discovered father, and especially not her fiancé. Too bad, she had decided. She was who she was. *Nothing* could change that. And today, she needed the "old" Miah more than ever to get through the next hour.

The chauffeur intruded on her thoughts. "Where would you like to go, Ms. Mohairbi?"

Oh God, she'd been daydreaming, wasting time she didn't have. Her heart moved with uncomfortable quickness. "Chicago First Federal, Mehemet."

Miah tried relaxing, but the traffic moved with aching slowness while time seemed to spin off the dial of her wristwatch. Would the blackmailer keep his threat if she was late? Would he send his vile story to the editor of *The Clarion,* a local tabloid that thrived on exposés and half truths? Her father, the sheik, had warned her that a scandal in the States could affect her acceptance by the people of Nurul. She could not afford to let this story get out. Not even if it were a lie. She tapped her foot, feeling ill, helpless, muttering, "Hurry, hurry, hurry."

After what seemed an hour, Mehemet pulled into the bank's parking area. Miah was out of the limo and to the front doors before he could unstrap his seat belt. When she returned a few minutes later, he was standing beside the open back door of the stretch car with his dark face clenched, but he said nothing, only nodded.

Miah swept past him. She clutched her purse—with the ten one-thousand-dollar bills secured in a plain white envelope within—to her thudding heart. Mehemet had been hired by her father and likely ordered to keep watch over her. She was not making his work easy, and a flash of concern that the chauffeur might report her odd behavior to the sheik scraped her aching nerves raw. She didn't want to have to explain herself. Her actions.

She edged onto the seat, gripping her purse in both hands as if someone might reach into the locked car and snatch it from her. "The Brinkmire Cavalli Gallery, Mehemet."

As the words slipped from her, Miah realized she'd repeated this trip with Mehemet two other times in the past four weeks, first to the bank, then to the Brinkmire Cavalli Gallery. *Three times in the past four weeks.* She groaned inwardly. The blackmailer was draining her financially and emotionally. And the chauffeur had to notice that even though she always went to the bank first, she never bought anything at the gallery. Would he start to get curious? Mention it to her father? Her fiancé?

The ice chips in her stomach seemed to be forming into a solid block.

The gallery was located near Grant Park, the end building in a row of refurbished warehouses. It was a mid-size structure, four stories tall. The original second floor had been removed in order to create the high ceilings. The top two floors were used as offices and storage, the gallery occupying only the ground level. The main salon dissected into dozens of spaces that could be widened or narrowed depending on what was being exhibited at any given time. There were also several intersecting rooms that allowed a steady stream of foot traffic to pass through without causing a bottleneck.

Miah need not have worried about that this afternoon. She seemed to have the place almost to herself. Her spike heels clicked on the tiled floor, echoing the quick, fearful *thud* of her pulse in her ears. She'd cut this close. Too close. Was the blackmailer here already? Struggling to swallow, she picked up her step and hurried through the salon toward the interlocking rooms, her destination the back exit. She raced past exhibits by the newest up-and-coming artists, through the room displaying paintings by established favorites, and one full of antique weaponry, guns and swords.

Toward the back of the building, near the public bathrooms, she stopped and glanced around, making sure no one was watching or paying particular attention to her. But she seemed to be alone, the eerie silence broken only by her footfalls. How she'd love to be able to ram one of her pointed heels into the extortionist's shin. She ducked into a narrow hallway, striding to the single waste bin near the door. She plucked the envelope from her purse and dropped it into the bin.

Divesting herself of the money seemed to suck the air from her lungs. She tried to inhale, but it was as if her throat had closed. A panic attack? She glanced up at the exit door. No. Going out this way would probably set off the security system. A prickling sensation hit her neck—that uneasy sense that someone was staring at her.

The blackmailer.

She spun around. A woman stood at the end of the hall, eyeing her questioningly. She wore a security uniform. "Can I help you, miss?"

"No." Miah was amazed she could find her voice, but the woman seemed to have startled away her panic. She tucked her purse under her arm, gesturing toward the trash bin. "I—I was just throwing out a tissue."

Though the panic didn't return, the sense that she was being watched lingered as Miah retraced her path back to the main salon. She cast periodic glances over her shoulder, studied the faces of those she passed. Was he nearby? The nasty puke who seemed to know details about her life that were no one else's business—such as the fact that her recently opened checking account contained enough money to pay the exorbitant amounts he demanded for his silence?

Outside, the heat struck her with the force of a blow, and she realized she was so tense that a light breeze could probably blow her over. She needed some TLC. Needed Cailin. Her best friend.

Needed a tall thirst-quenching beer. Needed one last afternoon to be the wild woman she'd been before January. Tomorrow, her life changed forever. Today, she could indulge some of her favorite things, could forget a blackmailer's demands. His threats. Could bank the fires of worry about her mother. Stave off the apprehension she felt about the marriage.

She instructed Mehemet to leave her at Finnigan's Rainbow—a family-owned and operated bar and grill— on Michigan Avenue in the heart of the shopping district, and take the rest of the day off.

Cailin was working the bar with her brother, Rory. Both wore Kelly green polo shirts and black pants. He grinned at Miah and hollered above the din, "Princess, what brings you slumming on the eve of your wedding?"

Princess. Miah slid onto a bar stool. She had to admit that aside from the money for her mother, the fact that she would be an honest-to-God princess after saying "I do" touched a chord inside her, as though something internal had aligned, connected.

Cailin snapped her brother's backside with a bar towel. "She's not officially a princess until tomorrow, you doof."

The Finnigans all had fiery red hair and mischievous blue eyes. Cailin was the only girl, a natural beauty. She greeted Miah with a smile. "Hey, girlfriend, nice to see you looking like your old self."

"Thanks." Miah caught her friend's gaze darting to the door. Bobby "The Buzzard" Redwing, Cailin's ex-boyfriend, had been hassling her. Miah had no more interest in encountering the Buzzard than Cailin; he was a reporter for the very tabloid to which she feared the blackmailer would sell his story of Grant Mohairbi.

She drew a shaky breath. She had to lose this mood. Quit thinking about the blackmailer. Determined to do just that, she forced a smile. "Hey, Rory, can 'almost royalty' get an ice-cold one and a slice of pizza in this dive?"

Cailin laughed and drew the attention of a couple of men at the end of the bar. She had a knockout figure, round where Miah was lean, skin like peaches and cream. Rory set a frosted mug of foaming beer before Miah, then went to fetch her pizza, leaving Miah and Cailin to chat. But the first thing out of Cailin's mouth was "Uh-oh."

Her gaze fixed on something over Miah's shoulder. Miah tensed. "Is it 'The Buzzard'?"

"Nope. This one's all yours. *The Gorgeous One.*"

Miah's heart thumped. Talk about stress-inducing. He would not be happy to see her dressed like this. She gathered her poise and glanced around at her fiancé. Six feet of gorgeous male animal, the most handsome man she'd ever encountered. Hollywood should have come knocking on his door years ago. Prince Zahir Haji Haleem. His dark, heated gaze landed on her like a sensual stroke played over her body. There was something possessive in that look, something that sent heat into her belly and fire through her blood.

She swallowed hard against the knot forming in her throat. It scared her, this heat she felt every time he was near. If his look, his casual touch could make her this flustered, this hot, he might just burn her up during serious intimacy. And she didn't doubt for a minute that this man—who had, before their engagement, been linked in tabloids with several of Chicago's top socialites, married and single, and who had so obviously majored in Pleasing Women 101—would be more than proficient at lovemaking.

Miah was no prude herself, no innocent. But she felt such shyness around this man. This stranger. Could she actually go through with marrying him? The thought brought an image of her mother's smiling face, and Miah knew she not only could, she would. Nothing must cause her mother's smile to vanish.

She took a swig of the beer, then thumped the mug onto the bar, slipped off the stool and, on her three-inch sandals, crossed to where he waited as though he'd sent her a silent command to come to him.

"Hello, Zahir."

"Miah." His gaze did a lazy climb from her gaily painted toenails, up the strappy heels and skimpy clothing to her face. She clenched her hands against the blush his sexy perusal brought to her flesh, lifted her chin and stared him in the eye. "Like what you see?"

He smirked. "Every man in the bar seems to."

"And you object to that?"

"I believe objections, were I to have any, would fall on deaf ears." He wore a black, Armani three-piece suit. His raven hair curled against the virgin white of his shirt collar. He smelled of a spicy autumn afternoon, and seemed somehow able to defy the heat.

"I like color," she said. If he had his way, she'd be covered from head to toe in flowing veils all fit for a funeral. But that she would never do.

"Color likes you back." He caught her chin in his big hand, startling her.

The blush swept her body again, gaining heat this time as it reached her face. She could pull away, but sensed the room watching them. She whispered, "What are you doing?"

He leaned closer, as though to kiss her. Her breath jammed in her throat at the raw sexuality in his very touch, his very nearness. The pad of his thumb traced the soft flesh above her upper lip. "Foam...from the beer."

"Tha—thank you." She took a faltering step back. "How did you know to find me here, Zahir?"

"Actually, I wasn't looking for you, love." His voice was a mix of Northeastern crisp and Middle Eastern mellow. "I had no idea you were here. I was passing by and spotted that tabloid reporter—what's his name—Redwing, outside." He glanced at the door as though he half expected The Buzzard to burst through it, camera flashing. "The last thing I want is him getting wind of where and when the wedding is coming down."

Coming down? That was a strange way to refer to their wedding. She lowered her voice. "Bobby Redwing has been hassling Cailin. He's probably not after you or me."

"In the past, he's been very persistent, very good at ferreting out...secrets," Zahir said in a distracted voice as though he were speaking to himself. He touched his chest near his heart and an odd expression played around his alluring mouth. Then he seemed to shake himself and flashed her a too-quick, too-bright grin. "*You* don't have anything to hide, do you, love?"

Miah flinched. "No. Nothing."

Nothing except a blackmailer's secret.

"What about you, Zahir?" *What don't I know about you?*

His gaze flicked away from hers, a sure sign he *was* hiding something. Miah felt the uneasiness returning, the second-guessing. She was marrying a man she didn't know. A stranger. One who could have secrets she didn't even suspect.

Maybe *dangerous* secrets.

Chapter Two

Javid blew out a taut breath and stepped from the dark interior of Finnigan's Rainbow into the blinding afternoon on Michigan Avenue. Pretending to be Zahir was taking its toll. He hated lying, even necessary lying. Just now, he'd have sworn Miah knew, sworn she was going to expose him right there in the pub. He tugged sunglasses from his suit pocket and glanced around, but saw no sign of Redwing. This game of hide-and-seek he was constantly playing with that damn snoop was wearing thin.

Tomorrow. It would all be over tomorrow. Thank God. He'd survived more than one tight situation in recent days, but none that had left him this rattled...and that was *her* fault.

Heat sizzled off the sidewalk, several degrees cooler than the fire in his belly, a fire for a woman he didn't want to want, a woman he wanted so badly he ached. He took long strides away from the pub, berating himself with every step, unable to abolish the image of her long luscious legs in that scrap of hot pink, her shapely feet in those high-heeled, mind-numbing sandals, the way that green top made her amber eyes shimmer like spun gold.

"Damn it all." *Miah Mohairbi was an assignment. The daughter of the devil himself.* She was also a vixen. He'd never met a woman quite her equal, and he'd met a lot of women since he'd been old enough to pay attention to his hormones— women here and in the Middle East, women at Harvard during college, women around the globe at each stop on his worldwide travels as Anbar's Goodwill Ambassador.

Miah was unique. Beautiful, yes, but she was so much more than that. She had a sharp mind, a wicked tongue, style and defiance. She could be hard one moment, tender the next. To his chagrin, he found the conflicting aspects of her personality endlessly intriguing. If only circumstances were different. If only she were not Sheik Khalaf Al-Sayed's blood child.

Thank God this torment ended tomorrow. After that, he could guarantee Miah would hate him—once she discovered he'd been lying to her, posing as his twin; once he helped arrest the father she seemed to adore, once he exposed Al-Sayed to the world for the heartless bastard he was.

An odd tightness twisted his heart at the thought of breaking hers. He checked his watch, then glanced around for Redwing. That damn reporter had made him late, but he hadn't dared risk being followed to the Langston Building. He'd ducked into Finnigan's Rainbow to avoid him and had run smack into Miah. The memory of meeting her unexpectedly like that, of her dressed like that, threatened to distract him anew.

His beeper went off. He stepped out of foot traffic and into a shop doorway to view the readout. "They" were waiting for him. Keeping an eye out for Redwing, Javid walked past the Langston Building, then circled back, went inside and took the elevator to the penthouse. The automatic door slid open on Solutions, Inc., the fictitious corporation that fronted for Chicago Confidential, an elite division of the Federal Department of Public Safety.

The outer office smelled new, but had the ageless elegance of corporate lawyers' suites—thick carpet, brocade waiting room chairs, cherry-wood receptionist desk, file cabinets and paneling. Picture windows framed the Chicago Harbor.

Liam Wallace, the building maintenance man, had one slender hip hitched on the edge of the desk, his head bent toward Kathy Renk, Solutions's receptionist. Javid couldn't see what they were doing, but when he cleared his throat, they jumped apart as though he'd caught them necking.

Kathy's apple-size cheeks glowed pink, and Javid wondered if he *had* caught them necking. The idea amused him, since the two were usually bickering over some inane thing or other. Not to mention their obvious differences. Liam was all of twenty-two, with ambitions to strut fashion runways parading the latest designs by Armani and Klein. He had the looks, the sculpted body, the hollow cheekbones.

Kathy, some seventeen years his senior, smoothed her blouse over her generous figure, gave a nervous tug at her short brown hair that was flecked with blond highlights. She had Meg Ryan features and a smile that never quit.

She beamed at him now, her face still red. "Mr. Haleem, they're expecting you. You want the usual?"

"Please."

"You've got it. Diet pop. Rocks."

As he headed to the inner office, Javid heard Liam hiss, "*It's* not crazy."

"No." Kathy snorted. "*You* are what's crazy."

Vaguely wondering what this newest spat was about, Javid let himself into the special ops room. He'd have thought that by now he'd be used to this room, but it always amazed him, always made him feel as though he'd stepped into the cockpit of *The Enterprise,* the *Star Trek* spaceship, with its wall-to-wall blinking lights, switches, screens and dials. Every kind of electronic device imaginable. Even some unimaginable. Certainly things Javid didn't understand, but that made chasing after terrorists a whole lot easier than the bad guys liked.

Andy Dexter, the tech whiz whose genius had assembled this room, was not present. In front of each chair at the round table was a built-in laptop screen for briefings.

The only incongruous sight in the room was the antlers mounted on the wall, a gift from the head of Montana Confidential to the head of this new unit.

Javid closed the door. Four voices stopped in middiscussion, all heads turning toward him. Javid greeted each agent by name. When not on undercover assignment for Chicago Confidential, the three men and one woman seated at the round table pursued successful careers, most unrelated to law enforcement. Javid took an empty chair, apologized for keeping them waiting and explained his delay.

"Redwing didn't spot you coming in just now, did he?" Vincent Romeo asked, his tone as unrelenting as his frown. Javid had learned that the head of operations seldom cracked a smile. His mind ran at warp speed, always attending to business—and this unit's business was serious. Vincent reacted accordingly.

"I doubled back on my route," Javid assured him. "No sign of Redwing."

"Good." Whitney MacNair Romeo, Vincent's gorgeous redheaded wife had been learning the ropes when Javid first met her. These six months later, she had earned her stripes and done the unit proud. Her family came from the same area of Martha's Vineyard as his grandparents and mother, and her accent roused old memories. Not all of them good. "We can't risk exposure at this point."

Exposure. Javid thought again about Miah and flinched. "I'm damn glad this will be over with tomorrow."

The agents picked up their discussion where Javid had interrupted it—something about the chief guard in charge of watching Zahir. At the mention of his brother's name, Javid sat back in his chair, his mind rolling back to how it had all begun for him at about the same time the Chicago branch of Confidential opened its doors.

Their first assignment: stop a suspected terrorist attack on Quantum Industries, a multinational oil distribution giant, the largest buyer and seller of oil worldwide, whose home offices were based here in Chicago.

Since the inception of the war on terrorism, Javid had devoted himself to promoting goodwill worldwide on behalf of Anbar, on behalf of the decent citizenry of the Middle East, and to the pursuit and capture of suspected terrorists. He'd personally helped expose a few cells of the vicious fiends—which had led to his discovery that his own brother was behind an attack in Iceland on one of Quantum's satellite offices.

He touched the spot above his heart where the scar remained, a raised and angry *X,* a "forever" reminder of the evil within his twin.

The attack had been a prelude, he'd learned, to something bigger targeting at Quantum's home base, but ultimately, the target was Anbar, Father and himself.

Quantum was the top buyer of Anbar oil. Javid had to do whatever was needed to ensure Quantum's ongoing safety. He sat straighter in his chair and steepled his fingers. Zahir had the opposite agenda: he would like nothing better than to see Anbar go broke.

Javid had approached the Chicago Confidential agency in March, seeking their help to stop his brother from committing any other acts of terrorism against Quantum. He'd shared his information with the agents and had been working, on and off, with them to bring about Zahir's capture, to try to find some way of stopping whatever Zahir and his henchmen had plotted for Quantum.

In the end, it was Zahir's own men—mercenaries he hired—who'd tried to hijack one of Quantum Industries's corporate jets and kidnap one of their vice presidents, Natalie Van Buren. Javid tapped his foot to the beat of the pulse at his temples. The evil plot was thwarted by one of Chicago Confidential's own agents, Quint Crawford, who was now engaged to Natalie. At the time of Zahir's arrest, the agents had suspected he was working with Khalaf Al-Sayed, but they had no tangible proof that would hold up in a court of law.

While connections were sought, Zahir had been incarcerated in a secret safe house. Earlier, Chicago Confidential had learned of Zahir's betrothal to Khalaf's newly found daughter. Since the time of Zahir's arrest, Javid had been impersonating his twin, gathering what personal information he could on Khalaf. Javid had had as little interaction with Khalaf as possible, knowing *he* was the one who could expose him, *he* was the one who knew Zahir, *he* would spot the differences, know he was dealing with a fake.

But Khalaf had been as elusive as a desert breeze.

Each time the agents had thought to arrest him, he'd failed to show up where expected. Since he would not miss Zahir and Miah's wedding, the agents had decided to take him into custody there.

"I'd like it a hell of a lot better if you were getting married on land." Lawson Davies intruded on his dark musings.

Law, as he preferred to be called, was a high-paid corporate lawyer who worked for Petrol Corporation, Quantum Industries's closest competitor. His suit was a serious pinstripe, tie subdued, eyes intelligent, green. He yanked off his wire-rimmed reading glasses, eyeing Javid as though he'd just presented a distasteful brief.

"A yacht for God's sakes. Makes this whole task more risky."

"Unfortunately," Javid said, "the 'where' of this affair was already set before I came on scene."

Vincent's expression was as serious as a thundercloud. "And Khalaf's insistence on security makes this a 'do it their way' situation."

"Y'all are makin' too much out of this," Quint Crawford drawled. Quint, a long lanky cowboy, had Texas oil in his blood, and embraced the accoutrements of his ranch lifestyle— boots, big black Stetson, silver belt buckle. He never took himself too seriously. "If you want to brand a calf, you gotta go to the corral."

"That's right." Whitney's hand went to her bright red hair. "The wedding takes place on a yacht, so we'll be on the yacht."

Quint punched the brim of his black Stetson higher on his forehead, his blue eyes twinkling. "I, for one, can't wait to see the prince say 'I do.' Seems like getting hitched is contagious."

Vincent glanced at his wife, Whitney. Only then did

his expression and his tone soften. "Don't knock it until you've tried it."

"I'm not knockin' it." Quint had a secret smile. "Heck, I'm all for it."

"Hey," Javid interjected. "There isn't really going to be a ceremony, remember? So, make sure you take Khalaf into custody *before* I end up married to his daughter."

"I've seen the charmin' Ms. Miah," Quint added, his infectious grin widening. "Worse things could happen to a man."

"Just make sure you do your job, and everything will work out as it's supposed to." Even Javid could hear the peevishness in his voice. He cleared his throat and reined in his emotions. "Too much could go wrong. So far, I've avoided Khalaf as much as possible. But he's no fool. If he discovers I'm not Zahir, our mission will be compromised."

Vincent nodded grimly. "We aren't underestimating the risks. We're on top of everything."

Andy Dexter burst into the room, slamming the door in his rush. His energy seemed to zing off the walls as though he were as electrified as his equipment. He didn't bother with a greeting. He hurried to his chair, waving something that looked like a miniature floppy disk at the group. "Just picked this up from Ramses, my Egyptian informer. It's a camera flashcard."

He inserted the disk into his computer and directed all eyes to their individual monitors. A parking lot appeared in the first frame, followed by a quick sequence of others, moving like a slowed-down motion picture. A dark sedan occupied a deserted space before what seemed to be a park and an indeterminate body of water.

Javid asked, "What are we looking at?"

"Khalaf," Andy answered. "Ramses has been following him since the sheik 'disappeared' last week."

There were no people on the screen.

"So, where's Khalaf?" Quint asked, his black hat dipping forward over his shaggy brown hair.

"In the car."

"Who or what is he waiting for?" Law plunked his glasses back onto his nose.

"No one. He's already in that car, meeting with someone."

"Who?" Javid asked.

"Come on, Dexter." Vincent groaned. "Don't make us play twenty questions."

"That's just it." Andy shrugged. "Ramses didn't know or see who Khalaf was meeting. He thought *we* could figure it out."

"What has this got to do with anything?" Whitney sounded as impatient as her husband.

They watched a white stretch Lincoln approach the dark sedan, saw Khalaf emerge from the sedan, but couldn't see inside the dark car, couldn't see who he'd been meeting. Khalaf got into the Lincoln and drove off. The taillights of the dark sedan lit up as the engine was started.

"This is all very interesting, Andy, but I'm already running late." Law checked his watch, pulled off his glasses and shoved back his chair. As he started to stand, hands planted on the table, his gaze landed once more on his screen and his mouth dropped open. "Oh my God."

"What?" Vincent glanced between Law and his own screen. "What?"

"Stop the film," Law barked, putting his glasses back on. "Can you run it backward, Dexter?"

"What the hell are we looking for?" Quint echoed Javid's thought.

"The back license plate of that dark sedan," Law informed them.

Andy found the desired sequence and freeze-framed it. They all saw it then. Petrol Corporation's logo, a small world globe inside the loop of a giant red *P*. Khalaf had been meeting with someone in a car that belonged to Quantum's chief rival, Lawson Davies's employer.

Quint sat back and swore under his breath. Vincent demanded of Davies, "Whose car is it?"

"I don't know. They aren't assigned." He peered closer at the screen as though he could find the answer written there in secret code. "Could be anyone in the upper framework of Petrol."

"Which means if we take Khalaf tomorrow," Quint said, "we won't be cutting off the head of this nasty snake."

Whitney glanced at Javid. "But if we don't arrest Khalaf tomorrow, that means…"

Javid felt all eyes on him, felt the bottom dropping out of his stomach. "No."

"Oh, yes, dude," Andy said with his loopy grin. "Come tomorrow, you're gonna have to marry the daughter for real."

Chapter Three

"'Happy's the bride the sun shines on...'" Miah peered out the porthole of the 222-foot yacht. Sunlight glistened off Lake Michigan, a huge sheet of glassy water on this cloudless day. It was nearly noon. The ceremony started at twelve-thirty. For a marriage to be happy the vows should be said on the upsweep of the hands of a clock, her mom had told her.

"Happy, huh! I'm marrying a man I don't even know." Miah grabbed the lacy veil, crossed to the full-length mirror in the master stateroom and began attaching the crown-piece to her gleaming mane of jet-black hair. Her amber eyes, enhanced with subtle shades of bronze and gold, reflected the butterflies in her stomach. "A man who looks at me like I'm a possession. A man I suspect is harboring dangerous secrets."

Am I nuts?

As if he stood beside her, Zahir filled her mind, and instead of the shudder her last thoughts should have brought, an unbidden allure flooded her veins, warmed her skin. *He* roused this heat, this erotic fire in her heart, this sweet awful need in her belly. A new fear edged along her nerves, stroked her spine and drove the heat higher—the fear that she might lose control, the fear that desire would consume her.

"No." She shook herself. "No."

She'd been with sexy men before, had had great sex before, and never lost herself. This man was no different from the others. And nothing and no one could control her unless she gave them that right. *That* she would never do. She'd made this decision. She'd agreed to marry Zahir all on her own. It was the right choice. For her. For Mom.

It was the *only* choice.

Miah jabbed the last pin into her hair with too much force and winced in pain as it pierced her scalp. Great. All she needed was blood all over her veil. She glanced at the clock. Where was Cailin? What was keeping her?

She twisted in front of the mirror, checking the back of the dress, making sure all twenty-five gold-colored satin buttons were fastened. She turned to the front again, smoothed her hands down her hips, then studied her image. A designer original, the pure satin, body-cleaving gown flowed from her shoulders to swirl around her feet like melted candle wax, flattering her lean, five-nine form, enhancing the good, downplaying the not-so-good. The deep white fabric gave her tawny skin a golden glow, as much as the touches of gold at her waist, neckline and threaded through the veil gave her eyes a sparkling light. Everyone had suggested dull old white on white. The golden touches were Miah's compromise.

Compromise. Her new byword. Lately, everything she did required a trade-off of some kind or other.

A discreet knock on the cabin door broke into her musings. "Miah, it's me."

"It's about time." Miah tore open the door. "I was starting to wonder if you were going to show up."

"My God...you're stunning." Emotion welled in Cailin's blue eyes. "Oh damn, my mascara." She blinked away the tears before they spilled. "You just look so awesome. I cannot believe it. In another hour, you'll be a bona fide princess." She curtsied and dipped her head. "Her Royal Highness, Princess Miah of Nurul."

"Idiot." Miah laughed and pulled Cailin inside, shutting the door behind her.

Her friend wore flip-flops, cutoff jeans, a halter top and a grungy baseball cap—and somehow made the look sexy. She ripped off her hat and glasses in one motion. Her face was flushed. Probably from rushing. Or maybe she'd run into Redwing.

"Bobby didn't follow you, did he?"

"No. Though, I know 'The Carrion' would love to get an exclusive on your wedding."

"The Carrion," actually *The Clarion,* had earned the vulturous nickname for its exposés based on lies and half truths, and for hiring scumballs like Bobby "The Buzzard" Redwing as reporters. "As though I'd like my wedding photos in that tabloid rag."

Cailin chuckled wickedly. "I brought T and J with me, just in case Bobby tried anything." T and J were Thomas and James, two of her four brothers, both heavy-weight boxing contenders. "If he *was* lurking somewhere on the pier, he's gotta be real sorry by now."

"Ouch. Serves him right. The last thing I need is him showing up."

"Don't fret. If by some miracle he did evade T and J, he'd never make it past the security you have aboard this floating mansion."

"They give you a bad time?"

"They insisted on searching me." Cailin made a face,

then gestured at her outfit. "I told them it was obvious I wasn't 'carrying concealed.' I let them go through my purse, but none of that hands-on stuff."

"Well, that explains the flush on your face when you came in." Miah laughed, and pointed to an ornate screen beside the bed. "You'd better hurry. Your finery awaits you there."

Cailin kicked off her flip-flops and slipped behind the screen. Miah could hear her clothes hitting the floor, then the swish of silk against skin. Cailin's voice drifted to her, sounding muffled, as though she had something over her head. "I noticed the name on the yacht is *Anjali.* Isn't that…?"

"My birth mother's name—yes."

"Then, the yacht belongs to your father?"

"I'm not sure." There was still much she didn't know about her birth father. "He said it belonged to friends. He has a lot of friends in this country."

"And enemies, too, apparently." Cailin alluded to the security and the fact her wedding was taking place on a private yacht in the middle of Lake Michigan, instead of some easily accessible, public chapel.

Miah disdained the persecution many Middle Easterners had suffered in recent times. "His life hasn't been easy."

Her father, Sheik Khalaf Al-Sayed, had entered the world as the second son of the Emir of Nurul. Nurul was a small country, bordered on one side by the Red Sea, on the other by Saudi Arabia. His older brother eventually succeeded to the throne and, shortly thereafter, married Princess Anjali.

Khalaf and Anjali fell in love and had a secret affair. When Miah was born, Anjali confided to him that the child was his. They decided to run off together. As proof of her commitment to him, Anjali signed a contract betrothing her newborn daughter to a man of Khalaf's choosing. But, as her birth father told the story, before he and Anjali could run away, rebels overthrew Nurul, slaying Khalaf's brother and Anjali. Servants saved Miah's life, secreted her out of the palace and spirited her to America.

Khalaf barely escaped with his own life. He took flight to Imad, a small country northward across the Saudi Desert on the Arabian Peninsula. Over the years, he made Imad his home, rising in political favor there to become their emir. At first he thought Miah had also been killed, but once he learned the truth, he began his twenty-five-year search for her. Fate arranged that the good people of Nurul overthrew the rebels at about the same time Khalaf found Miah.

Cailin sighed. "It's such a romantic story."

"It's a tragedy." Miah recalled the blackmailer's claims, then shivered as though from a premonition of more tragedy to come.

But Cailin was the one who claimed to be fey, to have the ability to sense things in advance, a gift passed through the females in her family. She stepped from behind the screen.

"Zip me, please."

The maid-of-honor dress, a solid satin shift, moved on her hourglass shape like liquid gold. Miah worked the zipper, then Cailin stepped to the mirror, fluffed her fiery shoulder-length curls and wiped a speck of lipstick from the corner of her mouth.

Her gaze met Miah's in the glass. She seemed to weigh the wisdom of something she wanted to say. Then she caught her left thumb in her right fist and began kneading it, a nervous habit she had. She blurted out, "I know 'The Gorgeous One' is the fantasy of our youth come true, but if I were you, I'd be terrified of marrying a man I hardly know.''

"I've gotten to know him.''

"I *thought* I knew Bobby The Buzzard.''

Bobby Redwing was a physically abusive brute. "Zahir is *not* Bobby. He's kind and gentle. Hey, *I'm* the one who's supposed to have cold feet, not you.''

"Maybe I'm all wet, but something about this whole thing—'' She worried her bottom lip.

"Your run-in with the security guards has your imagination working overtime.'' Miah thought she'd gotten a handle on her uneasiness, but having Cailin voice concerns started the butterflies moving in her stomach with renewed vigor. She could do nothing to change what was about to happen. *Would* do nothing to change it. But she could change the subject. "You have a lot of nerve, Cailin Finnigan, looking so great. The bride is supposed to outshine the other women at her own wedding, but that's not going to be the case today.''

"Diversion tactics are wasted on me.'' Cailin's frown deepened. "I've got four brothers who are way better at it than you. Maybe what I'm feeling is just a reaction to the state of the world. Are you going to be safe in Nurul?''

"As safe as when I'm traveling in America. Very safe. This is my heritage, Cailin. I *belong* in Nurul. I feel that in my heart. Besides, if not for a quirk of fate, I would never have been in America.''

"I'm going to miss you.''

"I'll be in Chicago as much as the Middle East. More, given mom's health. You'll see me so much you won't have time to miss me.''

Her mother swept into the room, looking anything but

ill. She might be a toy angel in a solid gold silk suit and
a pillbox hat. Her eyes brimmed with joy, her tiny hands
went to her throat. "Oh, Me-Oh-Miah, you are the most
beautiful bride. It's time, darling. The judge is ready."

THE JUDGE STOOD at the aft end of the great salon buf-
feted by baskets of white roses and twin shoulder-height
candelabra crowned with flaming six-inch gold-colored
candles. Miah carried a bouquet of white baby roses tied
with a lacy golden ribbon. In fact, white rose arrange-
ments tied with golden ribbons dominated the salon. The
floral scent filled her nostrils with such sweetness that
she might have been in a garden.

A floating garden.

The boat was a half-mile offshore, far enough to offer
privacy, close enough to see the harbor front from the
large windows on both sides of the salon.

The guests were seated on padded folding chairs—
glad, she supposed, to be indoors on this stifling day.
Outside, the temperature hovered near one hundred degrees Fahrenheit with one-hundred-percent humidity. Inside, it was a controlled and cool seventy-two degrees.

The guests included their nearest Mohairbi relatives,
an aunt and uncle on her mother's side of the family,
associates of the groom, her father Khalaf's American
friends, and security. She'd been disappointed that Zahir's parents could not leave Anbar at the moment—but
they would, he'd assured her, attend the royal wedding
in Nurul.

Of course, the scheduled trip to Nurul, her coronation,
and the royal wedding were all subject to change if a
donor became available for her mom.

But for now, all she had to concentrate on was reaching the judge without tripping over her feet. A string

quartet began a lilting version of the "Wedding March," and Miah's heart skipped as she lifted her gaze to the man standing next to the judge.

Zahir. He wore a white tuxedo with gold cummerbund and tie, his raven hair curled against the crisp white collar of his shirt. The suit seemed to add inches to his six-foot frame, expand the glorious width of his broad shoulders, emphasize his narrow waist and hips. His sheer beauty stole her breath, leaving her unprepared for his gaze catching hers, holding hers. The look of wonder and appreciation in his dark brown eyes sent a jolt of heat spiraling from her heart to the tips of her limbs, to settle like a hot coil in her most private place.

Her grip tightened on her bouquet. And the butterflies in her stomach took flight.

"Ready, Me-Oh-Miah?" Lina asked softly.

Miah smiled at her mother, who was giving her away today, took her tiny hand and thanked God for the hundredth time that they were sharing this day. She intended to make it one her mom would never forget. She *would* be "the happy bride" Mom expected—even if it stretched truth to the limits.

Miah nodded and whispered, "Oh, yes."

The "Wedding March" began. Cailin moved down the white carpet dropping golden rose petals; Miah and her mother followed after her. The very air seemed to shimmer. Perhaps it was light dancing off Lake Michigan, or the sudden light-headedness Miah felt. She clung tighter to her mother, her feet moving on their own. She spied her father in the front row.

Sheik Khalaf Al-Sayed was hard to miss as he alone wore formal Moslem attire. Diminutive in stature, he had a kinetic presence. His face was lean and leathery, lined from the trials of his life, and his eyes were deep-set and as black as his thick mustache.

He nodded as they moved past him. Cailin took her place at the other side of the judge, and Miah stopped and kissed her mother's cheek. Lina stepped back to allow her to move beside her groom. Zahir's subtle, spicy aftershave reached out to greet her as he took her hand. His touch was warm, pulsing, reminding her that for all the business aspect of this marriage, at the end of it was a thriving wholly masculine male who exuded a raw and heady sexuality.

Her pulse kicked a beat faster, moving the blood through her veins with a disturbing speed, making her more aware of everything—scents: the flowers, Zahir; touches: his, gentle ones, firm ones; breath: his, feathering her face, her lips.

She repeated her vows and slipped a wedding band on his tapered finger, glancing at Zahir as though rapt, actually feeling rapt, unable to pry her gaze free of his.

Vaguely, she heard the judge pronounce them husband and wife and state that Zahir could kiss his bride. He drew her to him then with all the skill she'd known he would possess, pressing her unresisting body to his, lowering his head with deadly accuracy, his mouth finding hers as though from memory.

His lips were pliant, hungry, demanding, dominating. Her knees weakened, and she melted into him, deepening the kiss on her own. The guests began to clap. Miah stiffened, pushing away from Zahir, her face as hot from passion as from embarrassment at having an audience witness her loss of poise.

He leaned closer and whispered, ''We'll finish this later, love.''

Miah laughed...at him, at herself, at the situation.

MIAH'S LAUGH held a throaty, sensuous tone that roused a carnal awareness in Javid. Her lips were the richest wine, the sweetest berry, forbidden fruit. She *was* a vixen. One moment playing hard to get, the next compliant, teasing. She had inherited the worst of her sire: his cunning. His charm. His treachery...as evidenced in the engagement ring she wore. A ring given to Nana by Grandfather Hayward for their twenty-fifth anniversary. Zahir had to have stolen it, for Nana had been looking everywhere for it and was heartsick at its loss.

When this was over, he would be sure to take it back to Nana.

Meanwhile, Javid decided, if he wanted to stay one step ahead of his bride, he'd best keep her off balance. He handed her a champagne flute, but when Miah started to drink, he stopped her. ''No, love. Like this.''

He twisted his arm through hers, offering his glass to her lips, taking her glass to his.

She frowned.

He grinned and whispered, ''From this day forward you are all mine.''

''I'm not a possession, Zahir. If ever I am 'all yours,' it will be because *I* choose to be,'' she whispered back.

Her defiance, as much as the brush of her body against him, as much as her gentle jasmine scent underscored by something wholly feminine, wholly Miah, started a deep pulse within his lower belly, filled his mind with imaginings of actually making love to her, something he could not, would not, in all good conscience do...no matter how great the temptation.

With difficulty, he forced his attention off his new bride and cast a surreptitious glance over their guests, but it was the sense that someone was watching him that set his internal radar on alert. He had studied his brother, learned his mannerisms, his peculiarities of speech, his walk, the way he held himself. He played his role well—but was it sufficient?

He supposed he'd know soon enough.

Javid and Miah moved to stand near the candelabra to receive their guests, who offered best wishes, kissed Miah and shook Javid's hand, then filed to the buffet table.

Khalaf came toward them.

Miah's father had a lean, wiry build, swarthy skin and a large, straight nose above a full black mustache. In contrast, his daughter towered over him by a good three inches, and nothing in her exotic face spoke of her sire. Javid surmised Miah took after her mother—which explained what Khalaf had seen in Anjali, but not what she had seen in Khalaf.

"You seem different somehow, Zahir." Khalaf narrowed his keen black eyes, peering at Javid like a chemist viewing a disease through a microscope.

Javid's breath hitched, but he warned himself not to panic. He had honed the arts of diplomacy and tact, and wielded both with the same daring he'd used as a boy handling Grandfather's treasured dagger. He gentled his smile and his voice. "Oh? Perhaps it is marriage that agrees with me."

"It is too soon to tell that." Khalaf's steely gaze raked over him, and a nerve twitched in Javid's jaw. "It is the suit, I think," Khalaf said at last, folding his hands over his formal robe. He sneered. "Too Western for my tastes."

"Ah…I thought perhaps it was my clean-shaven face." Javid stroked his chin, bare of the beard and mustache Zahir usually sported.

"Yes, this is the first time I have seen you thus shorn." Khalaf gave a disapproving shake of his head.

Javid's shrugged. "I prefer much that is Western."

Khalaf scowled with disapproval. "Do not forget who you are, my friend."

"I will never forget that." Javid touched the spot behind his left ear where a fake scar had been applied. Zahir had carried a scar there since the fateful day they'd dared play with Grandfather's swords.

"Good, good." Khalaf clasped his hand and smiled, revealing a mouthful of uneven, yellowed teeth. "We are family now, Zahir. United against our enemies. Soon, we will overcome the wrongs that have been done to us."

"Soon," Javid agreed, returning his father-in-law's knowing look, despite the fact that he had no idea how Khalaf and Zahir intended to overcome those enemies. Or why the sheik was so certain that the United States wouldn't place sanctions against Nurul when it discovered this newly formed familial connection. Javid could not, however, come out and ask Khalaf. Especially not at this time, no matter how quickly he felt his window of opportunity closing.

Felt time running out.

Whatever Khalaf and Zahir planned would happen within the next couple of weeks, between now and their departure for the Middle East. Javid felt it in his bones. He would have to get Khalaf alone, carefully pick his brain. Before it was too late.

With a tight band of frustration gripping his chest, he watched Khalaf kiss Miah, seeming to be a gentle, kindly father delighting in his daughter's joy. The deception soured Javid's stomach. God, how he ached to see this man behind bars, caged like the animal he was.

The sound of a high-speed motorboat approaching the yacht intruded on this thought. Shouts erupted outside. China cups rattled on saucers and voices inside the cabin collided. An outer door burst open and Khalaf's private bodyguards raced inside, consulted the sheik, then hurriedly hustled to the launch at the aft deck of the yacht before Javid could protest.

The launch was gone in the next moment, the powerful motorboat slicing across the water at twice the speed of the boat approaching the yacht.

Quint Crawford ducked into the salon, his head all but brushing the ceiling. He wore a security uniform, a baseball cap and his cowboy boots. He said to Javid, "Looks like paparazzi. How do you want it handled, sir?"

"Oh my God, it's Bobby!" Cailin headed for the door. "I'll get rid of him."

"No." Javid stopped her. "If Redwing sees you, he'll only become more persistent. I'll talk to him. Security will keep him from boarding. Everyone, please go on with the celebration."

"Zahir…?" Miah moved as though to stop him.

"Visit with our guests, love," he whispered. "I'll be right back."

Javid and Quint hurried out into the heat of the afternoon.

Quint grumbled in his Texas drawl, "Damn reporter scared Khalaf off like a sidewinder in a windstorm."

"I thought Andy has Ramses waiting on the pier to pick him up."

"That's the plan. You get anything out of the varmint?"

"Nothing helpful." Javid followed Quint to the aft deck to join the other Confidential agents, disguised as security, who were positioned there. The speedboat didn't slow as expected, but raced past with a spray of water.

"Hell, that's not Redwing," Vincent groused, his brow pulled into its perpetual frown. "Just some damn joyrider."

"False alarm, folks." Law tugged at the sleeves of his uniform as though he were adjusting a dress shirt with French cuffs.

Vincent nodded grimly. "You can put your weapons away."

A smile started to relax Javid's tensed face, but vanished at Quint's "Look out!"

Javid froze. The speedboat had circled around and was coming back. The driver wore a ski mask, a rifle at his shoulder. Quint tackled Javid at the same time he heard the teak paneling near his head explode. Screams issued from within the salon.

"Miah."

As Javid fell, a second blast went off. He felt a sharp pain in his forehead, then something dripped into his eyes.

The agents returned fire on the passing boat but were helpless to do more than watch it speed away. Until the launch returned, they were stuck on the yacht.

"Miah!" Javid pushed against Quint's weight. "Miah?"

"She's okay, pardner. Whitney hustled all the guests down to the staterooms. Now, you stay down." Quint moved off Javid and both men sat on their haunches.

Javid swiped at the warm liquid spilling down his face. *Blood.* "The bastard grazed my scalp."

"I don't think so." Quint flicked the brim of his baseball cap the same way he usually did his Stetson— missing it, Javid figured. He drawled, "Looks like a piece of paneling jabbed you. Cut's not deep, just messy."

He helped Javid into the deserted salon and settled him down on one of the folding padded chairs.

"Oh my God, Zahir." Miah appeared at his side, taking the chair next to him, dabbing a wet linen napkin to his wound, not seeming to notice or care that blood spilled on her wedding gown. Her golden eyes were dark with terror. "What just happened? Why was Security shooting at the person in the speedboat?"

"Because he was shooting at us, ma'am," Quint supplied.

Javid scowled at him.

"Tell me what's going on, Zahir." Miah lifted the napkin and narrowed her eyes. "Why would someone shoot at you? Try to kill you?"

But he had no answer. There was no way Khalaf was behind this. He'd never have disrupted his daughter's wedding. Or taken off as he had. So what was going on? Javid was sure of only one thing. Someone had just tried to kill him.

But was it Javid they wanted dead? Or Zahir?

Chapter Four

Zahir wrapped his hands around the steel bars of the prison cell where he'd spent the past few months, and swore in Arabic, then English. This was Javid's doing. When he got out of here, he would find his twin and kill him, plunge a dagger through his heart as he had been prevented from doing so many years ago.

This time no one would stop him.

Like a caged panther, he paced the six-by-six cell, past the rust-stained toilet and sink, the too-short cot with its lumpy mattress, rubber pillow, scratchy blanket.

His captors thought to break him with these obscene conditions, this vile treatment. Zahir laughed to himself. "Fools."

To survive in his world, a man learned many things, lessons taught through physical and emotional pain, endurance in the face of the unendurable. He'd spent his thirty years honing his senses on such trials. His fingertip found the scar behind his ear and the old hatred heated his gut. It was the first wound Javid had inflicted upon him, but not the deepest.

He had survived both, though at the time, he'd thought he'd die when his father displaced him as rightful heir to the throne of Anbar and bestowed it on that hyena,

Javid. He'd wanted to kill Javid, there and then. Their father, too. He'd been saved from acting on his fury by Sheik Khalaf Al-Sayed of Imad, a man with a like mind on the subject of Anbar, and toward Zahir's brother and father.

Khalaf had made him an offer he couldn't resist.

He'd allowed Father to believe he was sorry for his misdeeds, and Father had promised to keep Zahir in the lifestyle he'd become accustomed to, as long as he kept his nose clean and did nothing more to disgrace Anbar. To hide his covert activities, Zahir continued living as a playboy—until Javid told Father about his association with certain terrorists. Zahir had, naturally, denied all involvement with the cell, but Javid had provided proof, and Father had blocked Zahir's access to every single Haleem bank account.

At the time, Zahir vowed to exact immediate vengeance on his family. But Khalaf had taught him revenge, if swift, could taste as bitter as prematurely picked dates. The secret was to let your enemy relax, to study your prey like the cobra, find their weakness, let them think you had gone away, that they were safe from your vengeance. *That* was when you struck. Zahir, a fast learner, came to realize the wisdom of planning. Of patience. He strove for control of his patience now.

He closed his eyes, savoring how close he and his partner were to controlling a huge percentage of the world's oil supply.

He and Khalaf would be a rich and powerful force to reckon with, not only in the Middle East, but in the whole world. And Javid would finally pay for his treachery. But it would all be for naught if he couldn't figure a way out of this place.

He heard movement and the murmur of voices behind

the door at the end of the hall. His captors. He considered shouting *"I am not a terrorist! I am a Prince of Anbar! I have diplomatic immunity! I demand release this minute!"*

But they would ignore him, these jackals, as they had ignored his pleas for release from the first. Their mistake. They had no idea with whom they dealt. Their ignorance *would* cost them in the end.

If he were being held in a public facility, a Chicago Police Department jail, he would have been allowed a phone call, a lawyer, and he'd have been processed and out hours after being arrested. But his captors seemed to be a secret, undercover organization, one of those set up by the American government to search out and bring down terrorists. He had to get out of here. Had to warn Khalaf.

But how to escape?

He studied the cell, decided it might be easier to get out of this place than out of a regular Chicago jail cell, and tested the bars at the window and door. What worried him was that he'd lost track of time during his incarceration. Had not seen a newspaper or television newscast. Didn't know how close the wedding was. He reefed on each individual bar, but found them all solid. He knelt by the sink, gripped the moist drainpipe, and yanked.

His jailers refused to speak to him of the world outside this cell; their talk consisted only of their questions. Always their questions. He would never tell them what they wanted to know. Would never betray his and Khalaf's plans to demolish Quantum Industries...not even if they tortured him.

The pipe refused to budge, was rusted tight. He swore again in both his native tongues. He had to get out of here. But how? He growled and flopped down on the cot. The springs creaked in protest. *The springs.* He scrambled to his feet and lifted the mattress. The frame was a crisscross of stretched wires. Nice thick, sharp wires. Zahir smiled, sank to his knees and began the arduous chore of loosening one eight-inch length.

As he worked, his mind went to his impending nuptials. To Khalaf's daughter, his betrothed. Miah was merely a means to an end, a pawn on his path to untold riches and power, but he would enjoy bedding her. Often. If not exclusively. He would also enjoy beating some of the fight out of her. Curbing her sharp tongue. Her wild spirit. And the sooner, the better. But first things first. He gyrated the wire, twisted harder, felt it give.

Khalaf had to be frantic at his disappearance, beating the underbrush looking for him.

Unless...

His hand stayed on the wire as an unthinkable idea gripped him. No. But, yes. Javid *would* play his own game against him—*would* impersonate him.

Would Khalaf realize?

Would Miah?

The wire snapped free.

Zahir's head jerked at the sound of the hall door wrenching open. He heard the rattle of dishes on a tray. He sprang to his feet, dropped the mattress into place, shoved the weapon up his sleeve and crossed to the sink.

You are dead, Javid. As dead as this agent who brings my lunch.

Chapter Five

"You have to tell me what's going on, Zahir. My mother's heart can't take any stress. I can't have her exposed to, to, to…" The feeling she'd swallowed chips of ice hit Miah with renewed vengeance. There was no way to protect her mom from what had happened, no way to hide the blood splatters on her wedding gown. On Zahir's tuxedo. All she could do was deal with the aftermath.

"If I had answers for you, love, I would give them to you."

He had dragged her to the master stateroom and now stood by the door as though guarding it, or blocking her exit. She spied Cailin's cell phone on the bed and grabbed it. "Then, we'll let the police figure it out."

"No." He rushed to her, snatched the phone and thumbed the off button. "We aren't calling the police."

"Give me that." Miah grabbed for the phone, but he held it out of her reach. Furious, she growled, but stopped fighting him. "Look at us, Zahir. There's blood on our wedding clothes. Someone was shooting at you. You might have been killed. We *have* to call the police."

"No." Zahir's dark eyes hardened like the slivers of

bullet-blackened teak she'd tweezed from his forehead earlier.

"The harbor patrol, then," she insisted. She wanted the person who'd shot at her groom, who'd ruined the joyous day she'd planned for her mother, who'd given her mother the very stress she'd vowed would not touch her. *And she wanted that person now.*

"No, love. This must be handled privately."

"Privately? Privately!" She supposed his calm tone was meant to soothe her. It had the opposite effect. She moved at him and poked her index finger against his chest as she spoke, each strike a punctuation of her words. "Bullets were fired. That's against the law. A matter for the cops."

"Miah, you know your father has enemies." He tossed the phone to the bed, then caught her shoulders in a gentle, firm grip, holding her away from him. "He told you that. It's why we were married aboard this yacht."

"Her father, the coward." Lina shoved into the room, Cailin following on her heels.

Cailin threw up her hands in a helpless gesture. "She insists she's okay."

Miah rushed to her mother, but she could see all signs of her initial shock had vanished—likely lost in her outrage at Khalaf. Grant Mohairbi was a mighty idol to live up to; today Khalaf had fallen miles short. Miah checked her mother's pulse, her coloring, finding her complexion pasty, her lips too blue, her pulse erratic.

Lina said, "I'm fine, darling."

"No, you're not."

"Yes, I am. Don't you fuss. Cailin assures me no one was shot. Zahir's injury is minor and bandaged. But your lovely day... Are *you* okay?'' Her eyes grew round. "Oh, no, look at your dress. It's ruined.''

"That's not important.'' Miah wished she'd changed clothes. She tried steering her mother to the bed.

Lina would have none of it. She turned to Zahir, her shoulders squared, her spine stiff. "Tell me, please, is it the tradition of Middle Eastern men to run off and leave their children to face their enemies while they save their own skins?''

Zahir pressed his lips together. Then he shrugged and gestured with his hands as though it were obvious. "Miah is *my* wife now. *My* responsibility.''

Miah's hackles shot up. *His. His. His. What was it about this man and possession?* If he thought the ring on her finger was a ring through her nose, he was dead wrong. "I've been taking responsibility for myself for a long time now. And getting married hasn't changed that, thank you very much.''

"I only have your best interests at heart, Miah.''

His words were pointed, as though he were telling her more than she was understanding—like someone who says "trust me,'' when they're keeping vital facts from you "for your own good.'' Miah bit down a quick retort. Instead of instilling trust, he'd raised both her curiosity and her suspicions.

She took a mental step backward and forced herself to draw a steadying breath. Too much had happened too quickly today. She was reacting. Overreacting. Not thinking. Not reasoning. She gathered her calmest voice and asked, "How will this incident be handled 'privately'?''

"One of the security guards got some of the registration numbers off the side of the boat,'' he said. "Our people will start there.''

Our people? He hadn't sounded as though that meant the security guards, but Miah now recalled the exchange she'd seen between Zahir and the rangy officer who'd helped him into the salon. She'd thought it strange at the time—a silent dialogue, as though the two were well-acquainted, more than employer and employee. Her husband *did* have secrets. And given that someone had tried killing him, there was no longer any question as to whether or not those secrets were dangerous.

"The speedboat looked like the one owned by *The Clarion,*" Cailin said. She sat on the bed, kneading her thumb. Twin dots of pink colored her cheeks as though she felt responsible by association. "Bobby used to borrow it. We went out on it several times. But buzzard that he is, I can't believe Bobby would fire a shotgun at a yacht full of people."

"I'm sure it wasn't Redwing," Zahir said, his expression kind.

"You can't know that," Miah snapped. "The shooter wore a ski mask and was just far enough away, the boat moving just fast enough, that no one could have gotten more than an impression of him."

Zahir lifted his eyebrows and shook his head as though he thought her comment careless and hurtful to Cailin. Miah's face heated. She crossed to the bed, sat beside her best friend and grasped her hands. "I'm not saying it *was* Bobby. Just that we can't eliminate him as a suspect at this point."

Cailin nodded, her usually mischievous blue eyes full of concern, but Miah knew the concern wasn't for Bobby. Cailin didn't harbor romantic feelings for her ex. Cailin's defense of him had nothing to do with that. It was Miah she worried about. Miah could see it in her gaze, feel it in her heart, as though her friend were telling her to be careful.

Had Cailin "seen" something, some danger to Miah that had her more worried than she'd admitted earlier? Cailin wouldn't tell her if she asked. A shiver of fear traced Miah's spine.

"We need to get Mom ashore. Back to the penthouse."

"Fiddlesticks," Lina said with a stubborn insistence that had seen her through difficult times throughout her life. "We're safe from any more snipers now that the harbor patrol is watching over us and, I'm not leaving without a piece of your wedding cake—which you two have yet to cut."

Miah started to protest, but her mother cut her off, eyeing the bloodstains on her dress and Zahir's tuxedo with distaste. "But first you'll both need to change into something clean. Our guests have had enough excitement this afternoon." She gestured Cailin to come with her and headed for the door, saying over her shoulder "Hurry, now."

The soft *click* of the door latch sounded like a boom to Miah. She stared at Zahir, *her husband,* and felt as though every nerve in her body were painfully aflame. She had brought a change of clothes—an ecru summer suit that her mother had helped her select, insisted she buy—but she could not imagine undressing with this man in the room, even with a screen between them. "I, er…"

Zahir nodded as though sensing her discomfort and pointed to the door. "My suit is with my valet. Down the hall."

With that, he left the stateroom.

Miah blew out a relieved breath, deciding she'd better

change quickly before Zahir returned and caught her in her underwear. The thought raised her internal thermostat, and as her soiled wedding gown slipped to the floor, she couldn't help wondering if she was this self-conscious now, how would she handle the inevitable intimacy later tonight?

EXHAUSTION QUICKLY SNATCHED Lina's energy, but not before Javid watched her calm the nerves of guests and relatives, and see her daughter and new son-in-law through the cutting and eating of the cake and a round of celebratory toasts. By the end of the afternoon, he understood why Miah adored her. He felt a deep respect himself for this tiny woman with the big spirit. She refused to let her fragile health spoil her daughter's special day. But he was also profoundly worried at the toll her stubborn burst of bravado had taken. She looked worn-out, aged, her eyes sunken, the skin beneath bruised, her lips blue, the lines at the corners pronounced.

Javid insisted Security escort Cailin to her car, then accompany Miah, her mother and him to Lina's penthouse. They rode in silence, Javid lost in thought, trying to figure out what had happened, who'd been in that speedboat, who the shooter wanted to kill…and why.

By the time they arrived at the penthouse, he still had no answers, but was glad to find Dr. Forbes already there. The doctor and Lina retreated to her bedroom, and as soon as the door closed behind them, Miah turned questioning eyes to Javid.

"Dr. Forbes does not make house calls."

"He made an exception…after I explained that it would be easier on your mother if she didn't have to expend any more energy."

Miah's amazement at the doctor's willingness to

oblige his patient gave Javid pause, and he realized he took for granted that most people responded to even outrageous requests if enough money was offered as an inducement.

"Thank you, Zahir." Her hands went to her chest. "I couldn't stop fretting about her."

"I understand." His own mother was just as important to him. "She's a very special lady."

His compliment seemed to please her, but nothing else he said eased her worry. He watched helplessly as she silently paced the vast living room, until Dr. Forbes emerged from Lina's bedroom. The physician's expression was serious but not grim. They strode to the foyer with him.

"I warned you that your mother should avoid stress at all costs, Ms. Mohairbi, er, Mrs. Haleem. She wouldn't tell me what happened, but whatever it was, it has taken its toll. She will have to stay in bed for the next couple of days, and I caution you again—please consider her condition before allowing her near anything that might cause her stress."

Javid saw Miah blanch and felt a sudden fierce urge to wrap her in his arms and assure her Lina would be fine. But he knew only a heart transplant would cure what ailed his new mother-in-law. He curled his hands at his sides. "I assure you, Doctor, what happened today was beyond our control, but I'll see to it personally that nothing like it happens again."

Miah's eyes widened with disbelief, but the doctor seemed convinced. He thanked Javid and left.

Miah shook her head. "How do you intend to keep your promise to Dr. Forbes?"

"Easy, love. You and I will stay as far away from

your mother as possible…at least for the next few days.''

''But I can't leave her. She needs watching over.''

He took her left hand in both of his, the pad of his thumb rubbing her ring. ''That's what nurses are for. The one I hired will be arriving any minute. And I am also going to make sure your mother relaxes about you. I've canceled the honeymoon suite at the Sheraton—I cannot risk that our plans are known by your father's enemies. You may tell her that we can be reached, if she needs us, at the Presidential Suite in the newly constructed Royal Princess Hotel.''

''A royal hotel for a royal couple,'' she said, giving him a grateful smile.

Javid smiled, too.

JAVID'S WORLD TRAVELS had taken him to hotels of every size, shape and caliber. He'd slept on satin sheets, threadbare sheets, in bug-infested dives and pristine palaces. The Royal Princess Hotel was on the high end of the scale, a twenty-five-story glass, brass and marble extravaganza set on the shores of Lake Michigan.

From the outside, it glittered like a diamond against the night sky. Inside, subdued elegance reigned. Javid and Miah were whisked upstairs without checking in—another privilege of wealth. His personal bodyguards had escorted them from Lina's penthouse, stayed with them every step of the way, and now took up positions on either side of the door to their suite.

Rather than being eased, Miah seemed less than delighted at the bodyguards' presence. Javid didn't understand her attitude. Security was part and parcel of royal life, another thing he took for granted. She would get used to it—eventually.

Miah started to move into the suite, but Javid caught her arm. "Oh, no, you don't. There's tradition here to uphold."

"Oh?" Miah frowned. "Something I don't know about?"

"American tradition." Before she could think about it or offer a protest, he swept her off her feet and into his arms. She weighed less than he'd imagined, but for all her lean length, there was no mistaking the glorious creature in his arms was one-hundred percent woman.

Her surprised laugh spilled against his ears like a lilting, lovely song that sent shimmers along his nerve endings and yearning through his veins.

Vases filled with jasmine scented the air, blunting any lingering odors of new construction. The furniture was all white wood, the fabrics raw silk in shades of cerise and gold.

Javid asked, "It meets with your approval, love?"

The suite consisted of a living room, a small bathroom with a shower, double doors that opened to a bedroom with a hot tub and French windows that led onto a deck overlooking the lake. The tiled master bath had a view of downtown Chicago and a tub large enough for two.

"It's incredible, Zahir." She gently shoved against him and he set her on her feet, sensing in her an anxiousness, a hesitancy. Was she still distressed about her mother? About the shooter? Or having wedding eve jitters?

The last he understood. He had a few of those himself. He ran a hand through his hair. "Our luggage was delivered earlier. You'll find your clothes and other items have been placed in the dresser or closet and on the bathroom counter."

"Okay." Her face darkened. "I'm not sure I like

complete strangers handling my personal property. Or that I'll ever come to terms with it.''

"You will. It might take a little while and...it will require an open mind."

She glared at him.

He hid his laugh behind his hand. "We're having dinner in the four-star restaurant on the roof. You might want to wear something festive."

Recalling her clothes at the pub yesterday, Javid figured she'd be delighted with his suggestion, and her grin didn't disappoint.

She pulled off her suit jacket. "Is there time for me to wash off some of today's 'excitement' first?"

"Of course." Despite his promise to himself to remain a gentleman with Miah, the thought of her washing any part of herself sent a jab of desire through him. He swallowed over the knot forming in his throat. "Plenty of time."

Miah went into the bedroom and closed the doors. Javid stood rooted in place, the fantasy she'd elicited blossoming with a will of its own, until his breathing deepened and his blood began a slow boil. Damn. He shook himself. Swore again. Forced himself to move.

He had a small window of opportunity here in which to call and find out if the Confidential agents had discovered anything new about the shooting. He crossed to the desk phone and dialed Vincent Romeo's private number. Romeo's curt bark came reassuringly quickly.

Javid perched a hip on the desk, picking up the pen and pad supplied by the hotel. *Was that water he heard filling the bathtub? A tub large enough for two?* "Have you found out yet who tried parting my scalp today?"

"No. But Andy is working his magic with the registration numbers on the boat. Hopefully, we'll find a link to someone or something that will help us connect the dots.''

God, it *was* the bathtub. He tried not to envision Miah stripping off the ecru suit, dropping a lacy bra and silken panties to the tile floor. ''Meanwhile, what am I supposed to do?''

''What should you do?'' Romeo interrupted Javid's vision with an uncustomary laugh. ''Aren't you on your honeymoon?''

''This isn't funny, Vincent.'' The water stopped running and Javid's attention jerked toward Miah. Was she stepping into the tub now? Her long naked legs slowly sinking beneath fragrant bubbles? Damn it all. ''I don't know what to do.''

''Whatever comes naturally, of course.''

Javid clenched his jaw at the laughter still imbuing Vincent's voice, but the more he tried to banish visions of Miah in that damnable bathtub, the sharper they came. His mouth filled with saliva.

''I'd like nothing better than to do what comes naturally with that delectable woman. Hell, she might even be so inclined. But she's not in possession of the facts needed to make that choice. She thinks she's married Zahir. This whole thing is a lie. *I'm* a lie. The duplicity, the dishonesty goes against everything I believe in.''

''Yeah, but it's necessary. Have you found out if she knows anything of Khalaf's plans? Who his contact is at Petrol?''

Javid considered this a long moment, but Miah was too much a puzzle still. ''I'm not sure if she knows anything, Vincent.''

''Well, figure it out. It's important. Meanwhile, act like newlyweds. Go out, be seen, see the town. We'll page you the minute there's something to report.''

Javid hung up and glanced at the clock. He should be getting ready for dinner. He put his clothes into the bathroom off the living room. His forehead sported the butterfly bandage Miah had placed over his wound. His jaw was shaded with beard, his hair a mess. He shaved, showered and dressed, all the while pondering Vincent's advice. *Go out. Be seen. Do the town.*

Javid would follow that advice within reason. He wasn't taking chances with Miah's life. Not when they weren't sure whether or not she was in cahoots with her father. She might be a complete innocent. Which was it? Victim or vixen?

And how was he to discern the truth?

He opened the champagne, filled a glass and downed it in a single gulp. He'd faced death at his brother's hands without flinching, faced an assassin's bullets in stride, but his bride, a mere slip of femininity, had him totally unnerved.

He laughed.

"What's so amusing, Zahir?"

Chapter Six

"What's so amusing, Zahir?" Miah asked again.

He spun toward her, the smile still dancing in his dark eyes, in the lines of his intriguing mouth. He'd changed into a black tuxedo that, incredibly, looked better on him than the white one had. Her breath snagged at the back of her throat at the sheer beauty of this man she'd married.

He seemed unable to answer her question, his attention going to the "festive" beaded red slip dress she'd chosen and paired with diamond studs and red spiked sandals that added three inches to her height and gave her the sense of meeting him on equal turf.

But longing smoldered in his eyes, reaching out to her, luring her, filling her with heat, that damnable heat, and melting all illusion of equality, reducing them to male and female, the most primitive of magnetic equations. Had he moved to hold her, to kiss her at that moment, she would not have resisted, could not have resisted, could not deny it was what she wanted. But was she willing to finish what she might start? The tightness in her throat worsened. She decided whatever had made him laugh wasn't worth exploring. She just wanted to be where there were other people. Lots of other people.

"We should go."

"Are you hungry, love?"

There was no mistaking his meaning. He wasn't talking about food. Miah blushed. Did she want him? In every way a wife wants her husband? Yes. No. Oh God, she wasn't sure. Could there be total intimacy without total honesty?

"Cake is all I've eaten today."

"I like a woman with a healthy appetite." He grinned wryly and gestured toward the door.

Miah started forward, uncertain if the flutter in her belly was relief or disappointment or the need for food, so confused were her thoughts. As attracted as she was to Zahir, she feared his possessive side, feared giving herself to him would mean losing herself in some vital way she might never regain. They needed to set some ground rules, some basic foundation or other for how they would conduct this relationship. She had to define her place in it. He hadn't been willing to discuss it before the wedding, but before this night was over, he would have to hear her out.

He ushered her into the hallway. The bodyguards had multiplied to four. Two stayed on the door. Two went with them down the hall, one ahead, one behind. Their constant presence gave Miah the sensation of being boxed in. She'd thought extreme wealth would be freeing, but she was finding it was as constricting in many ways as poverty had been.

An open mind, Zahir had said. But how did one go about opening one's mind to being constantly watched? Constantly spied on…even if it was for one's own protection?

As the elevator rose to the roof, she heard the beat of a rock band thumping against the walls and she shook off her dark thoughts. She had never felt the need for pure mindless fun as strongly as she felt it now, and she anticipated with eagerness getting into the room full of diners.

Zahir took her hand in his, pulling her to his side, his heat sending a frisson up her arm and into her heart. He looked down at her, his breath a feather on her face as he fingered the wispy hair at her temples.

"I've been told Ambrosia's gnocchi is so light it could float off your plate." He peered deeply into her amber eyes. "That the imported wines are like sparkling liquid gold." His gaze dropped to her mouth. "That the sauce is a blend of lush, red tomatoes fresh from the Tuscany valleys." He stared at her lips as though they were the juicy, plump fruit of which he spoke, his glance a caress she could almost feel, and shivers spread from her neck to her stomach.

He acted as though they were alone, as though he'd forgotten about the bodyguards. How did he do that? How did he make her feel as though they *were* alone?

She spied a sign taped to the restaurant entrance and stopped, pulling back. "Zahir, we can't go in. It's closed for a private party."

"Yes, love. Our party."

She gaped at him. "We have the whole place to ourselves?"

"Yes, love."

"But the band…?"

"For us."

"You bought out the entire restaurant? Someone can do that?"

"For the evening, yes."

"Oh my gosh." An unfamiliar warmth filled her chest, a huge bubble of delight, of pleasure that expanded and burst through her. No one had ever treated her in such a special way. She'd agreed to this marriage in order to take possession of her inheritance, to claim her royal status, to gain an independence she'd never had. But Zahir was an unexpected bonus, as gorgeous on the inside as on the outside. An enigma, to be true. One minute harboring dark secrets, the next countering every bad thing that had happened this day with something wonderful.

He gestured to the exquisitely set table in the middle of the dimly lighted room. A magenta cloth draped to the floor, held in place with gleaming chinaware and a triad of candles intertwined with white roses. Floor-to-ceiling windows offered an unobstructed view of Lake Michigan, sparkling like black crystal beneath a full moon.

"Will it do, love?"

Miah flinched at how accustomed she was getting to the endearment, recalling that her charming husband also had that thing about her "belonging" to him. Her eyes narrowed with suspicion. Was he trying to reel her in with candlelight and sweet talk?

"It's wonderful. But please stop calling me 'love.' You don't know me well enough…to mean it."

"Perhaps tonight will remedy that."

A new anticipation shimmered through Miah. As if on cue, the music went soft and dreamy. She sighed, then made the mistake of glancing into Zahir's velvety brown eyes, so dark with need that her knees weakened. He seemed intent on pleasing her, on giving her the magic she'd expected when she'd discovered she was a princess, but had never quite felt until this moment.

One of the bodyguards moved ahead of them and spoke with the maître d', then nodded at Zahir and joined the other bodyguard outside the entrance, melting into the background.

Zahir pulled out a chair for her. Miah sat and clasped her hands, touching her wedding ring, determined to memorize every second of this evening. A waiter hovered, then spread crisp linen napkins in their laps and handed each a menu.

Zahir waited until the man moved away. "I'd order for you, love, but which foods you like and dislike is one of the things I want to learn about you."

So, they discussed food, placed their orders, talked about their families, their mothers, their fathers. Her fathers. Curiously, Zahir seemed to favor the subject of her birth father, as though he knew less about him than he should, given the length of time they'd known each other, but that topic made Miah squirm. Her mother had been outraged at Khalaf for dashing off, for seeing to his own safety in the face of danger without a thought to his daughter's. Her birth father had been the last of Miah's concerns this afternoon. Zahir and her mother were all she'd focused on. Even in the hours since the gunman had shot at the yacht, she hadn't allowed herself to think of Khalaf, but she could no longer hold the hurt at bay.

"You know, my dad—Grant—would never have run off the way my father—Khalaf—did, leaving us to face his enemies. Grant put others before himself—people who were not even *his family*."

The blackmailer's accusation crept through her mini-temper tantrum and increased her anger. She'd always believed her dad was a hero. Bigger than life. Someone to respect—not a liar or a sham, not, she supposed, human. Infallible. Certainly not the evil monster the extortionist portrayed. If only she could tell Zahir about the blackmail notes, if only she could trust him that much…

She reached for her wineglass with her right hand as Zahir touched her left hand, the pad of his thumb rubbing her engagement ring.

"I wish I'd met him."

"Yes. He was a great guy." She lifted her gaze to meet his, a knot forming in her throat as she recalled the Grant Mohairbi she had lived with and known, shoving down her doubts and uncertainties about him. "I'm looking forward to meeting your parents."

"They're going to adore you." He drank his wine.

"Has my father contacted you, Zahir, since the incident on the yacht?"

Her husband's eyebrows shot up. "Khalaf hasn't called you?"

"No. I—I don't suppose he knew where to reach us."

"I thought he gave you a cell phone."

"Yes, but I don't have the phone with me today. It's still in my bedroom at Mom's. He has your cell phone number, though, right?"

"Of course." Zahir nodded and pulled the phone from an inside jacket pocket, looked at the readout and grinned wryly. "It seems I've had mine off, though."

He turned it on. "Would you like me to phone him?"

But before she could answer, the phone rang, startling them both. Zahir laughed.

"Hello? Khalaf. Yes, Miah and I have only just realized that neither of us have had our cell phones on. I apologize for worrying you. We are both well. So, you were told of the shooter. No, no one knows who…yet, but I have people working on it. As soon as we know. Yes, I understand."

He told her father about the changed hotel reservations, where they were staying now. Then Zahir covered the mouthpiece. "He wants to speak to you."

Miah took the phone. "Hello, Father."

Khalaf said, "Zahir assures me that you are unharmed, my daughter. I am much relieved. And your mother? How is she? This attack cannot have been good for her."

Miah assured him her mother was doing as well as could be expected and would need a few days of bedrest.

He offered apologies and said in his raspy voice, "My bodyguards are overzealous. They thought only to get me to safety."

"I understand."

"Do you? My life has taught me it is often wiser to avoid a threatening situation—live to fight another day as it were—than to confront the unpleasant head-on. Your Irish lady friend had suggested to me earlier that she wouldn't be surprised if that reporter Redwing borrowed his boss's speedboat to try to get photos of the wedding. I'm afraid that I assumed the person in the speedboat *was* Redwing. So, I was not worried about your safety when I departed."

"It wasn't Redwing. Or any reporter."

"We know that now." He cleared his throat. "But at the time it seemed a good bet that it was someone from *The Clarion*. The editor seems obsessed with royals. I imagine he would relish being the only paper to have photos of your wedding. And given the lies this international tabloid often prints, it's better if we don't risk their publishing any stories about you and Zahir. We don't want to tarnish your image with the people of Nurul."

"Well, it would have been a real scandal if the gunman had actually hit anyone."

"I had no idea an assassin was aboard that speedboat or I never would have left you and Zahir to face him. I have offered Zahir extra security, but he assures me he has handled that."

"Yes." Warmth spread through Miah's chest, melting the hurt that had gathered into a snowball at the edge of her heart. Khalaf *was* the father she thought him to be. Kind and caring, generous and giving, the fairy godfather this princess needed. "The gunman meant to kill Zahir."

"Yes." He sounded odd, thoughtful. "Would that not be the best way to hurt me, by hurting my daughter?"

"So we've ruled out 'Big Tony' De Luca and his employees as suspects?"

"Yes. *The Clarion's* editor is a coward whose only weapon is printer's ink. I am certain the assassin who shot at Zahir was sent by one of my enemies. But do not dwell on this any longer, my darling daughter. This is your time for celebration and joy. May I speak again with Zahir?"

She returned the phone. Zahir frowned as he listened. "No, no idea. Where are *you* at present, Khalaf? I see. Of course. Yes. I will."

When he disconnected, he stowed the phone in his pocket, the thoughtful look lingering as though he were trying to make sense of something.

"What is it, Zahir?"

"Nothing, love—"

He patted her hand and she knew he was lying. Keeping more secrets.

"Khalaf wanted to make certain that your safety is my main concern. I assured him it is."

Her father had said he'd spoken to Zahir about that before asking to speak with her. So, what had he and

Zahir really been discussing at last? What was it that now had Zahir distracted? Not knowing brought that ice-chip sensation to her stomach again.

God, how she wanted to retain that sense of minutes before, that she and Zahir were growing closer, that she could trust him, could open up to him. But as her gaze fell on the bodyguards, the band and the restaurant workers, she realized the idea that she could define her place in this relationship was as much an illusion as the one of her high heels putting her on an equal turf with him, as much an illusion as the one of them being alone in this rooftop paradise. No amount of dancing, dining or dallying would secure a solid foundation for this relationship. Not with his lies and secrets.

Not with hers.

JAVID STEPPED after Miah into the elevator. He hated all this deception and deceit. Every time Miah called him Zahir, he hated it more. Every second they grew closer—pretending to be a man he wasn't with a woman he was starting to care for far too much—twisted the guilt tighter in his gut. He ached to tell Miah the truth, ached to take her in his arms…as himself.

Her soft floral scent seemed imbued in his senses, a sensuous lure like nothing he'd ever known. He blew out a breath. Hell, he'd had too much wine. Was dealing with too much need. Too much attraction to a woman he now believed was as innocent in this mess as she seemed to be—after Khalaf's last chilling words: *Protect her, Zahir. Miah must remain alive until we are established in Nurul.*

He'd done his damnedest not to show it, but it had staggered him then. It staggered him still.

The elevator stopped on their floor and they disembarked. At their door, one of the bodyguards stopped Javid and handed him a note. It read: "For the newly-weds, with love, Khalaf."

Javid questioned the bodyguard with his eyes. The bodyguard's answer was to open the door to the suite. Red rose petals spread from the threshold into the living-room and beyond. At Miah's exclamation of pleased surprise, he handed her the note. She read the message, sighed and hugged it to her chest as she went inside.

The main room was dim, the moon all that softened the darkness, but a golden glow beckoned from the bedroom. Javid shut the door on the bodyguards and followed Miah over the ever-widening rose-petal carpet, realizing as he caught up to her that the light came from dozens of candles arranged around the hot tub.

Céline Dion sang softly from hidden speakers. The king-sized bed had been turned down, rose petals rained across the spread, chocolates laid on the pillows, champagne opened, iced, in a bucket near the hot tub next to a platter of fresh fruit and cheeses.

Faced with this generous gift, it was difficult to believe that Miah's life could be in danger once Zahir and Khalaf "established" themselves in Nurul. She might be safe, he mused, *if* she cooperated. Agreed to be pliant. Amenable to whatever they ordered. He couldn't picture Miah's will bending to any man's. It was one of the things he found irresistible about her. That sassy, never-know-what-she-might-say-next quality she had.

But there was also that other little-girl delight she exhibited occasionally. She spun to him now, her eyes glittering with emotion. "It's incredible. I've never seen anything so romantic. It's perfect, Zahir."

Javid had the unsettling feeling that he was being sucked into a role he could not in all good conscience play. But he wasn't the only one being played. Khalaf had Miah starry-eyed, as if he were some sort of hero. She'd had almost the same look when she'd started talking about her adopted dad, Grant Mohairbi, who had actually been a hero.

He recalled now how her eyes had clouded as they discussed her dad, and he remembered wondering if he'd said something to cause that cloud, or if she'd thought of something only she knew about Grant that darkened her memories of him. She'd seemed about to share whatever it was, but in her hesitation, Khalaf had called. After talking to her father, she'd been less forthcoming, more reticent.

He'd done everything he could to warm her up—plied her with wine, danced to her favorite songs, shared the view and tender touches—when what he really wanted to do was wrap her in his arms and keep her safe from dangers she didn't even suspect surrounded her.

In many ways she thought herself street-smart. In many ways she was naive. Grandiose gestures by Khalaf had her believing that monster was a saint, had her convinced she was the apple of his eye. But Javid feared that Khalaf, unlike most Middle Eastern fathers, held no love for his daughter. She was a tool being used to further his power in Nurul. God help Miah when she learned the truth.

Miah kicked off her sandals and wriggled her bare feet in the thick carpet, sighing. She crossed to the wine bucket. Her hand trembled slightly as she filled the two glasses and plucked a grape from the basket. She popped the grape between her lush lips and bit down, sending a droplet of juice to the corner of her alluring mouth. The tip of her tongue slipped out, teasing away the juice, teasing Javid, stirring images in his mind, want in his veins. Mesmerized, he watched her eat, all innocence and enchantment, her subtlest movement a lure he couldn't resist, and the room seemed to heat to an unbearable temperature.

He doffed his jacket, tugged the knot from his tie, undid the collar button of his shirt and yanked open the French windows. He stepped out onto the balcony. A warm night breeze skipped across the moon-glistened lake to whisper against his skin.

Miah sidled up behind him, offering him one of the icy flutes of champagne, her head dipped shyly, hiding the amber jewels of her eyes with her thick black lashes. He took a deep swallow of the bubbling liquid, then accepted the grape she offered next, her unsteady fingers trembling slightly as they slid into his mouth. All resistance and logic fled from him; he set their glasses on the wide concrete railing and caught her to him. She came against his body as though she'd once been a part of it, fitting with such ease his breath jammed his throat and fire ignited in his belly. For what felt like long seconds, he held her to his thundering heart, a soft moan stealing from him, need stealing through him.

She lifted her gaze slowly, her glorious golden eyes dark with desire and longing, and, as though she'd rung a chime, Javid felt echoing emotions reverberating through his own body. His hands slid into her thick, sleek hair, claiming her, holding her as he dipped to gently brush his lips over hers, once, twice, three times, felt her breath catch in her chest; then their tongues met and his uncertainty drowned in a wash of urgency as she gave herself to him.

His hands began exploring the length of her back, his fingertips skimming the lush curves beneath the beaded dress. He felt her releasing the buttons of his shirt, tugging the tails from his slacks, her small hot hands on his belly, moving up into the dense hair on his chest. He located the zipper of her dress, slipped the garment down the curve of her spine, felt its beaded weight drop from her.

He traced the newfound silky smoothness, an endless stretch of bare back, a teeny scrap of satin panties. Need throbbed against the restraint of his clothing, harder and harder with every inch his fingertips explored of this glorious woman who was deepening their kiss, urging him on with sugared moans, honeyed sighs.

A sudden blaring bleat sounded against his ears, but until the bodyguards banged on the door of the suite, he was so lost in Miah that he thought the noise was inside his head. Then he realized it was an alarm.

A fire alarm.

"Oh my God, Zahir!" She covered her breasts, grabbed her dress from the balcony floor and dashed into the bedroom, trying in her panic to get the dress on.

Javid raced past her, snatched one of the plush robes from the hook on the bathroom door and brought it to her, along with a pair of flats. He helped her into the garment as she slipped on the shoes, then hurried her to the door. With the bodyguards leading the way and bringing up the rear, they joined the other hotel guests speeding toward the stairs. Voices, shrill and panicked, clashed in the wide hallway, only to quadruple in the stairwell. The lower they went, the more crowded the passage became. Progress slowed to a frightening creep.

"Is there a fire?" Miah asked.

"Probably a fire drill," Javid answered, squeezing her hand reassuringly, trying to soothe her. This day had been anything but the special one she'd expected, had

had every right to expect. He tamped down his anger and kept his tone light. "Hotels have them all the time."

"Really?" She hugged the robe to her neck, looking too damn vulnerable.

"Trust me, I've been through them in countries all over the world. You'd think after all the stairwells I've had to descend like this, that I'd learn to book a room on a much lower floor."

She rewarded him with a smile, and his need to protect her grew fierce. *Pray God, there was no fire.* He couldn't bear it if anything harmed Miah.

The descent took a good ten minutes, guests warning one another not to panic, not to push, not to shove, but there was jostling, bumping, crying and cursing. Once outside, pajama-clad guests huddled in the street, gazing at the hotel, quiet tension hovering over the crowd. Was there a fire? Was it a drill?

Javid sent his chief bodyguard to talk to the firemen who were returning to their trucks near the hotel entrance. He came back seconds later to report. "No fire. Someone pulled the bell on the restaurant floor."

Word spread quickly among the grumbling guests, who began pouring back into the hotel.

But Javid was still processing the fact that someone on the restaurant level had tampered with the fire alarm. Why? To get into *their* suite and plant something nasty? A possible fire had ensured he'd leave the room without security. He caught Miah's arm, halting her attempt to join the others heading back into the hotel.

She clutched the robe tight at her chest and eyed him questioningly. "Aren't we going in?"

"No."

"Why? What's going on, Zahir?"

"Nothing. I'm just not taking any more risks with

your life. I want you to go somewhere safe until I can join you.''

''But, Zahir. Our wedding night,'' she whispered, her meaning clear.

He didn't need reminding. In the cooling night air, he'd sobered, regained control of himself and realized he shouldn't have let it go so far. Miah trusted him. Thought he was Zahir. What he was was a jerk. A liar. Being her husband didn't give him the right to take advantage of her naiveté. Until he could level with her, he would have to make sure his passion didn't get out of hand. But God help him if this sham continued much longer...

He moved her hair from her cheek. ''We're not staying in that room tonight, Miah. And we aren't going to go to another hotel. I've gone to great lengths to keep our whereabouts known only to a few, but there seems to be a leak in that chain somewhere.''

''How do you know the fire alarm was set off to target us?''

''I don't. But after the speedboat incident, I can't afford to rule out that possibility.''

''But, Zahir, someone tried to kill you today. You have to come with me.''

''No. This may be nothing. But, in case it's not, I can't ask my people to put their lives in danger for me. If this is personal, I must face it personally. Please understand.''

A limousine pulled to the curb. Quint unfolded his lanky frame from the back seat and held the door for Miah. Javid said, ''You remember Quint from this afternoon? He's going to escort you. You can trust him.''

She put her hand on Javid's arm, and he winced inwardly at the fear in her eyes.

"Please, come with me," she said.

"I'll be there as soon as I've made certain our suite is secure."

"Then, promise me you'll be careful."

"I will be, love." He kissed her forehead and stepped aside, then watched the car drive away, Miah peering out the back window as though she'd never see him again.

Chapter Seven

Miah sank down in the deep leather seat, hugging the bathrobe to her throat, trying to purge the fear racing her veins, trying to convince herself to stop worrying about Zahir. He was in a hotel with hundreds of people. Surrounded by bodyguards. No one would risk another attempt on his life under those conditions.

But he'd been surrounded by security on the yacht and a lone gunman had singled him out.

Giving up on trying to assure herself of his safety, she turned toward the silent man beside her. "Will he be okay?"

"I expect so, ma'am," the man drawled. "I know he wouldn't want you worrying."

She stared at him, seeing little more in the dark car than his profile. "Just how long have you and Zahir known one another? Where did you meet?"

"Beg your pardon, ma'am?" The Texas drawl deepened. "Don't you mean, 'How long have I worked for Prince Zahir?'?"

His tactical sidestep did nothing to deter her. She'd seen the looks they'd exchanged. Seen the trust Zahir put in this man. That kind of reliance on an employee didn't happen overnight. "How long have you been in his employ?"

"Not that long, actually. Less than a year. I hooked up with him here in Chicago."

"Really? How did that come about?"

"He needed local security. That's my speciality."

"I see. It's just that the way you spoke to him after the attempt on his life this afternoon, well, it sounded less formal than I'd have expected given such a short...association."

"Unusual circumstances. But if I was out of line in any way, Your Highness, I apologize."

"I didn't say you were out of line. It's just that your exchange suggested to me that you're much more than boss and employee."

Quint cleared his throat. "I don't like to contradict a lady, ma'am, but whatever you think you saw, or heard, was only our mutual concern over the situation...and for your welfare."

"Of course. I see." Miah arched an eyebrow, unconvinced by the tall Texan and his tall tale. *Oh, Zahir, what secrets are you keeping from me?* She twisted her hands tighter into the robe, determined to find out. "Do you think the fire alarm was set off by the gunman who tried to kill Zahir today?"

He hesitated as though weighing his words, deciding what the prince would want her to know. "I don't think we can assume, or eliminate, that possibility without a thorough investigation of the facts. That's what your husband will be setting into motion now. That investigation. He'll also have a sweep done of the suite to make sure no one came in and planted nasty listening devices or other such unpleasantries while you were racing to safety."

She didn't like the sound of that. "Even after checking, how can we be sure it's safe to stay at that hotel? In that suite?"

"There is high-tech equipment for all kinds of things these days, even ones for detecting the presence of the other devices."

"So, tomorrow we may be returning to the suite?"

"I don't see why not, once it's been secured."

His assurances did nothing to ease the knot in her stomach or her fear for Zahir. She was amazed at how upset she was that she'd been pulled from her husband's arms and rushed away from her wedding night. Appalled that she'd been caught undressed, about to be gladly intimate with a man she'd been so shy with earlier, was so unsure of still. Embarrassed she'd been forced from her room in nothing more than flats, panties and this huge robe. *Some attire for a princess to wear in the presence of the hired help.* She checked the belt at her waist, the collar at her throat, but found no indecent exposure of skin. That made her laugh. She, who usually showed no concern over miniskirts and midriff tops. She felt another laugh coming and realized she was on the verge of hysteria. This should have been the happiest day of her life. The happiest night.

She glanced out the window and realized she recognized the neighborhood. "Where are you taking me?"

"To your mama's penthouse. It's secure."

"Oh God, I can't go to Mom's." Surely this was not Zahir's idea? He knew the doctor had warned them to keep her mother as stress-free as possible. "Her heart can't stand another distress coming so soon on the heels of the one this afternoon. And believe me, my arriving on her doorstep this late on my wedding night—without my groom and in a fair state of undress—will distress her plenty.''

''Perhaps if you sneak in—''

''My key is in my purse at the hotel. Sneaking in is not an option.''

''The doorman could—''

''No.'' She wasn't about to confront ''Snooty Stan''—as she and her mom had named the uppity night doorman—dressed like this. ''That's not an option either.''

''Then, what do you suggest?''

''I don't know.'' God, how she wanted someone to talk to. No, not just anyone. ''Cailin. I can stay at her apartment tonight.''

''Is that your maid of honor, Ms. Finnigan?''

''Yes.''

''Is her place secure?''

''Depends on what you mean by 'secure.'''

''I'm assuming your mama's penthouse is protected by a state-of-the-art security system and that no one gets past the doorman without an invitation, and I know Prince Zahir has men at her door. Does Ms. Finnigan have those precautions at her apartment?''

Since breaking up with Bobby The Buzzard, her friend had rejected moving back to the Finnigan family home in a suburb east of downtown, something Cailin considered would be a step backward. She'd leased a single-bedroom apartment in a renovated complex in a neighborhood that was an eclectic mix of nationalities and races. Corner shops and eateries displayed names like Wong's, Zinberg's, Papa Sergio's, Garcia's and Campbell's. The building itself was five stories high. The only security she knew of was the locked front door that required residents to ''buzz in'' their visitors.

She knew Quint would not consider this much of a precaution. "Cailin has four strapping brothers who will be at our beck and call should we need them."

"Well, now, see, that's a problem. I think we'd better stick to the original plan."

"I've just told you why that won't work."

"Your husband instructed me to take you to your mama's penthouse and he won't like me not following his orders. I'll need to call him. See what he wants me to do."

"Excuse me, but I'm not some child whose 'parent' needs consulting at every turn."

He acted as though he hadn't heard her. He pulled his cell phone from his pocket, then mumbled something. "Battery's gone dead. I'll have to get to a landline and speak to the prince."

"No. All this cloak-and-dagger stuff, necessary or not, is making me nuts." Miah drew in a stubborn breath. "You are my husband's employee—therefore I am assuming that you are also in my employ."

"I suppose, technically speaking, ma'am—"

"So, if I ask you to do something," she said, cutting him off before he could add a "but," "you'll grant my wishes. Right?"

He grumbled something unintelligible, but his displeasure was clear enough.

She didn't care, didn't need his approval. She instructed the driver that their destination had changed and gave him Cailin's address.

Minutes later as she stood next to Quint on the stoop of Cailin's building, waiting for Cailin to respond to the buzzer, Miah felt exposed, unsafe. She'd thought she would welcome shirking off the constant presence of guards, but oddly, the idea of Quint leaving, of no one seeing to her safety, left her feeling like a high-wire acrobat whose net had been snatched out from under her.

Puzzling the strange new feeling, she pressed Cailin's button again, and finally, Cailin's sleep-thick voice came through the call box. "I don't know who this is, but it had better be good."

"Cailin, it's Miah."

"I am definitely not in the mood for jokes."

"No. It's me."

There was a brief pause, then Cailin cried, "Oh my God, Miah. What are you doing here?"

Miah glanced around, feeling more like a target by the second. "Could you just let us in?"

"Us?"

"Cailin…please…"

The buzzer blared. Miah blew out a breath and pushed through the door. Quint accompanied her to the third-floor apartment. Cailin was waiting, pacing the hall in front of her open doorway. She wore a yellow sleep shirt beneath a robe that matched the brilliant blue of her eyes and showed off her shapely legs. Her feet were bare, her red curls tousled, her gaze wide with fierce concern as they swept Miah.

"What in the world?"

"I'll explain in a minute." Miah grinned soberly, realizing she'd half expected her friend to have "seen" the disastrous events of the evening in one of her visions. She accepted a hug, then started to step into the apartment. But Quint stopped both women. "Ms. Finnigan, I hope you don't mind, but I need to make sure your apartment is secure for the princess."

"I, er, wasn't expecting company. But knock yourself out." Cailin caught Miah's arm, her cheeks pink. She whispered, "I have underwear drying on every available bathroom surface."

"I'm sorry," Miah said. "But I couldn't go home like this. Mom can't take any more stress."

"No, of course not. Don't worry about it. Heck, I'm sure the cowboy has seen lacy undies before." Cailin's gaze went up and down Miah. "Are you okay?"

"Yes."

"Then, what the hell happened that has you traipsing around Chicago in your robe in the wee hours of the morning? Where is Zahir? Oh dear Lord, that gunman didn't find you guys, did he?"

"No. But—"

Quint interrupted before she could answer, telling them the apartment was as secure as could be—given what it was—and let himself out.

As soon as the door shut behind him, Cailin double locked it, then turned to Miah. "But what…? Where is 'The Gorgeous One'?"

"At the hotel."

Cailin frowned. "Doing…?"

Miah said, "Trust me, it's a long story, less interesting than it appears."

"Well, I have a brand-new tub of Cherry Garcia to discuss it over."

"Sounds like just the right medicine."

"The prince didn't turn out to be a jerk after all, did he?"

"No. In fact, Cailin, he's even more wonderful than I'd imagined. But…I feel like he's lying to me."

"About what?"

"Look, lend me a sleep shirt, and while I change, you get out that ice cream and two spoons. Then I'll tell you all about it."

"Top dresser drawer." Cailin pulled the ice cream from the freezer. "Hurry."

Miah took the first deep breath she'd been able to pull into her lungs since the fire alarm went off. The tension in her neck and shoulders ebbed away. Being in Cailin's residence always had this effect on her.

Cailin had painted the old wooden floors red, textured the walls a sunshine yellow and filled the rooms with plants and pottery and a few pieces of furniture: a table and two chairs in the kitchen, a futon, TV and antique trunk in the living room, a single bed and triple-wide dresser in the bedroom.

Space for clothes was a priority with Cailin.

Smiling, Miah strode into the bedroom, burrowing her hands into the pockets of the robe. The fingers of her right hand bumped stiff paper. She plucked a small envelope from the pocket. It was addressed to her—in distinct and familiar block letters she'd hoped to never see again. A cold sweat flushed her skin. *The blackmailer's handwriting.*

"Oh God, no."

She held the tiny envelope in a trembling hand, the lettering blurring before her eyes. When could the extortionist have had access to this robe that—until she'd donned it—had hung on a hook in the bathroom of her hotel suite? Had he been one of the people her father sent to scatter rose petals and set out the champagne and fruit? Or was he one of the bodyguards?

Quint?

No. He couldn't have; he hadn't touched her and none of the other guards had been closer to her than Quint. Then, someone else. Most likely one of the hotel guests who'd descended the stairs bumping and shoving into Zahir and her.

Miah sucked in a breath as realization struck. *The fire alarm.* She began to shake. Part of her felt a huge relief that no assassin had set off the alarm, that Zahir was safe at the hotel. The other part of her wanted to scream, to fold in on herself, to throw up. This evil person had disrupted her honeymoon in order to get close enough to thrust this note into the pocket of her robe.

Shivering, she tore open the envelope and read:

Bring fifteen thousand to the usual place and time tomorrow, or the day after the true story of Grant Mohairbi will be sold to the *Clarion*.

Miah's hand went to her mouth. More money? Oh God, he wanted more money? Her inheritance didn't kick in until she reached Nurul. Fifteen thousand would clean out her account.

Khalaf's warning that scandal in America could hurt her in Nurul rang through her head. She had to pay the extortion money. For herself, as well as for her mom. She couldn't risk this story hitting the press. She was going to have to find some way to elude Zahir and his merry band of security folk in order to get to the bank for the money and later to the gallery for the drop. It was a stroke of luck that she'd be staying the night here. None of his guards would follow her in the morning.

But the next morning, she and Cailin discovered Zahir had placed two bodyguards at the apartment door. Cailin drew back from the peephole and asked in disgust, "How'd they get into this building?"

"I'll tell you." Miah huffed with anger. "That darn Texan called Zahir on your bedroom phone, then stuck around until they showed up and let them in as he left. Damn controlling men."

She downed the last of her coffee. "I have to get out of here without them following me, Cailin."

"Why?" Cailin frowned. "You could be in danger, Miah. Shouldn't you take these guys with you?"

"No. I have something to do that I don't want Zahir to know about."

Cailin sighed and shook her head. "He's keeping things from you. You're keeping things from him. Obviously, I'm no expert on relationships, but even *I* know this is not off to a good start for a solid marriage."

"Please, I need your help, not a lecture."

"Help I can give. Always. But don't tell me later that I didn't warn you."

Miah donned a pair of Cailin's jeans that proved three inches too short for her long legs, and a T-shirt a size too large for her less-ample upper body. Cailin tucked Miah's hair into a baseball cap, then insisted she finish the look with large sunglasses. She stepped back and smirked.

"Even your Mom wouldn't recognize you in this getup."

"I doubt that." Miah laughed. "But as long as the bodyguards don't figure out who I am, I'll be happy."

She sneaked out onto the fire escape and made her way down to the ground, dropping the last few feet. After determining no one was following her, or paying her much mind for that matter, she ducked into Wong's Take-Out and called a cab.

She arrived at her mother's building half an hour later. The day doorman, Barney, a wiry man with hollowed cheeks, beefy arms and a ready smile, had none of the pretensions of Snooty Stan. Miah returned his gracious greeting, then explained about not having her key or her identification. Barney rode with her to the penthouse, vouched for her to the bodyguards and let her in. It was early; she'd planned it that way, knowing her mother would still be asleep. She entered, spoke to the duty nurse and stole into her room.

She raced to her closet, quickly selected a tailored suit her mother and Zahir would both approve of, dressed and applied makeup, brushed her hair until it shone, then stuffed her bank book into a spare purse. She had no choice but to leave past the bodyguards, but she guessed neither would follow or accompany her; both had been instructed to stay at the penthouse.

In the lobby, she found Barney had secured her a taxi. Miah gave the cabby the name of her bank and sat back, her hands knotted. She arrived twenty minutes before Chicago First Federal would open for the day. She ordered a latte in a coffee shop across the street and settled at a window table to watch and wait.

As soon as the bank opened, she made the withdrawal, getting the money in thousand-dollar bills. She put the cash into a plain business envelope, stuck the envelope into her purse, and started for the Brinkmire Cavalli Gallery, as she had done three other times.

She'd walked two blocks when a man's voice stopped her cold. "You have given my men the slip, Princess, but you can't get away from me that easily."

Zahir.

The heat from his hands seemed to sear through her suit as he firmly gripped her shoulders and spun her to face him. Her heart hitched, and fire flared in her cheeks. How long had he been following her. How had he found her? Had he had someone tailing her the whole time? Why hadn't she paid more attention? The envelope in her purse seemed to thump against her side as if it were a beeper set on "vibrate". She had to shake off the guilt she felt radiating from her. She put her hands on her hips and glared back at him.

"Good morning to you, too...*love*."

Her intended sarcasm had none of the distracting effect she'd been seeking. His frown deepened.

"What are you doing? Why did you leave Cailin's? Where are you going?"

He was dressed in another of his tailor-made suits, this one a dove gray, his dress shirt white, his tie silver with teeny wine-colored flecks. Not a strand of his raven hair was out of place. Only his eyes gave away that he'd spent the night in pursuits other than rest or sleep. Other than the pleasures a groom should have enjoyed.

Despite her anger, her heart went out to him. Thus far, this marriage was not exactly the bargain he'd counted on, either. Not caring whether or not public displays of affection were royal protocol, she reached up and touched his smoothly shaven cheek. "I'm very glad to see you, Zahir. I've been so anxious. Why didn't you call me?"

"I did. This morning. Your friend, Cailin, told me you were checking on your mother. I decided to meet you there, and discovered you'd been and gone."

"Yes. Mom was still in bed, still asleep. I told the attending nurse not to mention my 'visit.'"

"Why go there, then, if you were afraid to disturb her?"

"I had to get some clothes, of course." She bit back the anxiety that threatened. His interrogation was robbing her of precious time. Her palms dampened. "How did you find me?"

"You're very good at changing the subject, love." Suspicion hovered in his dark eyes—a cold steady gleam. ''The question is, what's going on? What are you up to, Miah?''

She swallowed against the certainty that he knew she was up to something. She felt trapped. The need to rush chewed her nerves. She had to drop the envelope. Had to have it there before the blackmailer arrived at the gallery to pick it up—or he would follow through on his threat. But how could she get rid of Zahir?

''I was just planning on doing some shopping, maybe visiting a local gallery or two. I didn't know how many hours I'd have to fill until I heard from you.''

''And you thought you should go out in public alone? Unprotected? Given what's been happening?''

Oh, yeah, great lie. If he hadn't been sure before that she was up to something, she'd just cinched it for him. Miah fought the panic building in her, with every sweep of the hands on her watch. ''Zahir, I've spent my whole life moving about in public without the need of escorts. I'm as used to that as you are to the bodyguards.''

His expression softened. He seemed about to stroke her hair, but stopped himself. Disappointment shivered through her, loss for the touch she hadn't received, he hadn't given. The tension pumping through her veins left her aching to step into his embrace, to open her heart and share her secret with him. But she didn't trust him enough for that.

''I can't help but worry, love.''

His words stung. If she could only tell him that the person who'd set off the alarm last night was not the gunman who'd come after him at their wedding, he'd likely relax a bit. But that was not an option. Her stomach pinched harder. For the time being, she had to act as though she shared his suspicions. ''Did you find something at the suite? One of the nasty devices that Quint mentioned to me?''

''Nothing.''

He sounded frustrated. She hugged the purse closer. If only he'd found something that could lead her to the identity of the extortionist. ''What about fingerprints on the alarm bell?''

''Only a couple of smudges that could indicate the person who activated the alarm wore gloves or used a hankie or something.''

''So, it's safe to return to the suite?'' She'd spoken so softly that her breath seemed to caress the air between them. Images sprang to her mind of their last seconds in that candlelit room, and Miah felt suddenly self-conscious with this man she'd been ready to give herself to the night before. In the glare of daylight, the glare of his suspicions, she was less certain.

''Yes, love, the suite is now safe, but we don't need to spend the day there. We're on our honeymoon. And so far, it hasn't been nearly as much fun as I meant it to be.'' He folded her arm through his, making her understand that he wasn't leaving her to roam around Chicago on her own. ''Let's have breakfast, then we can shop or visit those galleries you suggested.''

''That sounds lovely,'' Miah said, panic building in her. As they strode down the street, she checked her watch. Breakfast. The payoff. Zahir dogging her every movement. *Oh God, how was she going to manage this?*

Chapter Eight

Zahir lay on his jail cot, as unmoving as stone. His eyes were shut, blocking out all light as if he wandered at midnight in a starless, moonless sky, as unseeing as Habib, the old blind one who frequented the square in Bulzar, capital city of Imad. Habib had once been a vital, hale man, the bravest of the brave. He had daily risked his life capping well fires in the country's oil fields. Wildcatters knew the dangers inherent in their job, but Habib often boasted that nothing made him feel more alive than when he saw that boiling black smoke climbing toward the sun and he faced that deadly blaze head-on.

"Better than sex," he'd say, grinning with spoiled teeth. "I knew, of course, sooner or later, that devil would bite me back."

And it had. A misjudgment, a too-slow reaction and a near fatal explosion that had left him with a limp, without his sight, that had led to his present life as a beggar and a thief.

Zahir often took pity on the wretch, gave him pocket change, listened to his stories. For he had figured out that Habib was not the fool others took him to be. As per the human condition, people often spoke louder or shouted at those who were blind as if it were their hearing and not their sight that had been lost. Or they forgot he was there or ignored him, discounted him because he could not see. Therefore Habib gleaned knowledge that Zahir often found interesting and even more often found useful.

Last week, he'd recalled the old man telling him once that though he no longer possessed the gift of sight, he saw more clearly than when he had, much more clearly than men with all of their senses intact. He'd laughed and said, "'Tis a pity all mankind cannot lose the ability to see just long enough to learn what I have learned, that there is power in the other senses. Animal power. A reconnecting with one's instincts."

And so, in these past few days, Zahir had begun to teach himself the art of seeing like a blind man. Of honing the senses Allah had given him and that he'd heretofore ignored, for the most part.

It was working, too. He no longer merely heard noises beyond the door where his captives moved. Now, he could identify some of the movements, could tell how many people were in that outer room, could almost identify each individual by the sound of their footfalls, their peculiar scents, or, if the door was shut as it was now, by their inflections of voice.

This newly acquired skill would aid him when he could finally execute his escape plan.

Maybe today.

He opened his eyes and stared at the ceiling of his cell, but his concentration was such that he didn't see the cracked plaster, or the teeny spider in one high corner who struggled about its business building an intricate web.

The only intricate web he could see was the one he

and Khalaf had formed and would use to defeat those who had repressed them. He smiled at the thought of their triumph, at how good it would feel bringing down his enemies, making his father and Javid feel the pain they had caused him. They would both rue the day they'd cast him from the family.

But damn it, he had to get out of this hellhole. He drew the broken spring from its hiding place inside the mattress of the cot. He'd honed the edge to switchblade sharpness by stroking it back and forth on the concrete floor beneath the bunk. He touched the point to his fingertip and stared with pleasure at the drop of blood that instantly rose from the tiny wound.

His plan to kill the agent who'd brought his meal the other day had been thwarted when two other agents came in with his lunch. He'd eaten the bland, overcooked sole he'd been served, but had refused to answer the agents' repetitive questions.

He could detect the tension in their voices as he hadn't been able to do even a week ago. He would remember to reward Habib handsomely when next he saw the old man.

His gaze caressed the sharpened spring from tip to stern. Though he knew precisely where to strike a fatal blow with the bedspring, he could not risk taking on more than one person with only the sharp-tipped coil as a weapon. It was not a dagger or a sword. There was no hilt to grip. No way he could thrust it into his victim and retrieve it in a split second to use again. But the next agent who came into his cell alone was a dead man. Zahir would drop him like yesterday's garbage, strip him of his gun—and then find his twin.

For he was more certain than ever that Javid had taken over his life, had adopted the game he and Khalaf had planned on using. Convinced others that he was Zahir. Perhaps even married Miah. Javid would pay with his life for his treachery.

Zahir lifted the bedspring and vowed, "You won't have the last laugh, Javid. That is mine."

Chapter Nine

"You're not eating your breakfast, love. Is something wrong with your food?" Javid took a bite of his steak and eggs, waiting for Miah to explain why she was picking at the fresh fruit and yogurt she'd ordered, to explain what had her so distracted she was running her fork over her plate, creating little trails through the berries like an ant seeking an escape route.

"My food...?"

Vagueness flashed across her face, then cleared as she shook her head, sending her shimmering curtain of ebony hair over her shoulders; the soft rustle filled his ears, ignited his blood. She lifted her fork as though to take a bite of melon.

"It's fine. Sweet." She set her fork down, checked her watch. "I'm not very hungry. Maybe we should go."

He laughed and patted his flat stomach. "I've barely started, love, and I'm ravenous." What he most hungered for was Miah, hungered to shove his fingers through that lush hair, hungered to pull her close and devour those pouting, plump lips, to touch her, to find out how she liked to be touched, where she liked to be touched, to burrow deep inside her, to make her purr as she'd purred last night.

His thoughts sent desire raging through his veins, pooling hot in the deepest, most sensitive parts of him, rousing him with such need that he dare not move. Fearing he might actually shove the plates aside and ravish her right here, right now, he restrained the carnal urges with a painful effort and assuaged his appetite with a piece of steak smeared through poached eggs.

But he couldn't take his eyes off her, couldn't miss the anxiety that had her frowning and glancing at her wristwatch again and again. He had suspected she was up to something the moment he'd learned she had sneaked out of Cailin's to avoid the bodyguards he'd sent to protect her; he had seen confirmation in her eyes when he'd caught up to her, guilt in her lovely amber gaze. He took another bite of steak and eggs now, thinking she'd seemed like a child caught stealing a coveted toy. Hugging her purse to her side as though the stolen toy hid there. She'd paled when he'd suggested dining together, spending the rest of the day together. What was it she had to do that she didn't want him to know?

What could have come up between last night and this morning that had made her not expect to spend today with her groom?

He chewed, mulling possibilities. Nothing concerning her mother or she'd have stayed at the penthouse until Lina awoke. He cut another piece of meat. Nothing with Cailin or she'd have been with her friend when he found her. Maybe it had something to do with her father.

"Have you spoken with Khalaf since last night?"

"No." The question seemed to rattle her more than ever. Her eyes widened with distress. "Have you?"

"No. So, he doesn't know about the alarm or that you spent the night with Ms. Finnigan?"

"Not that I know of." She sank back with obvious relief. "I had no reason to bother him about that."

Javid's eyebrows arched. Why was she so relieved that he had also not "bothered" to inform Khalaf of the disruption to their wedding night? Because Khalaf would surround her with even more security? He glanced at his own men seated at a nearby table, so used to their presence he'd nearly forgotten they were there. She claimed she didn't like being watched. Was that it?

Or did she have something to do that she didn't want to be seen doing?

He sipped orange juice, studying her over the rim of the glass. Her gaze shifted between him and his plate as though willing him to eat faster. He could see she was about at her wits' end. About to insist they leave. Javid figured one more delay would be too much for her, that she'd either bolt or tell him what was going on. He began spreading jam on toast, taking his time, covering every corner from crust to crust.

"Did you pick up your cell phone this morning?"

Before she could respond, a man's shadow fell across Javid. He sensed the security men stiffen, heard them hit their feet. As Javid glanced up, instantly recognizing the intruder, he signaled his men to stand by. The man was not nearly as tall as Javid, but every bit as wide, as well built. His shiny shaved head, artistic black eyebrows, bold green eyes and perpetual smirk had made him a favorite on the wrestling circuit and a celebrity in his own right long before "Big Tony" De Luca gave up the ring to publish the sins and secrets of others in his yellow rag, *The Clarion.*

He'd traded physical violence for emotional violence.

But as if to prove the adage "what goes around comes around," life had kicked back at Big Tony the day his beloved wife committed suicide. Right now, De Luca's famous green eyes were bloodshot and hound dog sad. He wore a dark, well-cut suit and a black armband.

He tipped his head to Miah. "Princess." Then he turned to Javid. "Prince Zahir, I wanted to offer the two of you my best wishes for a long and happy union."

Javid tensed, wondering what this snake *really* wanted, wishing he had a clue as to how well Zahir knew De Luca and vice versa. Too much conversation could prove dangerous. Disastrous. Javid wanted De Luca gone before he said something amiss and De Luca realized he wasn't speaking with Zahir.

"As you can see, my wife and I are dining and would appreciate privacy, if you don't mind, Mr. De Luca."

"*Mister* De Luca? My, how formal we've gotten, Zahir. I assumed we were friends." Every word out of his fleshy lips was tenser than the last. "Or were you only my wife's 'friend'?"

"What are you suggesting, Mr. De Luca?" Miah asked, her cheeks red, anger flashing from her eyes.

"Please, Miah, I'll—"

"No. I don't like what he's implying. Did you and Angie De Luca have an affair, Zahir?" Her question carried across the restaurant. Diners' heads snapped up.

"Okay, that's enough." Fury pushed Javid to his feet. "Leave now, De Luca, or I'll have my men escort you out. Your choice."

"I meant no harm." De Luca gestured as though he were a wrongly accused innocent, and stepped back. "I just wanted to wish you both a longer marriage than mine."

Javid motioned for his men to make sure the publisher left the restaurant. Big Tony waved them off.

"I'm going. I'm going. But, Princess, you might ask

yourself how well you know your prince. He's not the upstanding citizen he claims to be. Marrying you can't legitimize scum like him. You can read about it soon in *The Clarion.*"

"What is he talking about, Zahir?" This time, Miah's voice was nearly a whisper and reed-thin.

"I have no idea." Javid's breakfast lodged like a brick in his belly. Whatever De Luca had on Zahir could blow this whole undercover operation. He had to meet with the Confidential agents ASAP. "De Luca earns his keep by manufacturing lies, and he seems to have a bone to pick with...me."

"Because of his wife?"

"Because he's an idiot. Angie De Luca may have found me attractive, but that's as far as it went. I promise." He signaled for the check, then shoved his plate aside, as anxious now as Miah had seemed earlier. "Why don't we start with some shopping, love?"

While she was trying on clothes, he could put in a call to Chicago Confidential and have Kathy Renk set up that meeting.

Miah shook her head. "I'd rather start at the Brinkmire Cavalli Gallery, a couple of blocks over."

"Oh, why is that?" Damn, he was in no mood to concentrate on art. He ushered her outside into the glorious day, his gaze automatically scanning foot traffic, alert to unexpected dangers as he hadn't been a few days ago.

Miah gazed up at him, hugging her purse to her chest. "They're featuring a new artist. One of his pieces has caught my fancy—a lovely statuette—but I'm not sure yet whether I want to buy it."

"Okay. The gallery it is." How was he going to get

away from Miah long enough for a meeting with the agents?

HOW WAS SHE GOING TO GET AWAY from Zahir long enough to drop the envelope? Elude the watchful eyes of the bodyguards? Miah bit her bottom lip. No one must see her leave the envelope. She could not risk someone other than the extortionist finding it. Taking it. She had no money to replace this payment if the blackmailer missed it.

The Brinkmire Cavalli Gallery was busy for a Sunday afternoon, and as they squeezed inside, Miah felt like a mouse facing a maze. More to break the weighted silence than to convey information, she said to Zahir, "This gallery is privately owned and operated and exhibits everything from the newest up-and-coming painters to antique weaponry."

"So, it has a little something for every taste?"

"Yes."

They fell silent again, and Miah realized he seemed as distracted as she, that he had seemed that way since Big Tony declared *"Marrying you can't legitimize scum like him."* What exactly had *that* meant? Was De Luca calling Zahir scum out of some bitter rivalry over his wife's affections? She realized she didn't know much about Angie De Luca. Such as, why *had* she committed suicide? Because Zahir had ended their affair?

She was surprised to find the idea of her husband sleeping with other women upset her. She knew Zahir's reputation. She'd read the articles. Seen the published photographs. But anything that went on between Zahir and other women before he'd become engaged to her was technically none of her business.

Except he's keeping secrets from you, the little voice

in her mind nagged. More than ever she needed to find out what those secrets were. But first things first. She scanned the faces of the other patrons. Was her black-mailer among them? Watching her? Waiting for her? She checked her watch. Oh God, she'd missed the scheduled drop time by ten minutes. The single bite of melon she'd managed to choke down at breakfast felt wedged in her throat.

"Where's that statuette you're considering?" Zahir asked.

"Uh…" Her gaze flew over the crowd again, and this time she spotted a man who seemed familiar, someone totally out of place in this upscale gallery. Was it…? That shock of red hair, the loose-boned way he held his shoulders as though slouching—the characteristics were inbred in the Finnigan clan. "Rory?"

Cailin's brother spun from the painting he'd been studying. His burnt-sienna eyebrows lifted. "Princess? This is the last place I'd expect to find the royal new-lyweds on their honeymoon."

"And this is the last place I'd expect to find Finni-gan's ace bartender." Miah stepped up and hugged him lightly. "I thought your taste in art ran to hot-rod cars?"

"Oh, that. I need something to talk about with the regulars at the pub." Rory smirked and shrugged. "But there's more to me than meets the eye. You just never looked close enough."

Zahir was scowling at Rory's flirtatious attitude. He laid a possessive arm on Miah's shoulder. "I've seen your friend at Finnigan's Rainbow, love, but we've never been introduced." He didn't wait for her to speak, but addressed himself to Rory. "Prince Zahir Haji Hal-eem."

"Rory Finnigan." Rory didn't seem to know whether

he should offer his hand or bow. Zahir extended his hand and the men shook.

Miah's need to drop off the money seared her nerves. She hadn't time for this inane exchange. She had to go. She was already late. The walls seem to press in on her, sucking the air from the room, casting her surroundings in a surreal glow, magnifying details—the bulge of a gun under a bodyguard's jacket; the diamond stud anchoring Zahir's tie; the thick, solid gold bracelet around Rory's wrist.

She started. If the bracelet was real gold, as it appeared to be, it had to have cost a lot more than Rory could afford on his salary. What had he said to her? *There was more to him than met the eye. She'd just never looked close enough.* She looked now. From haircut to shoes, he appeared to have stepped out of the pages of *GQ*.

He was right. This was not the Rory she knew. *That* Rory couldn't tell Armani from Calvin Klein if his life depended on it. Where had he gotten the money for this makeover?

Was Rory the blackmailer? Was the money to pay for his new image nestled deep in her purse? Miah's stomach churned at the idea. She had known Rory forever, trusted him as if he were her own brother. Would he betray her? Steal from her? She didn't want to believe it. Hated herself for even considering it.

But without more information, what else could she think? She interrupted his departing words. "Nice threads, Rory. Come into some kind of windfall lately?"

He blanched. Then flashed a smile of even white teeth. She thought of the Big Bad Wolf grinning at Little Red Riding Hood with every intention of eating her. Rory said, "A windfall? Like yours, you mean? Trust me, Princess, nothing *that* lucrative."

With that, he left.

Miah stared after him, realizing she could barely pull in breath from the tightness in her chest. There were too many areas of her life that had become gaping questions. Her mind whirled and dipped with confusion and ugliness. She wanted to go somewhere quiet and sit long enough to think about all this, but at the moment something more pressing called her.

"Where's the statuette, love?"

"In another room, but I have to do something else first."

With difficulty, she pushed away everything she was feeling to concentrate on her most immediate problem. The blackmailer. She had to deliver the extortion money *now.* "I'll be right back, Zahir."

Zahir gestured for one of the bodyguards to accompany her.

Miah flushed. "Really, Zahir, I'd rather go to the ladies' room alone."

Before he thought to argue with her, she scooted off. She made a line for the bathrooms, but strode past them to an exit door near the rear of the building. She checked to make sure no one was watching or following her, then ducked into a narrow hallway and hurried to the single waste bin near the door. She plucked the envelope from her purse and dropped it into the bin.

Seconds later, she was in the ladies' room at the row of sinks. A relieved sob spilled from her. Her knees wobbled and tears stung her eyes. She blinked them back, grabbed a paper towel, wet it and dabbed cold water on her heated cheeks. Her face was too red, too warm. Her heart pounding too fast. She dipped the towel under the cold water again and again, glad when the high color began to fade.

Lord, how long had she been gone? Zahir would be looking for her. She retraced her steps past the hallway where she'd dropped the money, some small part of her hoping to spot the blackmailer at the trash bin. But the hallway was vacant.

Maybe she should stick around. Find out who the extortionist was. Who was doing this to her. All she asked was one good look at the blackmailer. No, she had to get back to Zahir. She turned—and slammed into him.

"Miah, there you are." He steadied her.

She tensed as he studied her face, expecting him to comment on her red eyes.

Instead, he said, "Look, I know you wanted to see about buying that statuette, but could it wait for another day?"

"Of course." Miah felt a rush of relief.

"Good. I think we should go. This crowd makes me uneasy. We're too much of a target here."

"But what about safety in numbers?"

"Crowds won't deter whoever is after us. In fact, that might make the challenge more tempting."

"All right." As badly as Miah wanted to find out who was blackmailing her, she wouldn't risk Zahir's life.

They stepped outside. Mehemet waited at the curb beside their limousine. Zahir caught her arm, guiding her toward the car. A man shouted, "Prince Zahir!"

Zahir froze, his grip tightening on her arm, his head jerking toward the voice, his expression alarmed, his stance protective.

Miah's heart raced as her gaze found the source of her husband's distress. Bobby Redwing. The reporter was charging them with a camera, flashing shots as he neared. As usual, his flowery aftershave reached them before he did. He had dirty blond hair greased to his head like some fifties rock and roll singer. His eyes were large, baby-boy blue, his nose bumped. His Adam's apple, his most prominent feature, was huge and the source of his nickname. He didn't really smile, but curled his lip in a sneer, just like the nasty carrion he resembled.

"How the hell did he know we were here?" Zahir muttered.

Rory? Miah blanched at the thought. No. Rory hated the reporter for the way he'd treated Cailin. He'd never have sicced The Buzzard on them.

So, what *was* he doing here? Was Bobby the extortionist? Had he come to collect his blackmail money, then seen her inside the gallery with Zahir and decided to take advantage of her even more by using this as a photo opportunity?

"Back off, Redwing." Zahir pulled Miah close, shielding her in his embrace. She could feel his heart thumping, feel the tension in his body, but his words and his voice were calm, controlled. "Keep your distance."

The bodyguards moved like a fence around Miah and Zahir, but even that didn't stop Redwing. He said, "This is a free country, Your Highness. You've heard of freedom of the press. So, why don't you just relax and smile?" Bobby kept snapping photos as he neared, the flash blinding Miah.

"Give me that camera." Zahir went for Bobby, but Bobby danced to one side, then the other, chortling like a loon...until Zahir caught him by the shirtfront.

Then Bobby crowed, seeming oblivious to the fact that he was no longer controlling the situation. He held the camera as far from Zahir as he could. "Got me some nice front page material here."

Zahir ripped the camera from his grip, then released Bobby with a shove. Bobby landed on his butt, then sprang up with the speed of someone with more zeal than brains. Miah found it odd that Bobby didn't shriek at Zahir to give him back the camera. Zahir seemed not to notice. He just grinned and wrenched the film free, exposing it to the sunlight.

Bobby reached into his jacket to withdraw something. Miah caught Zahir's arm. "He's got a gun."

The bodyguards all went for their firearms. But Bobby laughed louder, holding a smaller camera up for everyone to see. Before Zahir could grab this one, he leapt out of reach, snapping several shots of Zahir with the exposed film hanging from his fingertips, his face a mask of rage. He caught the guards holding their guns on him, and Miah cowering beside her groom with the terror she felt frank on her face.

"Get that camera!" Zahir dropped Bobby's big camera and lunged for the reporter.

"Here, Redwing!" Big Tony sprang from the watching crowd like a football receiver going out for the long bomb. Bobby executed a perfect forward pass, tossing the small camera to his boss. De Luca scrambled into the limo and sped away.

Zahir held himself as stiff as the flagpole beside him, fists at his sides. Miah suspected he'd like nothing better than to punch Redwing. His voice, when it came out, was hard and dangerously low. "If you don't keep away from us, Redwing, I'll have you arrested."

"For what? Doing my job?" Bobby sneered.

"For stalking."

He laughed. "Threats won't deter me, your princeship. I've got the United States Constitution on my side.

I'm guaranteed freedom of speech, and the right to liberty and justice for all.'' Whistling, he started down the street, then stopped and tossed over his shoulder ''Can you claim the same for the citizens under your rule?''

Chapter Ten

Miah closed out the chaos of angry voices surrounding her. Zahir's. The bodyguards'. She shut her eyes and laid her head against the soft leather of the limousine seat, her fingertips kneading her temples, trying to ease the pain creeping across her scalp. Her mother wasn't the only one who could use a little less stress in her life.

Nothing like longing for something she couldn't have.

The stress in her life was spiraling upward, not downward. What she needed at the end of the day was a soft place to fall, strong arms to embrace her, keep her safe. Zahir should be that for her, but De Luca's and Redwing's accusations had stirred her suspicions of her husband more than ever. She really didn't *know* Zahir. All the information she had on him came from her father, and from *him*.

It hadn't occurred to her before now to question what she'd been told, to wonder whether either might have lied, perhaps embroidered the truth to win her over. She gazed at her husband, at his flawless face, the lines and planes of character, the black lashes dense against his tanned skin, his brow creased in a secretive scowl, *and she wondered now.*

Would she find him more interesting, or less, if she

unearthed his secrets? Could she keep her mother and herself safe if she didn't?

The limousine pulled to a stop, and Miah realized she'd expected they'd be returning to the Royal Princess Hotel suite, but that's not where they were. She peered out of the darkened limo window at the shop directly opposite. Tevo's Fine Jewelry. Her husband was grinning at her.

"Why are we stopping here, Zahir?"

"Because I have a surprise for you, love."

The last thing Miah wanted was another surprise. Even one as pleasant as this promised to be. She'd thought of nothing but the accusations hurled at her husband, while he seemed able to shirk off the charges without a second thought. Like a man with a clear conscience? Or one who knew the denunciations were true?

She joined Zahir on the sidewalk, her stomach in knots. The bodyguards stood watch outside while she and Zahir were buzzed inside. The windows and door all had bars as defense against break-ins and theft, though from what she glimpsed, the shop had a low-budget, austere appearance—as if nothing of value or importance was sold here. She cast a hesitant, questioning gaze at her husband.

"Zahir?"

Zahir laughed. "Trust me, love. Some of the world's most valuable gems have passed through Tevo's skilled hands. He doesn't need frills or expensive advertisements. He's an artist."

Tevo stood behind the single display counter. In his late forties, he had the baby face of a teenager, pale cheeks quick to color, discerning blue eyes, soft brown hair combed over a balding dome, and a jeweler's glass on a chain around his neck. But it was his hands she noticed, the long tapered fingers like fine instruments, the skin as abnormally white as if he wore gloves. He waved his hands dramatically.

"Ah, Your Highness. You have come for it."

"Yes, Tevo."

Zahir introduced Miah to the jeweler, who bowed in respect, then studied her. "I see now why you chose as you did, Prince Zahir. Her eyes are most unusual. Oh, yes, you chose well."

Tevo excused himself and disappeared into a back room. Miah took advantage of this first moment alone with her husband in hours. "Why, Zahir, did Bobby Redwing ask whether you guaranteed freedom of speech, liberty and justice for the citizens under your rule? Was he speaking of Nurul?"

Zahir's smile saddened. He closed the space between them, tenderly brushed a lock of hair off her forehead, his touch warm, reassuring. He leaned down to her, speaking in a low voice. "Promise me, Miah, that you won't waste a moment's worry on anything that sleazy newspaper claims. Or buy into Redwing's and De Luca's barbs."

"Is there any truth in their accusations?"

His gaze seemed to stroke her face. "Judge me for what you know to be true, what you see, what your heart can feel."

She wanted to believe the earnest gleam in his eyes, but she'd have preferred a more forthright answer. She pulled in a wobbly breath, inhaling his spicy aftershave, and realized she yearned to draw the scent of him into her, yearned to fold herself into his arms and accept his reassurances.

But she couldn't risk buying into lies. She ran a finger down his tie, felt the steady beat of his heart and drew strength in the connection, as small as it might be. "The whole world is aware of some of the inhumanities that occur in the Middle East. Especially to women. I don't want that kind of rulership for Nurul."

"Nor do *I*." His sensuous mouth tightened and his hand went to his heart, as though he were making a pledge, a promise to her, to himself, the gesture stirring something intense in his eyes.

She laid her hand on his, sealing the pledge. "I'll hold you to that."

"Do." He grinned and kissed her temple, then stepped back at the sound of the jeweler returning.

"Ah, here you go." Tevo laid out a black velvet cloth, then spread on it something that looked like a twisted, sparkling ray of sunlight. Miah stepped closer, transfixed by the simplicity of the delicate strand of small golden diamonds, a necklace as thin as string, as lovely as a Chicago sunrise.

"Oh, Zahir," she said, rendered breathless by the beauty of his gift.

"Your prince designed it himself." Tevo touched the necklace with his pale fingers, as though he couldn't believe he'd shaped this wondrous piece of jewelry. "I wanted it to be heavier, but he wouldn't hear of it. Said gems should enhance the beauty of the wearer and that the woman he had in mind was so beautiful she didn't need diamonds, but—"

"But she deserves them," Zahir finished.

Miah's heart fluttered with joy. She'd been watching Zahir as Tevo spoke. He seemed embarrassed under the jeweler's praise. He was indeed a puzzle, this man she'd married, an incomplete picture that became more and more intriguing with every revelation.

"May I?" Zahir gathered the necklace.

Miah lifted her hair as he hooked the loop at her nape. The strand of diamonds settled against her skin as though designed for the hollow between her collar bones. She spun toward Zahir. He seemed stricken with such a look of awe that her stomach dipped. He grazed his knuckles down her cheek, his gaze locked with hers.

"It's beautiful. You're beautiful."

Miah's heart swelled at the compliment, not because she thought she was beautiful but because he made her *feel* beautiful clear down to her soul, and overwhelmed her with desire. How could a man wield such power? She might not know him well, but she was falling for him more every minute she spent with him.

"Thank you."

Tevo said, "I have a mirror. Would you like to see?"

But Miah shook her head. She didn't need a mirror. She'd seen herself in Zahir's eyes; no glass image could improve on that reflection.

Zahir's beeper went off. She jumped, then laughed nervously. He gave her an understanding smile as he drew the pager from his pocket and checked the readout. His expression altered, as though dropping a mask, and his shoulders shifted, as though shedding some weight or facade.

The change was subtle but unmistakable. Miah's new sense of trust in him went south. She tensed. "Is something wrong?"

"Yes and no. Business. I need to meet with my contacts at one of the local oil distributors."

Obviously this wasn't a scheduled meeting. "Is there some kind of emergency?"

"Nothing to cause that frown, Miah. Tevo, my thanks."

Zahir ushered Miah out to the waiting limo. "Come

on, love. I think you should show off your necklace to your mother. I think she'd appreciate knowing that you're okay and seeing that you are, in fact, having a wonderful time.''

''Yes, I suppose.'' Why did she suspect there was more to this simple meeting than he was sharing? ''But why do I have the feeling that you want to make sure I'm somewhere you won't have to worry about me?''

''Is that so awful?''

From his perspective, she supposed it wasn't. But from her point of view, she'd be as penned as a dog in a cage—while he could run free. The lovely necklace that nestled her collar bones felt suddenly choking, a diamond-studded leash.

''Okay. The last thing I want is to cause you worry.'' Miah forced a smile. She had no intention of sitting at her mother's twiddling her thumbs. Her trust in Zahir was too easily shaken. Every time she felt she could believe in him, something or someone shattered that fragile confidence. She needed to know he was going where he said, meeting whom he said.

On the way up to the penthouse, Zahir said, ''Though the doctor assures me Lina is better I'd like to see for myself, if she's awake, or at least hear what the nurse has to say. She's been on site and will have noticed little things she might not have told the doctor.''

He'd been in contact with the doctor today? Her heart gave a crazy thump. He hadn't said a word to her, had known instinctively that she'd be checking in with the doctor and nurses. What a constant enigma was this man she'd married, surprising her, confusing her at every turn. Ribbons of warmth spiraled through her, one of amazement, one of awe, one of gratitude, one of affection—one of budding love.

The nurse met them in the foyer. After a formal welcome, she said, ''I must insist that you both be very quiet. My patient is napping. But her coloring is much better this afternoon, Mrs. Haleem. Her appetite, too.''

Something tight broke loose in Miah's chest. She pulled in a full breath. No matter what else was going on in her life, her mother's health was constantly on her mind. This was great news, and she beamed at the nurse. ''Thank you. Mr. Haleem is leaving, but I'll be so quiet you won't even know I'm here.''

''Well—'' Zahir touched her cheek ''—that's my cue to be off. I'll pick you up in a couple of hours.''

''Sure.''

As he closed the front door, Miah dashed to the back exit and took the service elevator to the lobby. She arrived in time to spy Zahir striding toward Mehemet, who held the door of the limousine open. *Oh, no.* She dug her nails into her palms. She hadn't thought beyond following him, hadn't made a contingent plan in case he went by car. Now what would she do?

Zahir glanced toward the building. Miah gasped and leapt behind a huge planted palm. Had he seen her? Her heart slammed her chest wall. She held her breath, waiting for Zahir to come into the foyer and demand to know what she was doing hiding behind potted plants.

She risked a peek around the palm. Zahir was dismissing the limousine. Maybe he was going to walk to wherever his meeting was. She stood rigid, hoping. But as the limo pulled off into traffic, she saw him talking to Barney, the day doorman. As she watched, Barney hailed Zahir a cab. Zahir climbed into the cab alone, the usual contingent of bodyguards absent.

Curious, she moved from behind the plant and waited until his cab drove away. Then she raced out to Barney.

He turned, surprised to see her. "Oh, Princess Miah. The prince has just gone."

"I know." Her pulse raced. "Barney, did you by any chance hear where he was going?"

Barney squared his shoulders. "Why, yes, the Langston Building."

"Oh, that's right." Miah struggled to keep the urgency from her voice. "Barney, could you get me a cab?"

TRAFFIC ON THE LOOP was hectic, bumper to bumper this afternoon. The Langston Building, a skyscraper in the heart of the city, was a block or so east of Michigan Avenue and hugged the Chicago River. Miah's cab arrived as Zahir was stepping from his. She fumbled in her purse for the fare, taking her time, watching Zahir glance in every direction as though making certain he hadn't been followed. It seemed a strange thing to do if he was there for a legitimate meeting with oil distributors. And why was he alone? Unprotected? He might keep secrets from her, but from his loyal guards?

With one last look around, he went into the building.

She paid her fare, then stole inside. This high-rise rented office space to all types of businesses in the upper levels, and shops, boutiques and restaurants on the ground floor. Today, the lobby was packed. Her pulse beat erratically as she scanned the crush of shoppers and workers, trying to find Zahir before he saw her.

There. By a bank of elevators. His raven hair glistening in the overhead lights. Several people waited with him. One was taller than Zahir, wearing a Stetson. Why did he seem so familiar? The tall man shifted, looking over the crowd around him, his glance furtive. Miah's pulse skidded as she got a shot of his profile.

Quint.

Acting as if he didn't see or know Zahir. Acting as suspicious as Zahir. He wasn't dressed for security, either. His suit was Western. Well-cut. Expensive. Did Zahir pay him so well, he could afford tailor-made or designer suits?

Or was Quint not who she thought he was?

As she puzzled this possibility, Zahir glanced at Quint. To Miah's amazement, he made no acknowledgment. Her curiosity bloomed larger. What were these two up to?

She strode to a newsstand near a wall of windows that overlooked the river, noticing that a few brave souls traversed the walkway, oblivious to the pounding heat. She purchased a magazine, then, holding her head low and the magazine high, she pretended to be enthralled by the article she was reading and sidled closer to where Zahir and Quint stood. A bell sounded. Elevator doors sprang open. Several people exited. Then those waiting with Zahir began boarding. A spry, elderly woman darted on and planted herself in front of the numbers pad as though she owned it, asking everyone which floor they wanted.

Zahir looked annoyed, but speaking loud enough for Miah to hear, said, "Penthouse."

Miah slipped from his range of vision, her hand going to the necklace. What should she do? She wasn't sure she could risk following. What if she got to the penthouse, and Zahir or Quint saw her?

She strode back to the windows and slumped against the wall, blowing out a frustrated breath. Now what? She might as well be outside, her brain frying in the cruel heat for the ideas that came to her. She glanced aimlessly over the lobby, and as her gaze landed on an information desk, inspiration hit. She straightened and headed for it.

As she approached the counter, Miah scanned the board over the clerk's head that listed all the offices and businesses in the building. As far as she could tell, the only company occupying the penthouse was Solutions, Inc. It didn't sound like the name of an oil distributor to her.

"May I help you?" the clerk asked.

He was a serious-looking young man with a clean-shaven face and long dark hair cinched at his nape. He was well-dressed and nice-looking enough to grace the cover of *Businessman's Monthly,* if he'd been a young executive.

His hazel eyes peered out from behind wire-rimmed glasses, tracing over her clothes, the necklace. He didn't lack a discerning eye. Or a huge ego. A leering smile dragged his lips apart. He liked what he saw. Clearly thought she felt the same about him.

Thank God for men with healthy and unhealthy egos, Miah thought. *There were times when a woman could use them to her advantage.* She slid her arm onto his counter and gave him a dazzling smile, then rounded her eyes to look totally guileless and in need of his "incredible" expertise. "I have a meeting in this building with an oil distributor and, for the life of me, I can't recall the company name, but I was sure it was in the penthouse. Is Solutions, Inc. an oil distributor?"

He leaned toward her and shook his head. "I don't believe there are any oil distributors in this building. I think someone has given you the wrong address. Perhaps you'd like to step back here and use my phone. Call your secretary or…?"

"Then, Solutions, Inc. isn't an oil distributor?"

He reached an index finger toward her arm. "Now, didn't I just tell you that, honey?"

Miah stamped down the urge to smack the man's hand

away. "Well, then, what kind of business is Solutions, Inc.?"

"Something to do with computers for big companies."

"Computers?"

"Yes." His hand landed on Miah's arm.

She tugged free and stepped out of his reach.

"Thank you," Miah mumbled. She returned to the bank of elevators, considered going to the penthouse and confronting Zahir and Quint, crashing into that office and finding out exactly what the hell they were up to. Because it sure as hell wasn't oil business. And it sure as hell wasn't computers. A prince didn't handle the buying of computers for his companies. He hired people to take care of details like that.

In the end, she wandered outside. The heat stole her breath, made her itch to shed these clothes, this frustration. She needed a drink and could use some of Cailin's insight. She wasn't that far from Finnigan's Rainbow.

She could walk but it was too damn hot. She hailed a cab and settled in, grateful for the air-conditioning, for the chance to get off her feet, even if only for a few minutes. A muted ringing jarred her out of her reverie. She pulled her cell phone from her purse, fearing it might be Zahir and that he'd realize from the background noises that she wasn't in her mother's penthouse. But the lighted panel showed her father's private number. Her tensed muscles relaxed.

"Hello, Father."

"Miah. It warms my heart to be so addressed."

Khalaf's words warmed *her* heart. She had missed the connection a daughter shared with her father, missed it more than she'd even known until he found her. She needed that connection now more than ever.

"Father, thank you so much for the wonderful surprise in our suite last night. It was incredible."

"Then, your honeymoon goes smoothly?"

She hesitated. Her honeymoon had gone anything but smoothly. She'd been wed over twenty-four hours now and the marriage was yet to be consummated. But she could hardly tell her father that. "It's wonderful."

"There have been no more 'incidents,' then?"

"None," she lied. She feared he'd see the fire alarm going off at the hotel as another "incident" connected to the shooting, but she knew otherwise and decided not to waste time with that.

"Where are you and Zahir now?"

She didn't tell him where she was. "Zahir is at a meeting with one of the local oil distributors."

"Oh?" Khalaf sounded surprised. "He ran off from his bride to take care of business? If he had contacted me, I would have seen to it. His honeymoon should not be disrupted for any reason."

She'd never have guessed what a romantic her father was from his appearance. But the roses, candles and champagne last night, and his willingness to take over business for Zahir today, allowed her a small window into why her birth mother, Anjali, must have fallen in love with him. "It was an emergency meeting."

He was silent for a moment. "Do you know where the meeting is taking place?"

"I think it's at a company called Solutions, Inc."

"I've never heard of this company. You say they distribute oil?"

"No. Computers."

"I am very confused, daughter. Why would Zahir meet with a computer company about oil distribution?"

Exactly. "I have no idea. I guess I'll have to wait until he returns and ask him."

"Yes. I think that would be wise. Meanwhile, I'll see what I can learn about this company...this Solutions, Inc."

"Will you? That would be great. Only, Father, please don't tell Zahir you learned about this company from me. Okay?"

"As you wish, daughter dear. This shall remain between us."

She heard a smile in his voice. The knowledge that she and her real father were sharing their first father-daughter confidence filled Miah with such warmth that she thought her heart might burst. Nothing and no one was ever going to take *this* father from her.

Chapter Eleven

Javid sat in the special ops room with his head in his hands, his temples pounding with tension. The past twenty-four hours had been pure hell. He'd married a woman betrothed to his brother—*an infatuating, mind-bending woman he was half in love with, a woman he was totally beguiled by.* He'd been shot at and nearly killed shortly after saying "I do," and he didn't even know whether *he* or his twin had been the assassin's target. He'd had his wedding night interrupted, *at a most inopportune time.* Had had his bride ripped from his side and had had to allow her to spend the night in an insecure building, *when he'd rather have passed the evening exploring every intimate curve and crevice of her ripe body, pleasuring her, being pleasured.*

Ah, Miah.

Instead of making a deeper connection with her, as he'd intended this morning, he'd been cursed and threatened and all but exposed. A door opened and his head jerked up. The Chicago Confidential agents—Law, Vincent, Whitney, Andy and Quint—filed in, and he thought of how he'd come to know and trust this group over the past few months. Together, they had gone through the fire and back, but this time, the flame was so hot, he feared it would burn them all.

Vincent was eyeing him, assessing him, trying for a handle on the situation. His black attire and somber expression brought to mind a funeral director. How apropos, Javid thought.

"You look like hell, Javid," Vincent commented as he took his seat at the round table. "Must have been some wedding night."

"You want to tell them, or should I?" Quint asked Javid, his crinkled blue eyes bright beneath the black brim of his Stetson.

Javid indicated he'd do the honors. "From midnight on, I was supervising a sweep of the Royal Princess Hotel and of our honeymoon suite, from top to bottom, looking for signs of a bomb or any other nasty device left behind by whoever set off the hotel fire alarm."

"Someone set off the fire alarm?" Whitney asked, sounding perplexed. Once again, her Northeastern lilt roused memories of his childhood, of his brother. "Why would that cause you to do a sweep of the hotel and your rooms?"

"Javid's convinced it was done in order to roust him and his blushin' bride from their suite," Quint said. "I'm not sure he's wrong."

"Why? Was something found?" Vincent's black eyes were fathomless, serious, matching Javid's mood.

Javid shook his head. "Nothing—that's the odd thing."

"Yeah, we searched high and low." Quint lifted his hat and ran his hand over his shaggy brown hair. "But came up as empty-handed as a beggar on Lake Shore Drive."

"Then, why are you convinced, Javid, that the point

was to get you and Miah to leave your suite?'' Whitney leaned toward him, her golden-red hair shifting forward, her gray eyes narrowed.

"I can't explain it." Javid tapped two fingers against the spot on his chest over his heart, the site of the old scar. "But I know it."

"Intuition? That's what you're basing this on?" Law mouthed the stem of his reading glasses, studying Javid for a moment, as he might a witness in court. "I mean, isn't it possible that a prankster or a drunk activated the alarm? I don't mean to sound insensitive to your situation, Javid. Nor do I mean any offense. You've every reason for wariness. And nerves. Hell, if someone had tried murdering me at my wedding, I'd probably be jumping at shadows, too."

Javid's muscles tightened, frustration knotting his belly. He couldn't hand them proof, nothing they could see, touch or call undeniable, but he knew it was more than paranoia. More than gut instinct. He and Miah had been flushed from their room for a reason. He just didn't know what that reason was. Yet.

"I have made enemies in my quest to shut down terrorists worldwide. I don't know if one of those enemies is after me, Javid, or if it is someone after Zahir."

"I think Law is suggesting the fire alarm was unconnected to the attempt on your life yesterday—a coincidence." Whitney's voice was a soft contrast to Law's deep tones.

Law shrugged off his suit coat as though settling down to defend his argument. "Is it such a far-fetched scenario?"

"No." Vincent's somber tone intimated he considered it probable, too. "But Javid did what had to be done.

Caution first. Lives depend on it. Quantum depends on it.''

Javid appreciated Vincent not dismissing his concerns out of hand. He might not be so generous if their positions were reversed. He had not one whit of proof to support his conviction that the alarm had gone off to get to Miah and him. But he believed it. For what purpose and by whom, however, remained a mystery.

Vincent's black gaze landed on him. ''I'm assuming you didn't call this meeting to discuss coincidences. Something more has happened, right?''

''Right.'' Javid ran a hand down his tie, reassured that he still appeared put together on the outside, even though he was anything but inside. ''This morning while I was having breakfast with my wife, we were interrupted by Big Tony De Luca. He made some barbed remarks about his deceased wife, Angie, and Zahir, then addressed himself to Miah and stated something to the effect that 'marrying her wouldn't legitimize scum like me.'''

''De Luca of *The Clarion*?'' Law had placed his suit jacket on his chair back and now rolled his shirtsleeves to his elbows as though readying to physically dig into whatever problem faced them.

''The same,'' Javid said. ''He intimated that she could read all about it in the next edition of his paper.''

''Read all about what?'' Quint's boot heels clicked together.

''I don't know.'' Javid glanced from one to the other of the agents as he spoke. ''I'm at a complete loss about De Luca's relationship—his wife Angie's relationship—with my brother. I brushed off De Luca's insinuations of an affair between Angie and Zahir by implying the woman had meant nothing more to 'me' than a social contact. That further incited Big Tony. Do any of you know whether Zahir and Angie De Luca were ever romantically involved?''

He looked for confirmation, but all the agents were shaking their heads. His hopes for a quick resolution died like roses in an icy wind, so much rotting mulch, more fertilizer for his frustrations. ''Andy, is there any way you could ferret out the truth?''

''You betcha, but it'll take a few hours,'' Andy replied, glancing up from his computer screen, his intelligent eyes unexpected in his boyish face. ''Talking about coincidences, though, it's kinda funny De Luca seeking you out this morning, since we've been checking whether or not the speedboat driven by the shooter yesterday was his.''

''Yeah,'' Quint drawled. ''De Luca's name just keeps poppin' up like a curious prairie dog peekin' out of his hole to see what he's missin'.''

Andy grinned his loopy smile. ''Too bad the lead was bogus. Big Tony's ride hasn't left its marina mooring since his wife's death last month.''

''Then, that's a dead end.'' Whitney pushed her hair behind one ear.

''Never was a good lead in my opinion.'' Law put on his reading glasses. ''We only checked it out because Miah's friend 'thought' it looked like De Luca's boat.''

''Her friend wasn't wrong about the look of the boat.'' Andy directed the agents' gazes to their monitors. ''As you can see, it was the same size and color as De Luca's. Unfortunately, it's one of Fiberform's best-selling models.'' Andy spouted statistics like a boat salesman. ''Police reports show a Fiberform like the one we're seeking was stolen the night before from a local stockbroker. It turned up yesterday evening, tied to a private dock along the river. I'm getting a copy of the fingerprint report from a source at the Harbor Patrol. I'll match them through ViCAPS if possible."

"They won't belong to De Luca," Vincent said, stony-faced, knowing that the Violent Criminal Apprehension Program couldn't help them in this instance. "Man's a coward. His weapons are newsprint and nasty words."

"But you can't deny he's a showman, dear." Whitney smiled at her husband. "When he was a wrestler, his moves were as staged as a Broadway dance number. Sounds to me like he's choreographing something or other now."

"Valid point." Vincent's smile was like a falling star in a midnight sky, there and gone. He turned toward Javid. "What the hell can he be up to?"

"I'm not sure, but then later on in the day, Miah and I were accosted by De Luca's ace reporter, Bobby Redwing."

"Oh, Bobby The Buzzard," Andy said, lifting his gaze from his computer screen as his fingers continued clicking away. Bobby's face appeared on everyone's monitor. "He's a nasty bird."

Javid nodded. "He asked me point-blank whether or not I could say that the citizens under my rule were guaranteed freedom of speech, liberty and justice for all."

"What's that supposed to mean?" Law tapped his glasses on the table.

"I'm afraid it means he and De Luca have unearthed the information about my brother's terrorist activities that we've managed so far to keep from becoming public knowledge."

Quint swore.

Javid said, "I was hoping we'd...you'd... Is there

anything, any influence we can bring to bear on De Luca that will get him to kill this story?''

Vincent's eyes were stormy. ''Unfortunately, we aren't the CIA or any 'recognized' undercover agency. If we were, we'd have the kind of influence you're talking about.''

Javid's gut burned. ''Then, what do we do? We can't ignore this threat. If De Luca prints the truth about Zahir, there is no telling what Khalaf will do. He may disassociate himself from Zahir.'' *Where would that leave Miah?* The thought of her in dire jeopardy sent razors of fear through him.

Quint added, ''Or it may escalate whatever their plans are to destroy Quantum.''

The room grew silent as this sunk in. Then Vincent glanced at Law. ''Have you gotten any leads on the Petrol connection?''

The lawyer pulled off his glasses, shaking his head. ''I've narrowed it down to a couple of vice presidents who consider Quantum the Antichrist, but whether either would resort to siding with terrorists to eliminate the competition...well, that I can't prove—not at this point.''

''So, just what is our next move, Vincent?'' Quint pushed his Stetson so far back on his forehead that a red mark showed where the band had pressed.

''Before Khalaf realizes what we're doing,'' Vincent said at length, ''before he can escalate his plans, we're going to escalate ours.''

WHAT I NEED, Miah mused as she pushed into the smoky, cool interior of Finnigan's Rainbow, *is a plan.* Her gaze was slow to adjust to the change in light. She stood where she was, blinking until she made out Cailin behind the bar...with Rory. Her heart skipped. All thought of a plan flew from her head. She'd been so self-absorbed, her mind so full of Zahir and his secrets, she'd forgotten about her encounter with Rory. Her suspicions of him. She ached to talk to Cailin, to spill her guts, but she didn't want Rory hearing any of it.

The pub was unusually quiet for a hot afternoon. Instead of going to the bar, as she normally did, Miah stood by the door until she caught Cailin's eye, then nodded toward the back booth and headed for it. It was her silent way of communicating to Cailin that she wanted some one-on-one.

Cailin arrived three minutes later with two frosted mugs of beer and slid into the seat across from her. Her bright red hair was plaited in a French braid, curling tendrils springing loose at her temples and nape. She wore a kelly-green polo shirt and black slacks that served as uniform for the pub—an outfit better suiting her brothers and father, who all worked here, than Cailin's buxom curves.

"I hate to say this, Miah, but you look awful, girl-friend. Worse than you did this morning. Is it your mom?"

"No. She's resting. Eating. Doing better."

"That's great, but something *is* wrong. What?" Cailin laid her hand on Miah's, but before Miah could answer, she jerked back her hand, her blue eyes rounding with alarm. "Oh, no. Did Zahir discover what you were doing that you didn't want him to know?"

Miah tracked a fingertip through the frosty film on her mug. "Actually, it's the other way around."

"Huh?" Cailin took a sip of beer.

"I discovered Zahir doing something he doesn't want *me* to know. Trouble is, I don't know what it is."

Cailin set her mug down with a *thump*. "Well, that's as clear as a blended margarita."

"I know, I know." Miah filled her parched mouth with a deep swallow of the cool beer, and sighed with the pleasure of it.

"I wasn't going to say anything, Miah, but Bobby The Buzzard was in here earlier bragging that *The Clarion* is running an exposé on Zahir, and when it hits the stands next week, you're going to find out you've married the Prince of Evil. Is that why you look like you've lost your best friend? Which you haven't, by the way."

"The Prince of Evil? Oh God, Cailin. What is that supposed to mean?" Were Zahir's secrets evil? The idea had Miah's stomach churning.

She wrapped her warm hands around the chilled mug, drawing several bracing breaths. As her stomach calmed, she filled her friend in on what had transpired earlier in the day, omitting her encounter with Rory, but including every insult fired by De Luca, every insinuation slung by Redwing.

"Did Bobby say anything more than that?"

"Yes, he said the final copy is on De Luca's desk, ready for his approval before printing."

Miah groaned. *The Prince of Evil*. Just the sound of it chilled her. Damn The Buzzard. Normally, she would ignore this kind of name-calling, especially given the source. But despite *The Clarion*'s penchant for printing lies, there was usually a grain of truth in all of their stories, and it was that modicum of annoying sand that felt like a huge rock against her heart.

"The thing is—" Cailin intruded on her dark thoughts "—De Luca's not going to get to editing that piece today. Bobby let slip that Big Tony would be out of the office the rest of the afternoon." Cailin took a gulp of her beer, banged down the mug and leaned across the table. "This might be our only chance, Miah, to find out what The Buzzard was talking about...before it hits newsstands."

Miah stared into her beer and saw again the editor of *The Clarion,* saw his vengeful eyes, heard his vile innuendoes. She looked at her friend. "What about De Luca's staff? They're not going to let us waltz into his office and help ourselves to whatever we like."

"That's no problem." Cailin gave her a smug-cat grin. "I know a way in that bypasses the staff."

"Really? Well, then, what are we waiting for?" Miah's pulse leaped, then faltered as she gazed around the pub. "Oh, can you get off?"

"Absolutely. This place is as dead as a funeral parlor at midnight. Sean and Dad are in the kitchen if Rory needs help any time in the next couple of hours. But business shouldn't pick up again until the dinner hour."

Miah drained her mug, wishing she'd had something stronger, something bracing, a jolt of that special Irish whiskey the Finnigans called "Courage." "Let's go."

Cailin ran off to tell Rory she was leaving. Miah stood, finding her knees unsteady, her nerves shaky. Zahir's image came into her mind, especially his warm brown eyes as he'd pleaded with her to judge him on his actions, on what her heart told her. Why couldn't she just do that? She gathered her purse. She knew why. After asking her to trust him, he'd turned right around and lied to her.

But as much as she wanted the truth, she also dreaded it. Something curled in the pit of her stomach, something reptilian and squirmy. Miah recognized it for what it was: fear.

THE CLARION OFFICES were located across the river from the Langston Building. Cailin led Miah to the river side of the building, an employees' entrance. "They change the code every month, but it should still be..." She punched numbers on the security keypad, and they watched the access light change from red to green. Cailin beamed. "Yes."

She opened the door and gestured for Miah to precede her. Miah stepped into a long hallway. The roar of heavy machinery indicated they were near the area of the building where the newspaper was printed. Cailin caught her arm and pointed to a closed door to their right. She whispered, "Private entrance to De Luca's office."

Miah grabbed the knob. It refused to budge. "Locked," she whispered in frustration.

"Yes, but it's one of those old-fashioned push locks, and I have the key." Cailin held up the one and only credit card she possessed. "You'll recall when I applied for this sucker, and actually qualified, I promised myself not to use it expect in emergencies. I'd say this occasion fits that criteria."

Miah shook her head. "I've seen this done on TV, but how do you know it will work?"

Cailin's smile widened. "I learned all of my criminal talents from Rory, bless his sneaky black heart."

Miah's throat tightened at her friend's light-hearted comment, her suspicions of Rory lifting again. Just how black was Rory's heart? No. She could not deal with that at the moment. One problem at a time.

The lock gave. Cailin pulled the door open on a carpeted stairwell. They scrambled in, quietly shutting the door and engaging the lock. The click sounded like a boom to Miah. Her pulse tripped. Above, they could see a wide-open space. They shared a tense glance, then, as though in silent agreement, ascended side by side. Miah was taller, gaining her the first glimpse of the landing at the top of the steps, at the private elevator.

Although they were alone, Cailin whispered, "Big Tony's office takes up a third of the top floor."

"Do we need a key or anything to use this elevator?" Miah asked, looking for such a thing but finding none. *Could it be this easy?*

"No key necessary. As far as Big Tony knows, he's the only one with access to this area."

"I guess he'll change *that* security breech after we show up." Miah pressed the button. The door slid open on an empty cage with a carpeted floor and mirrored walls. Her reflection showed she looked as pale as someone chilled to the bone—which was exactly how she felt.

Cailin, on the other hand, seemed too hot, her cheeks pink.

"You're sure De Luca won't be there?"

"That's what Bobby said."

Miah took a deep breath and they filed aboard, neither speaking. As the elevator rose, Miah's heart plunged. As much as she wanted information on her husband, getting it from this source seemed a complete betrayal of Zahir. But she *had* to know what he was keeping from her.

The elevator stopped; the door slid open. They stepped into a huge office with vaulted ceilings and massive windows offering views of the Chicago skyline and Lake Michigan. Miah did a slow, pivoting scan, startled by the fierce black-and-yellow decor, Big Tony's wrestling colors. In one corner, an actual life-size ring was set up with a bank of movie seats beneath. The furniture was ultramodern—molded plastic and leather upholstery.

"It's a little hard on the eyes, yes?" Cailin said.

Before Miah could answer, a greasy blond head bobbed up from behind the desk startling both women into silence. Bobby Redwing. A sickening heat flushed her body. Damn. *They should have brought Thomas and James.* To intimidate the little buzzard, if nothing else. As though he had no right and she and Cailin every right, she blurted out, "What are you doing here?"

Bobby blanched, a nervous laugh clawing out of his long neck as though they'd caught him stealing something from De Luca's desk. Had they? If so, what? His huge Adam's apple jumped, then settled, and his tense smile fell to a blustering leer. "What am I doing in the office of *my* boss? I think a better question is what are the two of you doing sneaking into a private office through a private entrance?"

"We...we came to see Big Tony," Miah said, gathering her nerve.

He looked at Cailin. "I told you he wouldn't be here this afternoon."

"Well, you were wrong," Cailin blustered. "We—we have an appointment."

"Oh, yeah?" Bobby glanced at something on the desk, then eyed them with renewed suspicion. "You wouldn't be here to take a gander at this story on the 'Prince of Evil,' would you, ladies?"

Cailin's hands landed on her shapely hips. "No. I told you, we came to see Big Tony."

Bobby looked her up and down as though she were a meal he was about to devour. "Yeah, sure."

Miah stepped forward, cutting off his visual line to Cailin. "Bobby, earlier today you and your boss made derogatory remarks about my husband. Then you went to Finnigan's Rainbow, where you continued shooting off your mouth, defaming Zahir."

"As I told the prince, America is a free country, Princess."

Miah pulled in an exasperated breath. To get what she wanted, she would have to verbally spar with this scavenger in reporter's guise. As he would do, she started with threats. "What you're saying about my husband is a pack of lies. If you print any of it, we'll sue you and walk away with every asset this piece of crap paper brings in."

Bobby smirked, eyeing her with a mix of pity and triumph in his eyes. "The only way you could win such a suit is to prove we were lying. But we have the truth on our side. We have hard evidence."

"Then, prove it. Show it to me now."

He strutted closer, his huge Adam's apple bobbing. "Why should I do that?"

Why, indeed? She considered offering him money, then recalled she'd given the last of her ready funds to an extortionist. Perhaps this man. Her palms felt damp. She could threaten to tell his boss they'd caught him in this office when he knew Big Tony would be out. Trouble with that was she didn't know what he'd been doing, and, arguably, she'd have to explain her own sneaky entrance into this office. Damn. She could think of nothing else to use to persuade him, except bluster.

"You seemed to want me to know earlier. Has something changed since then?"

"No, but—"

"Then, why not just tell me?"

His ugly grin reached his eyes. Clearly he liked having power over women. He seemed to be weighing how best to use her "need to know" against her.

"Tell her, Bobby." Cailin stepped between them.

The Buzzard's gaze shifted to her and his muscles

bunched as if he readied to pounce on his favorite prey. Miah feared for her friend. She grabbed Cailin and pulled her from Bobby's easy reach.

The only way to fight this kind of vulture was by using something he understood. Something he reveled in. "Just as I thought. You and De Luca don't have anything on Zahir."

"Oh, but we do. And it will make you rue the day you ever met the man."

"If you have such knowledge, then tell me."

"Again, why should I?" He glanced at Cailin and licked his lips. "What's in it for me?"

Miah lifted her chin. "What's in it for you? Why, the sheer pleasure of watching me squirm."

He took a step closer. "As pleasant as that would be…it's not enough."

Cailin's cheeks were as red as her hair. "Maybe Big Tony would like to know we caught you in his desk, looking as culpable as if you were stealing the petty cash."

That guilty look grabbed him again. He narrowed his eyes at Cailin. "You do and I'll—"

"Look, Bobby, let's deal, okay?" Miah clutched her friend's arm, squeezing, silently signalling her to cool it. "You show me this so-called exposé and your proof, and I'll not only give you my reaction to it, I'll give you signed permission to quote me."

Chapter Twelve

Against Cailin's protests that she shouldn't be alone, Miah dropped her friend at Finnigan's Rainbow, then returned to the Royal Princess Hotel. She clutched the sheaf of papers she'd gotten from Bobby against her dully thudding heart and moved jerkily into the suite Zahir had reserved for their honeymoon. She felt as if she'd never been here, never set foot inside these walls, never kissed her husband with abandonment on that very balcony.

The rose tinted glasses had been ripped from her eyes, tainting even the mild hues of this decor—vivid, stark, cruel.

In the bedroom, she found the bed made, the scented petals, robust cheeses and bubbling champagne erased as if they'd existed only in her mind.

As much an illusion as Zahir.

She sank to the bed, the papers heavy on her lap, and stared at the ring on her finger, the family heirloom he'd given her for an engagement ring. She'd been thrilled to wear it, proud to join such a grand lineage—but now, looking at it, she felt as blue as the sapphires, as green as the emeralds, as icy as the diamond. Glum and sick and cold. So cold. She'd been completely taken in. Her father had been completely taken in. They'd both believed in Zahir. In his goodness. She slipped the rings from her finger and set them on the nightstand, shivers racking her body.

She'd married a monster.

She unclasped the hook of the necklace he'd designed for her and spread it out beside the rings, its beauty no longer reflective of the man she'd been falling for, the man who had shown so much concern for her mother. For her. Bittersweet memories attacked her, clawing with sharp talons. How could *that* man also be the fiend in these pages Bobby had given her?

Yet, he was.

She flinched as her gaze caught sight of the photograph on the top of the stack. It was of Zahir standing over defeated innocents as though he were a big-game hunter touting his skills.

She ran to the bathroom and heaved.

When she came out, Zahir was there, his face a mask. But then, hadn't it always been that? He seemed to notice neither her distress, nor the ghostly pallor she'd seen reflected in the bathroom mirror, nor the tremor rattling through her body. How had she ever thought him sensitive?

He was scowling, his beautiful face clouded with fury. She supposed another woman, one less enraged, would be intimidated by that look. She stood her ground, glaring back at him. She could swear she saw a smile light his eyes, as if her defiance won his respect—some perverse admiration or other.

"Miah, you must stop taking off without anyone guarding you. It's too damn dangerous."

She dug her nails into her palms, finding strength in the pain, in this reminder that she was still alive to fight the evil that stood before her. "The only real danger to me is you, Zahir."

"Excuse me?" His brown eyes darkened to near black, his ebony eyebrows shooting up.

She managed to pull in a shuddery breath. "I went to see Tony De Luca this afternoon. I wanted him to know that we'd sue him if he printed lies about you."

He touched his diamond tie tack as if to assure himself it was where it belonged—the only outward indicator he wasn't as cool as his exterior suggested. "And did he promise you that he would run a story on me, love?"

She recoiled at the endearment, at the flash of one of the photos that zipped across her mind. "Actually, De Luca wasn't there. I spoke with Bobby Redwing."

Zahir's expression remained unreadable, but she was surprised to realize that she knew him well enough to detect worry in the depths of his gaze.

He said, "Is Redwing going to pass your threats on to his boss?"

Her jaw clenched and unclenched. "Bobby told me the truth about you, Zahir."

Zahir smiled and shook his head. "His version of the truth, no doubt."

It was all she could do not to fly at him like an enraged hawk, to pierce his vile hide until he bled like his victims, until he ached as she ached. "He called you a terrorist."

"He lied." His gaze intensified, heating like deep dark hot chocolate, issuing a silent plea for her to trust him, to believe in him. "I promise you, Miah, I am *not* a terrorist."

She would give him one thing. The man had charm, had his act down to a tee. He actually sounded earnest.

Innocent. But she knew better now than to believe anything he said.

"Bobby showed me proof." She snatched up the papers she'd left on the bed and shook them at him. *"This proof."*

He tried grabbing the papers, but she tossed them toward the ceiling like the debris they were, garbage so filthy she could not bear to touch it, to see it. For three whole seconds they stood in the blizzard, until the last page settled on the floor.

Zahir grabbed up a few of the pages, scanned them, then groaned, crushing the papers in one of his powerful hands. He rushed back to the bedroom door and slammed it, the bang like a gunshot. Miah's mouth went dry. Fear flickered through her. Maybe confronting Zahir hadn't been such a great idea.

He leaned against the door, blocking her exit, his chest heaving as though he'd run a great distance. But he made no move toward her. Her fear ebbed and she realized, afraid or not, she wasn't going anywhere until she'd told him what she thought of him, told him she was getting an annulment and gave him back the family heirloom ring.

Neither spoke, but as she watched him, she saw something odd—that same slight alteration in his expression she'd noticed at the jeweler's today, the strange shift to his shoulders as if he were dropping a heavy weight, some worry or other, some facade.

He lifted his hands like a surrendering bandit. "I couldn't tell you the truth. Not until I knew you could be trusted."

"Trusted?" Miah thought she was numb, thought herself incapable of sustaining another shock, but his words assaulted like a blow to her entire body. She shuddered with the force of it. "You thought I'd approve of the killing of innocent people?"

"What?" His eyes went wide and he jammed his hands through his hair. "Dear God, no. That's not what I mean. I said I'm not a terrorist. I'm an *anti*-terrorist. I hunt down terrorists and turn them over to the authorities."

She glanced wildly at the scattered papers, her gaze, as luck would have it, landing on the worst of the photos. She squatted and grabbed it. "What about this, Zahir? It's you. Pictures don't lie."

He didn't even try to take the photograph from her. Just stood where he was, his expression one of a man suffering a heart attack. His hand went to the spot on his chest, where they'd shared the pledge earlier at the jeweler's, as though it had some great significance to him.

"Oh, Miah, I have dreaded this day more than you will ever know, dreaded having to tell you…" He drew in a deep breath, then said on the exhale, "I'm not Zahir."

Miah's ears buzzed. Had she heard him right? She frowned so hard her face ached. "What did you say?"

"I am Prince *Javid* Haji Haleem of Anbar. Zahir is my twin brother."

"Bull." Miah laughed at the absurdity and glared at him. "Zahir hasn't got a twin."

"Yes, he does. Me."

His voice was so impassioned, his expression so earnest, her fury faltered. "Then, then, then, why didn't Bobby mention that?"

"How should I know? It's no secret. You could verify it through any legitimate newspaper or even on the Internet most likely."

No. It was preposterous. Unbelievable. "So, all this time you've been impersonating Zahir?"

"Only for the past couple of months."

Her skin burned. She'd met Zahir last January, had dated him, spent time with him during these past six months, but she'd never noticed when one twin took the other's place? No way. If that were true... No. *That* was too humiliating to contemplate.

"You expect me to believe that you've been impersonating your so-called twin for the past couple of months and I didn't know the difference?" She couldn't keep the skepticism from her voice.

His eyes went kind, warm. "I didn't do this to humiliate you, Miah. You must believe that. If you were fooled, it's only because you didn't know Zahir well."

He said it as though she shouldn't be embarrassed by that. She'd been played for a fool, tricked, lied to, betrayed. Embarrassment was the least of what she felt. She hugged herself, hating that he'd said something undeniable. She didn't know Zahir, didn't know him at all.

She strode out onto the balcony, gazed down at the sparkling lake, heard the roar of afternoon traffic in the distance, the cry of a gull. Normal sights and sounds driving home the point that while *her* private universe had come to a screeching halt, the rest of the world kept spinning. Tears of self-pity sprang to her eyes, but she bit them back, recalling what her daddy, Grant Mohairbi, had often said to her: "Be careful what you wish for, Me-Oh-Miah, you just might get it."

Boy, had she gotten it. She'd wanted to be a princess, had wanted to marry Prince Charming, had believed in the fairy tale with all her heart. Her now broken heart.

She would never be that naive again.

"MIAH, I CAN PROVE who I am...." Javid stood behind her, barely controlling the urge to touch her, speaking low, not wanting to startle Miah, recognizing the fragility of her composure. She'd had more than a vicious shock. Javid wanted to wring Redwing's scrawny neck until that bulging Adam's apple popped out of it. But he could hardly blame the reporter for ferreting out the truth about Zahir. He and the agents should have suspected it. Guarded against it.

Damn it all, *he* should have been the one to tell Miah, eased her into the truth when she'd come to trust him more. Instead, she'd been shattered. And she hadn't heard the worst of it yet. God knows what she'd do when he told her the rest. And he was damn well not going to let anyone else break it to her. She had to hear this from him.

"This is all the ID I have on me at the moment. I can get more, if this isn't enough." He dug deep into the secret pocket inside his suit jacket and extracted his passport, his diplomatic immunity papers and the letter from his mother about his grandmother's missing ring. He laid it all on the balcony table, then left her alone to study them.

When she came into the bedroom ten minutes later, he'd picked up all the papers Redwing had given her and locked them in his briefcase. Out of sight. He would have to take them to the agents later, but for now, he could no more bear to look at them than she could. Could not bear to look at the monster who bore his likeness.

Miah waved his ID papers at him. "If what you're telling me is true—and I'm not going to buy it without investigating you further, *Javid,* then, explain to me why you're impersonating your brother."

"Because my twin *is* a terrorist. *Is* the man in those photographs Redwing gave you." Javid sank to the bed and asked her to sit down, hoping she'd opt for the spot beside him, needing her near, aching to ease the pain from her eyes, from her mouth, a pain he knew issued from deep inside her. She chose a chair near the French doors.

He leaned forward on his thighs. "Not that you want to hear the story of my life, but there are a few facts you might find pertinent. Zahir is the older twin, and as such, he was the natural successor to the throne of Anbar. As far back as I can recall he was always impetuous, mischievous. As a child, my parents found it cute, but he never outgrew it. If Zahir were told not to do something, it was as if he'd been told whatever it was was the most desirable thing in life. The greater the risk, the more dire the consequences, the more irresistible that thing became to him."

"I take it you didn't share that trait?"

"No. Other than looking like mirror images, we are exact opposites."

"But you must once have been close—most twins are inseparable."

Javid shook his head, but he no longer hurt from the loss of his twin as he had years ago. "Zahir hates me. I think he always has, as though my existence somehow makes him less than he could be. He would kill me, given the chance. I have the scar to prove it." He touched the spot near his heart as he related the story of their sword fight.

Miah's eyes followed his fingertips and she blanched. "My God. He was that evil at fourteen?"

"Yes. It was the hardest thing I've ever had to face." *Until now.* "But I knew if I didn't accept that truth, he would use that to his advantage and find some way to end my life.''

Her hands went to her chest as though her heart were aching as his ached at the evil committed by people like his twin.

''A few years ago, Father discovered Zahir's involvement with certain factions suspected of terrorism. Zahir swore he didn't realize what his 'friends' were into and promised to break off his association with them. Instead, he became more proficient at hiding his misdeeds. But Father had spies of his own. He discovered Zahir, hiding behind a playboy exterior, was using family monies to finance these beasts. He stripped Zahir of his right to the throne, cut off access to family money and barred him from Anbar.''

''But why isn't that a known fact?''

''Because my father could not bear to have his private shame made public. He ripped Zahir from his heart as though he had never existed.''

''And the rest of your family? Your mother, your grandparents—how do they feel about him?''

''How do you expect? Can you imagine the guilt my parents feel at having borne a child who has wrought such horror on their friends and neighbors, their co-workers? You want to know why my parents and grandparents didn't come to our wedding? He didn't invite them. They have disowned Zahir. He has shamed us. Betrayed us. Betrayed the good and decent people of this world.''

She was gripping the letter from his mother in white-knuckled fingers. ''What brought Zahir to Chicago?''

''His next target. Quantum Industries. It is one of the world's leading oil distributors, whose home base is here.'' He explained Zahir's interest in taking out Quan-

tum Industries in order to do business with the more
agreeable Petrol Corporation.

"But how does Zahir plan to bring down Quantum?
Through stock manipulation or some such?"

"He likes a more direct approach."

"You mean, he'd rather blow them up than play the
stock market?"

"That's what I'm trying to figure out. Zahir hid his
true intentions like the pro he is. Pretending to be inter-
ested only in continuing his playboy lifestyle, he took
the Chicago social scene by storm, establishing himself
as a major player, all the while instigating the kidnap-
ping of one of Quantum's vice presidents, Natalie Van
Buren."

Miah thought long and hard, but she couldn't come
up with any memory of Natalie Van Buren being kidnapped, and *that* would surely have been heavily covered by all local media sources. "If Zahir had done that,
it would have been in all the newspapers, on TV. It
wasn't."

He sighed. "The attempt was foiled and the whole
incident hushed up. Zahir was taken into custody, where
he remains."

"Zahir's social conquests were well documented, so
I have to ask myself how such a darling of the media
escaped attention when he was arrested.

"Because Zahir wasn't arrested by any local or state
police. He wasn't missed because I immediately took his
place."

She smacked the envelope against her palm. "This is
just so far-fetched—"

"Look. Somewhere in those papers you got from Redwing, there is the mention of a scar behind Zahir's left
ear."

That stopped her. She'd seen that part of The Buzzard's report.

Javid lifted his hair and pulled off the fake scar, wincing as it came free. "I gave Zahir that scar, but as you can see, I don't have a scar behind either ear."

He could see she was starting to lose her grip on her denial, but was not yet ready to give it up completely.

She said, "If you've stopped Zahir from carrying through on his plans, why then was it necessary for you to step into his life?"

Javid grimaced as though he wrestled a difficult truth that had to be told. He shoved his hands into his hair. "Because Zahir was not working alone."

Miah felt an inexplicable sense of foreboding, instinctively knowing she didn't want to hear whatever he was about to say, but *had to hear it all the same.* "W-who do you suspect is working with him?"

"We couldn't prove it at first, couldn't find the connection—they'd hid it so well."

"They?"

"Zahir and...your father."

Grant? No. He died when she was twelve. Zahir would have been all of seventeen, too young to have been involved with Grant. "My...my father?"

"Khalaf."

"No! Don't you dare call my father a terrorist!" Tears sprang to her eyes. Vile images filled her head. The photographs Bobby had given her. The horrors perpetrated by terrorists, evil men. America attacked. All of those innocents killed. Families shattered. The whole country grieving. Outraged. Oh God, she couldn't breathe. "My father...*not*...terrorist!"

"I know you don't want to believe that, Miah. I know Khalaf told you a beautiful love story about himself and your birth mother, Anjali, but the truth is, Khalaf murdered your mother. He hired the freedom fighters who invaded Nurul. One of those men was Grant Mohairbi. Grant was under the mistaken belief that he was helping Nurul. But when he discovered what Khalaf and the rebels really wanted, what their true intentions were, he knew he'd been lied to. He rescued you, brought you home to America, adopted you, raised you as his own. He's the one who deserved your love and respect, the one who loved you for yourself. Now that the people of Nurul have regained control of their country, Khalaf wants to use you for his own purposes.''

''Liar!'' Miah launched herself at Javid, knocking him from the bed to the floor, pinning him there, fists flailing, banging his chest, as she'd wanted to do earlier, slapping at his face, his head, wherever she could reach. ''Lie! Lies! Liar!''

He didn't try to stop her or dissuade her. Just lay there letting her beat him until she collapsed against him, whimpering, weeping. Then his arms came around her and he held her with such gentle strength that it kept her from slipping over the edge into madness.

As Miah calmed, she began looking at her father in a new light. One that was clear and bold and painful. Since she'd met him, all Khalaf had said and done had been geared toward getting her to Nurul. She should have questioned why he wanted the daughter he'd so recently found ensconced in a country so far from the one he ruled. Should have questioned why he'd been so anxious to marry her off. But she'd seen nothing beyond her own desire to be a cherished daughter. She looked now at the unloving things Khalaf had done…like saving his own neck the day of her wedding…like embracing Zahir as a son.

Khalaf had handpicked Zahir to be her husband. He had to know Zahir's family had disowned him and why. Had to know of his association with terrorists. Was probably the one bankrolling Zahir's activities. She shuddered against Javid.

But the man in her arms was *not* Zahir, the monster in those reprehensible photographs. This man understood that kindness reached where reason could not; this man knew what she needed when she did not; this man turned all of her lies into truth; this man reached into her heart, sang to her spirit, caressed her soul, this man in her arms. She raised her head and gazed into his eyes, warm brown, full of such concern for her.

And she knew the truth then, knew it in her soul. Grant had rescued her where Khalaf would have killed her. *Grant had been a true hero. The father who'd cherished his daughter. The father of her heart. The man she'd always thought him. A man like this man.*

She reached a hand to stroke his face. His lips. He kissed her fingertips, caressed her face, her back, cradled her against his chest, against the pain of disillusion and broken dreams.

And Miah felt herself catching fire.

Chapter Thirteen

So cold was Miah that she felt the first flickers of heat licking against her core as pain, the kind of confused intense ache of thawing fingers over a campfire, as though she needed to pull away from the too-hot heat, all the while wanting to draw nearer to it, draw it over her, into her, through her.

"Oh, Javid." *Javid. Javid. Javid.* The name rang new and sweet inside her head, chiming like a Sunday morning church bell, a call to celebration, a cleansing, a washing away of the hideous fear that she'd aligned her fate with a fiend.

She lifted her head away from his and looked deep into his eyes, such a dark, beautiful shade of brown, a rich mink with a band of slate around the irises, the lashes thick and velvety, as black as the night. Mesmerizing eyes. Sincere eyes.

Listen to what your heart tells you about me, love.

She hadn't listened then.

She listened now.

Listened to her heart's happy thrum as Javid gently gripped her head in both hands and pulled her lips to his, lightly, then bolder. Need shimmered through her, and Miah listened, and knew—on some primal level she had always trusted this man, despite her misgivings, despite his secrets, despite hers.

With this knowledge came other awareness, that of his body taut and hard beneath hers, that of her body atop his, pressed to the length of him, of the heat that burned slow and steady within, of the dissipating cold, of the budding joy. She yearned to lose herself in the wonder of it, to lose her shy resistance, to lose the restraint of their clothing, to loosen their reined-in passions.

"Make love to me, Javid. Please."

He shoved his hands into her hair, stared longingly into her eyes. "Are you sure, Miah?"

"Oh, yes." She reached for his tie, tugged the knot free, then used it as a winch to lift him, bringing his mouth to hers again. He tasted of mint and man, his tongue rough against hers, every stroke eliciting fiery shivers through her veins, her extremities. *Oh, wicked, wicked tongue.*

He moaned, such pleasure in the sound, such pleasure in his touch, she found herself moaning in echo. He rolled her over, cradling her head in one large hand, the small of her back in the other, sweeping her to her feet with the grace of a ballet move, kissing her as they rose, steadying her, then stepping back and shucking his coat.

Miah caught the ends of the tie again, tugged his head to hers again, his mouth to hers again, needing the connection, craving the heat he stirred and stoked within her, the promise of exquisite joy. She dropped the tie and drove her hands into his dense, wavy black hair, amazed to find the texture coarse yet satiny against her fingertips. She found his neck, burrowed her hands beneath his collar and wanted the shirt gone. She struggled with the buttons.

Javid stepped back and ripped the shirt free, tossing it to the floor.

Her first sight of his naked torso tangled her breath in her throat. His skin was bronzed perfection dappled with curly, silky black hair across his chest, downy on his anvil-hard belly. The only imperfection was a large *X* shaped pucker of white flesh on his chest, a small spot where the hair did not grow. Reverently, she touched the tiny indentation that looked as if something had been cut from him, surgically removed like a malignant tumor, and she knew it had. At least, emotionally. Somehow he'd survived severing the bond formed at conception with his twin, a connection no other sibling could feel— a pain she could not even imagine—to become a strong and righteous man.

Javid's hand covered hers, locking her palm against the beating rhythm of his life's blood, and she felt an odd sensation that the old scar connected them in some way she didn't fully understand.

"You're beautiful," she whispered. "Like a masterpiece painting."

"You've been spending too much time in art galleries, love."

Javid laughed, and the sound surrounded her in a bubble of pure pleasure as he pulled her to him, his arms encircling her, her arms encircling him. His words, though, brought anxiety. But she pushed them to the back of her mind, to fully enjoy the experience to come. The first stroke of her hands against the defined muscles of his back sent a shot of current through her as if he'd spilled the finest whiskey on the flames searing her insides, exploding the fire higher, hotter. Her nipples beaded, twin pearls pushing against the cloth that separated them from his sight, his touch, his mouth, his flesh.

As if he wanted this, too, Javid caressed her shoulders, her back and her jacket, then her dress pooled at her feet. His magical hands made her feel more, lifted her higher, brought her closer to a place she'd never been. "I want more...of you."

"Oh, love, I want all of you." He pulled her to him, his mouth hungry on hers, his tongue delving, twining, plundering. His hands ran the length of her back, boldly cupped her bottom and pulled her hips to his, his fierce need pressing her belly. The heat inside Miah went liquid, as thick and rich as melted gold.

The tip of Javid's tongue stroked the delicate flesh near her ear, then he nibbled kisses down her neck, her arms, over her belly, and somehow she was naked and he was lifting her, lying her on the bed, stepping back, his gaze drinking her in with the fevered intensity of a parched man swallowing water. His brown eyes darkened to smoldering black coals.

"You're the beautiful one, love. You steal my breath."

She couldn't speak, couldn't take her eyes from his, had never experienced the feeling of inner beauty that he made her feel, had never sensed the power that such appreciation gave her, the confidence, the contentment, the trust to open herself completely to him, every vulnerability exposed. He would not hurt her. Would take the gift of her love in the reverence with which it was offered.

She raised her arms to him and Javid came naked to her, his greedy mouth meeting hers, his kiss long and deep, as his hands fondled and roused her beyond anything she'd thought possible. He nibbled her neck, her earlobe, then the other earlobe, kissed the hollow of her throat, caught one sensitive nipple in his mouth and

sucked hard, nipping it with his teeth, eliciting cry after
cry of pleasure from her. He relinquished that breast for
the other, giving it the same attention, until desire was
a wild, crazy pulse, a vibrating, coiling spring that only
he could release.

He smoothed his hand down her belly, and Miah
arched in response, casting aside the last of her shyness
with him, urging on the fingers he twined in her dense
curls, sighing his name again and again, and finally, finally, he found the hot, wet, waiting juncture of her legs,
stroked the swollen, sensitive bud, slipped a finger inside. His touch brought an immediate, rocketing climax,
brought his name singing from her lips. "Javid, Javid,
Javid..."

Miah soared above the world, flying on a cloud of
pleasure, the sensation like nothing she'd ever known.
She wanted to float like this forever, but too quickly felt
herself drifting back to earth, felt the satisfaction was
somehow incomplete. To her surprise, the need hadn't
diminished but was building again, and she knew then,
she craved what she hadn't had...him. All of him. She
wanted to touch him, to taste him, to hold him inside
until he felt as incredible as he made her feel.

She sat up, opening her arms to him, hugging him,
kissing him, pressing herself against him, feeling his still
thundering heart, hearing his rapid breathing, her own
lungs picking up the pace again. She eased him down
on his back, his head on the pillows, and began an intimate assault of his body, experiencing every angle and
plane, each new discovery thrilling. As her mouth explored his neck, his flat erect nipples, his rock-hard six-
pack, her fingertips stroked the velvety hair on his chest,
petted the thin line of fur that spanned his belly, delved
into the thatch of curls surrounding his stunning erection.

Awed at the size of him, at the overpowering draw of his need for her, Miah touched him timidly at first, but desire overwhelmed her, quickened her breath, her pulse, stripped her patience, and her fingers wrapped him with growing boldness. She gasped softly at the sheer sleek feel of him, as though God had sculpted him from the purest marble, and yet, this was no cold, lifeless length of stone she held throbbing hotly in her palm.

"Oh, love, oh." Javid groaned louder with every lift and plunge of her hand, his voice raspy with passion. "Miah, Miah."

He caught her upper arms and gently pulled her up the length of him, then rolled her onto the mattress and moved between her thighs. She spread her legs, inviting him inside. His heat met hers like a flame meeting a torch, the explosive touch startling, exquisite, then he plunged in deep, deeper, then stilled, his gaze locked with hers. And Miah smiled with a delight that seemed too much for her heart to hold.

"Oh, Miah, love…"

Javid's mouth found hers again as he lifted his hips, easing out of her, then into her, thrusting slow wicked stabs, then quicker, deeper, the need refusing to wait, to be put off longer. Miah lifted her hips to meet each thrust, felt herself stretching to accommodate him, to take all of him into her.

The coil inside her began to unwind with dizzying speed, and she cried his name as he brought her higher and higher, then both of their voices rose together like an ancient song, blended, harmonized, the sharpest notes—reached as one honeyed aria—accompanied a wild explosion of exquisite sensations, a spiraling burst of joy and pleasure, racing to her fingertips, her toes, her scalp.

Javid collapsed onto her but made no move to disengage himself. Miah didn't want to lose their connection either. She needed this sense of wholeness, the feeling that all would be right with her world from here on out. They spent the night making love. In the hot tub, in the bathtub, on the balcony and in bed. Miah had never known such sensations, had never been with any man who was at once tender and gentle yet fierce and bold. He was indeed a master at pleasuring a woman's body, but she could see it was *she* whom he wanted to pleasure, not just any woman, and that was an irresistible elixir.

Morning and reality dawned too early, and Miah knew she could no longer cling to the feeling that all would be right with her world from here on out. Nothing was right with her world. Not her mother. Not the blackmailer. Not her birth father. Not the man she'd been betrothed to. She glanced at Javid, still sleeping beside her, and her heart felt the heaviest weight. Not even this lovely man and his lovely lovemaking.

She'd been lied to, betrayed…even by Javid.

She got out of bed, stole into the bathroom and showered, then dressed. When she came out, Javid was just rousing. "Love, where are you going?"

"Nowhere." He'd finally earned the right to call her "love." "We're going to talk."

"Okay." He stretched his arms wide. "Come back to bed and we'll talk about anything you like."

"No. I won't be distracted." Her cheeks warmed with memories of how very distracting he could be.

He plowed his hands through his hair and sat up, eyeing her, seeming to realize she was serious, and tipped his head to one side as though trying to figure out just what she had on her mind. To his credit, he didn't ask.

"Okay. I'll bath and dress, but you've rendered me ravenous, love, and if I don't also eat something soon, I'll be too weak to think straight."

"I'll order breakfast." Miah grinned and headed for the phone. During the night, she'd held tight to the fact that she'd begun to fall, not for a monster as she'd thought after her encounter with The Buzzard, but for a good and decent man. A man who'd shared his secrets, a man who'd bared his soul. But this morning, what he'd told her about others had begun to sink in, and though she was still trying to make sense of it, to process it, she also realized there were some major holes in Javid's story.

Like his relationship with the mysterious Quint.

QUINT WAS THE LAST MAN Javid expected Miah to want to discuss. Khalaf, yes. Zahir, yes. Himself, even. But Quint? No way. "Quint, huh?"

He'd figured, if anything, the serious expression in her golden eyes had been about what had gone on between them. That was the main thing occupying *his* thoughts. Hadn't she considered it the most incredible sex of her life? He had. He glanced to where she stood at the balcony. Her back was to him, her arms hugging herself as if she were cold, but he sucked in a noseful of humid air and knew she couldn't be. Today already promised to be another scorcher.

Breakfast had been spread out on the table beneath a sun umbrella. Javid helped himself to coffee from a silver carafe, then gazed at Miah again, his attention caught by the sheen of her raven hair, the glow of her tawny skin. He pulled out a chair and sat, resisting the urge to go to her, to take her in his arms, to soothe the tension from her tight muscles. And in that moment, he realized sometime in the night she had lain claim not only to his heart, but to his soul.

The set of her shoulders, however, told him something wasn't right. Had she suddenly—in the cruel light of day—come to regret their lovemaking? Did she not feel what he felt—that if he made love to her every hour of every day for the rest of his life it would never be enough?

She glanced at him and he realized her eyes held no such thoughts. She was still too wounded, running on emotion, distrustful…even, he saw, of him.

Javid drank coffee, plucked a piece of bacon from his plate, chewed on it thoughtfully, feeling as helpless as a leaf against the storm of her disillusionment. Miah came to the table, lifted a glass of orange juice and held it so tight, he feared it would break. There seemed only one thing he could do and that was to keep his true feelings for her to himself. Until his investigation ended and Khalaf and his partners were arrested, their intended acts of terrorism averted, he would not add to Miah's concerns, would not speak to her of their future.

"Javid, are you going to tell me who Quint is, or not?"

"Ah, Quint," he said, as evasively as before, sipping his coffee, nibbling a croissant.

"Yes, Quint. Who is he…really? And don't bother making something up. Because I followed you yesterday to the Langston Building and saw you both pretending not to know each other while waiting for the elevator. Why would you do that if he is in your employ?"

He choked on his coffee, then cursed under his breath as he dabbed his wet face with the linen napkin, scrambling for an intelligent response, knowing he needed caution. She was one surprise after another—some of the surprises more pleasant than others.

"You followed me?"

"You said you were meeting with an oil distributor, but there are no oil distributors in the Langston Building. What possible business did you have with a computer company?"

What was she talking about? "A computer company?"

She sucked in an impatient breath. "Does Solutions, Inc. ring a bell?"

Javid felt himself pale. He closed his eyes and groaned, then looked at her. She was waiting. What could he tell her? He'd sworn to keep Chicago Confidential a secret. He couldn't break his word. But lying to her was not an option either. Not after last night. He blew out a resigned breath. The agents weren't going to like it, but he was on his own to make the best out of a bad situation. "Sit down, and I'll tell you."

She took the chair opposite, still clutching her glass of orange juice with white knuckles. He explained who and what the Chicago Confidential agency was, that he'd approached them in March to help stop Zahir from committing acts of terrorism against Quantum Industries, that he'd been working with them ever since. "Quint is one of the secret agents."

"Oh my God." Miah paled, looking suddenly sick. "Oh, Javid."

"What's wrong?"

"After I left the Langston Building yesterday, Khalaf called my cell phone. I asked him if he knew what business you'd have with a computer company. He said he would investigate Solutions, Inc. and get back to me."

Javid swore under his breath. This put a definite kink

in the works—something else, besides The Buzzard's photos and report on Zahir—to discuss with the agents ASAP.

"I'm sorry." Miah's hands were on her chest.

He hated the alarm in her eyes. The fear. "You know what, love? There are precautions in place for just such a possibility. So don't fret. All the same, I think I'll call Quint right away." He patted her hand as he rose. "Let him alert Kathy Renk and Andy Dexter."

He excused himself, made the call, then returned minutes later. Miah was picking at her food. He said, "We're going to meet in a couple of hours."

She glanced up when he sat down. "I'm going with you."

He shook his head. "That's impossible."

"No, it's not. I've been lied to and betrayed by everyone, including the Confidential agents. Including you. That ends today. I am your best hope to get to Khalaf, and I want him as much—no, more—than you. More than all of you. He murdered my birth mother. If Grant hadn't saved me, he would probably have murdered me, too. Or used me my whole life in ways that I can only imagine." She shuddered. "I want in on this. I deserve it."

He could think of several arguments...including her welfare and safety, not to mention the agents coming totally unhinged at this new wrinkle. "It's not an option."

"Make it one."

"I don't have the—"

"Call Quint back. Ask. If they balk at the idea, tell them I'm threatening their complete exposure to the very person they're trying to stop."

Not for one minute did Javid believe she'd follow

through on this threat. But he didn't want her more involved than she already was. "You don't know what you're talking about. How dangerous this is."

"Oh, but I do. Every American knows how dangerous terrorists are, and though I was not born here, I am and always will be an American in my heart of hearts. I'm also Middle Eastern, with a name and face that has garnered me more than my share of suspicious looks and ugly slurs."

He was also American and Middle Eastern. Had suffered some of those same slurs and looks. "I understand."

She touched his hand. "My dad was a firefighter. He lost his life saving others—just as courageous men and women across the country have done in the face of terrorism. Right now, I'm in a position to make a difference. To help save Americans from further atrocities. To show that not everyone with a Middle East heritage is evil. You can't deny me this."

He understood exactly how she felt, had lived a day like the one she lived now. She deserved to follow through on what she felt was her right, her purpose. "Okay, I'll make that phone call."

But the phone rang before Javid reached it. The man on the other end spoke rapidly in a tone that brought chills to his stomach. He said nothing, just listened, struggling to keep his expression from revealing the worry spreading through him. "I see. We're on our way."

He hung up, crossed to Miah and caught her hands in both of his. "That was Dr. Forbes."

"Mom? Is something wrong?" Alarm shot across her face, but quickly dissolved into denial, into hope. "Please tell me a donor has been found."

"I wish that were so. The news isn't good."

Miah went ashen. "Tell me."

"She's being rushed to the hospital. The doctor is meeting the ambulance there."

"What happened?" She held onto him as though he were all that kept her erect.

"Apparently something upset her this morning. All the nurse knew was that an envelope arrived addressed in block writing. Whatever was in the note upset her badly. She kept calling your deceased father's name."

"Oh God. Oh God. Oh God." She tore loose from his grasp. She raced into the bedroom, found her shoes, jammed her feet into them, hopping. "That bastard. If she dies..."

"She's still alive."

Miah seemed to not hear him. She scanned the room looking for something, her chest heaving. Her golden eyes were crazed. "I paid him, but he sent a note to Mom, anyway. Told her all those lies about my dad, Grant." She spied her purse and pounced on it, talking more to herself than to him. "The damn liar."

"Who?" Ja id hurried into his suit jacket, scooped his wallet, watch and other items from the nightstand into his pocket. He followed on Miah's heels as she raced for the door. "Who sent your mother a note? Khalaf?"

"No. The blackmailer."

Chapter Fourteen

Javid hurried after Miah, catching up at the elevator and finding her flanked by two of his bodyguards. He pulled his cell phone from his jacket and dialed, ordering the limousine.

But Miah didn't wait for Mehemet to arrive. The second the elevator reached the lobby, she took off, tearing past the check-in area and scooting outside to a waiting taxi. Javid caught her by the arm. "You can't take a cab."

"The hell I can't." She wrenched from his hold. "My mother needs me."

"I know, I know." She was in shock, not thinking straight. "But Mehemet is pulling up now. See, love?"

"Fine." She flew to the limo and climbed in.

Javid instructed the bodyguards to follow in a separate car. He wanted Miah to himself for a while. Needed some answers. He joined her in the limo, ordered the chauffeur to get to Northwestern Hospital on the double, then closed the privacy window.

His heart and his pulse seemed to be pumping on overdrive. He could only imagine how Miah was feeling. "Do you want to tell me about this blackmailer?"

She didn't answer. Didn't even respond. Might not

have heard him, he realized, from the look on her face. Her hands were clamped together as though she were praying. God knows he was. He tamped down the fury that burned his gut and silently cursed the unknown extortionist who had added to the hell this woman was going through, the person who may have caused her mother's death.

The motion of the car sent him lurching sideways, then back. Mehemet drove Michigan Avenue like a NASCAR driver at Daytona, changing lanes as though the limo were a race car, but Javid knew it wasn't swift enough for Miah. Nothing could be. He'd never felt so helpless. Her hands were white knuckled, her face set with worry—no, fear—her skin an unhealthy gray.

He could only imagine how she must be feeling, and thanked God his own mother was healthy. Losing her would kill him. He'd grown fond of Lina Mohairbi and didn't want to lose her, either. The urge to assure himself as well as Miah had him slipping his arm around her shoulder, pulling her to his side. Her body came against his, stiff, unyielding, as though she were incapable of taking comfort from another person.

He kissed her temple. "She's going to be okay."

Miah's head came up sharply and there was such hope in her golden eyes, Javid wanted to bite back his words in case he was wrong.

She asked, "Did Dr. Forbes tell you that?"

He drew a ragged breath; he couldn't lie to her. "The doctor was cautious. He hadn't seen Lina yet. But I'm sure once he has he'll say the same."

He watched her face collapse and wished he could find some way to replace the hope.

"I can't lose her now, Javid." She waved her hands in frustration. "Not after all of this…this…"

Javid's throat tightened. He glanced at Mehemet and squeezed Miah's hand. The privacy glass was still in place, but the chauffeur might have the intercom on. Javid wasn't sure what orders Khalaf had given him, but knew eavesdropping wasn't beyond the realm of requests.

Just in case, he drew Miah near and spoke close to her ear. "Love, I know you're upset, but even so, you must remember to call me Zahir whenever we're in public."

"Oh my God." Her gaze darted to the chauffeur, then back to him. "Did he hear me?"

Javid studied Mehemet. The chauffeur seemed to be concentrating on his rush to get them to the hospital, not on the rearview mirror. "I don't think so. But we have to be more careful than ever now. Oh, and you really should wear your rings."

He'd gathered her jewelry from the bedside table and put them in his coat pocket. He offered the wedding and engagement rings to her now.

"I'll return your grandmother's ring when this is over," she whispered. Then she gazed up at him and shuddered. "The thought of calling *you* Zahir makes me ill."

"Then, use an endearment or nickname—just not Javid." He recalled how his name had sounded coming from her as they'd made love and added, "Unless we're alone."

She nodded, her expression still dark, her eyes distracted, her manner anxious. "What about your meeting with the agents?"

Javid lifted an eyebrow. At least he'd distracted her for a moment, thawed her frozen mind. He suspected she'd deal better now with what lay ahead of her. As

Mehemet pulled up to the Emergency entrance, Javid hoped he'd fare as well.

"I'll make the phone call after we know how your mother is."

MIAH FELT as if she couldn't breathe. All the lies and betrayals, all the secrets still to be kept. Her nerves were raw, her stomach jittery. She wasn't sure she could stand the tension, the not knowing, for another minute. "Why doesn't the doctor come...Zahir, and tell us how she is?"

"He's probably running tests, Miah." Javid stroked the side of her cheek, the gesture reassuring and tender. "Take encouragement from that. It means she's still alive."

Miah nodded, feeling vulnerable, exposed. Her gaze flicked to the bodyguards who stood at the edge of the waiting area. She'd never been more aware of them, never disliked their presence more. This was an extremely private time, not a time for strangers' eyes and ears.

As she looked at them, they seemed to multiply, and seconds later, she understood why. Khalaf, outfitted in military dress, came around the corner. His weathered face was solemn, full of fatherly concern. "Daughter, I came as soon as I heard."

Inwardly, Miah shrank in disgust, her stomach lurching. She struggled not to show her true feelings, knew the danger in which that would place Javid and herself...even her mother.

With a strength she didn't know she possessed, she found a smile and plastered it in place. "Father, thank you for coming, but how did you know?"

"I have, of course, made your mother's health a priority. Has Dr. Forbes told you anything yet?"

She felt Javid's eyes on her and suffered an insect-in-a-jar feeling as she accepted the sheik's outstretched hands into her own. Surprisingly, for a man with such a cold heart, he had warm, rough hands. Odd that she hadn't noticed before, but these were the hands of a man who didn't just dictate orders, he handled some of the dirty work himself.

Javid said, "Dr. Forbes is in with her now. We haven't spoken with him yet."

Khalaf peered up at Miah. His black eyes steadied on her like dark beacons that saw more than the average person suspected. "Elias Forbes comes highly recommended, Daughter."

"Yes, I know." She nodded, swallowing hard. "I'm just afraid—"

"Well, maybe I can ease some of your distress," Dr. Forbes said, coming into the waiting room. His long face was flushed, his gray eyes guarded but not grave.

Miah's knees went rubbery. "How is she?"

"Better than I had hoped. I believe with rest, she'll pull out of this." Beneath a white clinical jacket, he wore a tailored suit and dapper tie. He tapped a pen against his palm. "I'd like to keep her a couple of days, monitor her."

"Of course." Miah wanted to believe the doctor. Wanted to give in to the relief his words offered. But she wouldn't. Not until she saw for herself that her mother was as good as he said.

"What brought this on?" Khalaf asked, his compact body held rigid.

Miah was struck by the contrasts in the personalities of the three men. Each had powerful presence, but the sheik, small in stature, was as black and white as a midnight sky on the fullest cycle of the moon, the doctor was as tidy, yet shadowed, as dusk, and Javid was a summer sunrise, enchanting, promising, brushed with the truest tones God had created.

The doctor nodded toward Javid. "As I told His Highness, she's had a shock of some kind, something to do with her deceased husband."

"May I see her?" Miah's throat was dry.

"She's asking for you, but you must only stay a few minutes, and I caution you not to do anything to upset her."

"Don't worry." Miah hoped only to relieve her mother's mind.

But as she hurried from the waiting area, she heard the doctor telling Javid and Khalaf "She needs that donor soon."

The Cardiac Care Unit ward was shaped like a giant *U* with a nurses' station in the center. Her mother had a private room. Lina Mohairbi's tiny frame might belong to a child, she looked so small in the large bed, machines surrounding her, attached to her, beeping and buzzing. Her lips were blue and her eyes closed. *But she's alive,* Miah reminded herself. She approached the bed and touched the back of her mother's hand with a finger. "Hey, Mom."

Lina opened her eyes. "Oh, Me-Oh-Miah, I'm sorry I gave you such a scare, darling."

"Shh. You're okay. That's all that matters."

"Oh, that awful note...it said the most horrid things about my Grant."

"None of it is true, Mom. None of it."

"Well, *I* know that, dear." Her mother gave a feeble laugh, as though the shocking claims in the blackmailer's note hadn't almost killed her, as though reassuring Miah were the important thing now. "Grant Mohairbi was the finest man I've ever known."

"He was, Mom." Miah squeezed her hand. "He truly was."

"But that note said those lies were going to be printed in *The Clarion*. All of our family and friends will see them, everyone at Firehouse 12. They'll remove Grant's photograph from the wall of honor."

"No, no, they won't. If *The Clarion* dares to print those lies, we'll sue—and we'll win and Dad's photograph will stay right where it is."

That seemed to please her. She closed her eyes for a moment, and Miah could see she was worn-out. Miah started to leave, but Lina said, "Who sent the note, Miah?"

"I don't know." *But I'm going to find out and make him very sorry for hurting you.* "You rest now, Mom. I'll be back to see you later."

MIAH STORMED into the penthouse, Javid stopping long enough only to make sure the bodyguards stayed at the door. The nurse had gone. The rooms had an empty feeling, the sense that something had happened suddenly, sending the occupants scurrying out. A half-finished soda on the coffee table. The television still running. Miah switched it off, then swept into her mother's room. Her gaze went to the bed, to the pillows propped against the padded headboard, indentations of Lina's small head still showing. The blankets and sheets were tossed back as though she'd left in haste.

A pile of notes spilled across the covers and onto the floor. Miah plowed through them, finding the one she sought wedged between the bed frame and the nightstand. She read it quickly, then crumpled it in her hand. It had been addressed to her. The other cards, she noted, were congratulations and wedding well-wishes from family and friends. Somehow this note had gotten mixed in with the others and her mother had read it by accident. All the same…

Miah shook with rage. "I want this bastard, Javid. I want to put my hands around his neck and squeeze until he feels the life draining out of him. Until he feels as if he's going to die, so that he'll know how he's made my mother feel."

Javid stood in the doorway, leaning against the frame. At her declaration, he lifted his eyebrows. "I realize you are capable of many things, love, but I hadn't considered you a violent woman. Perhaps now you'll tell me what you know about this blackmailer, and what demands he's made on you."

Miah glanced over his shoulder. "Are we alone?"

"Yes. I've checked each room. No one here but us."

"Are you sure no one's bugged this place?"

"It's clean. I had my men do a sweep of it today." He lifted her hand and kissed her fingertips.

The kiss sent heat flushing through her limbs. She couldn't look at Javid without thinking about the night they'd spent making love, without recalling the wild abandon with which she'd offered herself to him, the hot sensations he'd roused in her—that memories were rousing now.

As if he were thinking the same, Javid said, "About last night—"

"Last night was wonderful, Javid." Miah cut him off, not wanting to hear that he considered their lovemaking nothing more than a night of great sex. "I've no regrets. No expectations. I just want to get through this hell in one piece. I want my mother well and my birth father in the cell adjoining your brother's. And if we can find out who this blackmailing bastard is and put him in cell number three, all the better.''

"I agree. So, fill me in.''

Miah made them coffee, which they sat at the kitchen table to drink. She told him everything she knew about the extortionist, including the note he'd managed to put in her robe pocket on their wedding night after setting off the hotel fire alarm. She placed the rumpled note on the table between them. "This is his fifth demand for money. But I don't have any more money. He's drained my account.''

"Your account?''

"Khalaf placed one-hundred thousand into an account in my name in January,'' she said, shuddering a bit at how pleased she'd been at the time. What a mess this was. "As soon as the royal wedding took place in Nurul, I would then be a princess for real and would receive my full inheritance. I suppose that's no longer going to happen. What will happen to Mom if I can't claim my money?''

Javid covered her hands with his. She gazed up at him, searching his eyes as though the answer were there.

"First of all,'' he said, "I would never let your mother go without the medical treatment she needs, and that includes covering every expense involved in having and living with a heart transplant. Secondly, I don't know what nonsense Khalaf was pulling with you—likely trying to get you to go along with his plans—but you're a princess no matter who you marry. Before you marry. You don't need a husband. You never did.''

"What?''

"That's right. You don't need to be married to claim

your monetary inheritance, either. The money is there. It's yours. It always has been. It was just that no one knew where you were to give it to you.''

Fury hit her again, but this time it came in a wave of cold acceptance, resignation. "So, Khalaf has been controlling me and my money, too.''

"So it appears. I'm sorry, Miah.''

"If that wasn't so sick, I'd laugh.'' But then, the joke was all on her.

Javid's gaze was sympathetic. "Khalaf will do whatever he needs, use whomever he has to, to get what he wants.''

"Which is what?''

"To be the most powerful ruler in the Middle East, to control the oil supplies of the world. You are his key to obtaining these things.''

"No. I *was* his key. We're no longer playing by his rules.''

"Don't underestimate him. We've got to let him think he's still calling the shots until we can find out what his plan is for Quantum Industries and stop it before he can execute it.''

"How do we do that?''

Javid tapped the blackmail note. "Let's take out one villain at a time, okay?''

"Okay.''

"This note demands that you bring fifteen thousand to the Brinkmire Cavalli Gallery tomorrow morning.''

"That's the usual drop-off spot, but I don't have any money to pay him. My account is drained. I don't know how to get Khalaf to give me more. I don't even know if the original deposit was from Khalaf's own personal money, or if he has access to my inheritance and took the money from that.''

"It would be his own money." Javid stirred cream into his refreshed coffee. "I doubt he could touch your inheritance."

Javid stopped short of saying what they were both thinking, so she said it. "You mean, if he had access to my inheritance, he wouldn't have had need of me."

He nodded. "I'm sorry."

"Don't be. He means nothing to me." But she couldn't put aside the horrible fact that a monster's blood ran through her veins. She thought of the scar on Javid's chest, of how it signified a severing of the invisible cord between himself and his evil twin, and she realized that she too had a scar—only hers could not be seen. Javid's was over his heart. Hers was on her heart.

With Javid's help, she had survived the cutting of the cord that bound her to her father emotionally. The healing, however, would not begin until Khalaf was paying for his crimes. "Is there any way you can check on my inheritance for me?"

"Not personally, but I have sources who could."

"Would those sources be Chicago Confidential agents?"

He smiled at her. "The meeting has been rescheduled for this afternoon. I've gotten permission to bring you."

"Good."

"As to the extortionist, I've been thinking of a way that we can set a trap for him. After tomorrow, he won't be blackmailing anyone again...not after I'm through with him."

Chapter Fifteen

Zahir scrubbed his body with the scentless soap provided by his jailers, the shower water beating cold against his flesh, making every nerve alive, alert.

Today was the day.

"Hurry it up, Prince. I've got better things to do than train my gun on a naked man," the guard barked, glancing up from his X-rated girly magazine.

The shower was a blue-tiled alcove without curtain or door, part of a huge bathroom that had obviously been remodeled some time or other in the past couple of years. The guard sat on a metal chair just beyond reach of the spray of water, his hand threaded through his gun, the barrel pointed at the floor. Zahir did not doubt for a second that if he had to, the guard could move with the speed of lightning. He was quick and big. Not much larger than Zahir, but beefier, a gym fanatic from the look of him.

They were alone this morning. The guard had assured the others that he could handle Zahir by himself. A man convinced his size made him invincible. Zahir lowered his head and smiled to himself. Such men were fools. They did not understand that wit and cunning more often came out the victors in a war with brawn.

And, of course, there was always that element of surprise.

Zahir cut off the flow of water. "I'm done."

"Then, cover yourself." The guard tossed him a towel, and Zahir used it to dry himself, then wrapped it around his waist. The guard stood, folded the chair and leaned it against the wall behind him, backing out of the way and gesturing with the gun for Zahir to move to the counter where his clothes waited.

Zahir began dressing, boxers first, then socks, then a white T-shirt. "What's the date today?"

The guard didn't answer.

Zahir had expected this response. The guards never answered his questions. Just demanded he answer theirs. *What do you and Khalaf have planned for Quantum Industries?* He answered their questions as they answered his. With silence. "Is it Monday? Tuesday? June? July? August?"

He chatted, keeping the guard distracted as he patted the jumpsuit they'd insisted he wear after he'd been strip searched. His fingers found the reassuring bump in the breast pocket. The bedspring. He'd worried the guard would go through his clothing and find it, had considered leaving it and taking the man out in his cell. But he couldn't guarantee the guard would go into the cell with him. So, he'd had to take the risk.

He closed his eyes, willing his mind to that state of blind awareness he'd learned from Habib, casually slipping on the jumpsuit, detecting the guard with his senses. Hearing the magazine slap against the man's thigh, the glossy paper making a *thawp* on the heavy denim fabric, the sound loud in his mind. He could smell the paper. Smell the man—his musky aftershave and deodorant, his cocky confidence, the very blood pumping heavy in the vein of his neck.

Zahir zipped the jumpsuit, stepped to the mirror and finger-combed his wet hair, pretended to straighten the front of the jumpsuit, and palmed the sharpened bed-spring.

"Listen, pretty boy, don't waste that effort on me." The guard chortled. "But you know what—unless you start *singing* soon, you'll be put someplace where there are plenty of nasty fellows looking for a 'girlfriend' pretty as you."

Zahir lunged and jabbed the bedspring into the man's throat puncturing the carotid artery. The guard's large blue eyes went wide with surprise, and the gun fired, blasting a hole in the floor, sending tile chips flying. Zahir swore, his gaze flashing to the door. What if some-one heard the shot? He had to hurry. But the guard hadn't gone down. He growled and lifted the gun. Zahir karate-chopped his wrist, then kneed him in the groin. The gun clunked against the floor. The guard's face slapped the tiles and blood oozed from the neck wound, dyeing the grout crimson.

"I prefer to choose my own lovers, insect food." Za-hir spat out the words, bent down, found and emptied the man's wallet of cash—a measly fifty bucks and change. Zahir had an emergency stash of money and credit cards in a locker at the bus station, but how far was he from there? He might need cab fare.

And he needed to get the hell out of here. Quick. Before someone showed up to investigate the gunshot. He picked up the gun, kept one eye on the door, both ears alert, and exchanged his jumpsuit for the man's jeans and shoes. He stuffed the gun into a pocket and discovered a set of car keys and a second clip of bullets.

Holding the gun up, ready, he left the bathroom, moving with speed and caution through what, he assumed, had once served as a master bedroom, but was now set up as a workroom with desks and chairs, phones and file cabinets, a coffeepot and a TV. He stole to the outer door on panther feet, listening like a blind man. Hearing nothing. The door opened into a larger room, a living room without furniture. It appeared to be an empty house. Sunlight filtered in through mini blinds that covered a picture window. He peered through the slats.

He'd been mistaken. He wasn't in a house, but a warehouse, in the middle of a run-down industrial park. He hastened to the door, stepped outside and was immediately assaulted by the heat and fresh air, the bright sun stinging his eyes. He stopped long enough to listen. No sirens coming. No sound of vehicles, except in the distance. He ran to the parked car, jumped in, jammed home the key and, seconds later, exited the industrial park.

He drove through a warren of streets and roadways, uncertain where he was, fear rousing sweat on his forehead. What if he ran headlong into the very people from whom he was trying to escape? As the thought came, he spotted the freeway in the distance, watched a jet lifting toward the sky—and had his bearings. He exhaled his first breath of relief. He was somewhere near O'Hare.

Excitement winked inside him and he allowed himself to look at it, embrace it, feel it. *He was free. He was free.*

He drove until he spied the skyline of downtown Chicago, then began taking roads that would lead him closer. Soon, he reached a busy two-lane street, then a four-lane thoroughfare. Several blocks later, he pulled into a mini-market. He went in, bought sunglasses, a baseball cap and a copy of *The Clarion*. Even though he'd murdered someone, he didn't expect there would be a BOLO—Be On The Lookout—or statewide hunt for him, his name and photograph plastered over TV and in every newspaper. He hadn't been held by the regular police. His *jailers* would be looking for him, no doubt of that, but it would be a covert investigation. He had to take as many precautions as possible.

He abandoned the guard's car, walked three blocks, called a taxi to take him to the bus station. Once there, he collected the bag he'd stored there, hired a different cab to take him downtown, then another uptown, then one to midtown where he was dropped off at a loft he'd bought under an assumed name. Even Khalaf didn't know about this place. The only one who'd ever been here was Angie De Luca…and if he had to, he'd make sure she never told anyone about it.

He'd set up this hideaway so that he could stay here indefinitely, if need be. There were closets and drawers packed with every item of clothing he might ever require, a Sub-Zero freezer fully stocked, a wine cupboard replete with his favorite years and labels and an office with Internet accessible computers and untraceable, fully charged cell phones.

He located the key he'd hidden beneath a floorboard, punched in the code on the security pad, then opened the door, stepped inside and reset the locks and the alarms. The loft smelled dusty, unused. Zahir inhaled as though sniffing a fresh, sweet bouquet of jasmine. "Ah."

He switched on lights and heard the automatic blinds closing at the windows. He set the newspaper on the kitchen counter, shoved a frozen dinner into the microwave and strode into his bedroom to change into his own clothing. Four months. He'd been locked up for four whole months. His life taken over by Javid.

Rage had started to boil in his gut the moment he'd read the date in *The Clarion,* but it was the article inside about the secret, royal wedding that had ignited his full fury. He returned to the kitchen, opened a bottle of Merlot and poured himself a glass.

In the office, he booted up his computer. "What I don't understand, Javid, is how a jackal like you convinced Khalaf you're me. I truly hope you've enjoyed your time in my shoes, brother, because that is about to end."

He lifted the photograph of Miah. "And you, my love, will soon be in *my* arms, where I'll let you do your best to earn my forgiveness for marrying my brother."

He selected a cell phone and dialed Khalaf's number.

Chapter Sixteen

It was the first time Miah had ever seen Javid dressed in something other than a suit and tie. His undercover outfit consisted of blue jeans and a white T-shirt, a Chicago Cubs baseball cap and mirrored, aviator-style sunglasses.

"Do I look like a tourist, love?"

She bit back a smile. If anything, Javid looked like a movie star trying to look like a tourist in order to walk in public without being besieged by fans. But that wasn't what he wanted to hear. "No one will give you a second glance."

He pulled off the glasses and his dark eyes warmed to a rich cocoa. "Not even you?"

Heat shot through her, brought back the memories of the night before, the second night they'd spent making love. Her body was sore in ways she'd never dreamed possible, alive as it had never been, and if she gave in to the lure in his gaze and the echoing response in her belly, they would spend the day here in their suite, instead of where they needed to be. She should move away, back away, but his gaze held her.

"Would you prefer that I save my glances for you or for the blackmailer?"

"Always for me." He lifted her chin with his fingertip, brushed her lips with his. "I don't want you in the gallery when he shows up to collect his blood money. That's my game."

She didn't like that he thought of this as a game, didn't want him risking life and limb to catch the extortionist. "Please, Javid, promise you'll be careful."

He kissed her again, cupping her head in both hands, then gazed at her. "Blackmailers are cowards. It's not likely he'll be carrying a weapon, especially in a public place. Too many eyewitnesses. It's one thing to be caught removing something from a trash bin, quite another to be seen attacking someone."

"Promise." She reached up to caress the side of his face.

"Don't worry about me." He nuzzled her hand. "You've enough to deal with this morning. My men will be scattered about and always nearby. Besides, there should be very little danger."

Why did she have the awful nagging sense that he was wrong about the level of danger? That something horrible lay ahead of them this day? "Will any of the Confidential agents be there?"

She'd met the agents yesterday afternoon and been amazed at the high-tech know-how they were providing in their personal war against terrorism.

"They told you, they have bigger fish to fry. We're after a minnow, they're out to hook a Great White." He released her, crossed to the chair, gathered her purse and handed it to her. "Now, you'd best get going if you intend to visit your mother."

It was ten a.m. She'd already called the hospital twice and spoken with Dr. Forbes once. Her mother had spent an uneventful night, had rested well and was doing better this morning. She could probably come home in another day if she kept on this way, but Miah wanted to see for herself and was going to visit her before going to the gallery. Javid had arranged for Mehemet to drive her and a couple of bodyguards there.

She'd also called Cailin, who'd been less than happy with her evasive answers to the hundred questions she had about Zahir. She'd finally gotten her to accept the elusive "Nothing is as it seems, Cailin, and I'll explain *that* and everything else when we can sit down together. Meanwhile, don't believe everything you see or hear on the news or elsewhere. Just believe in me. Okay?"

Cailin had promised she'd sit tight, but not for long. So, Miah had better make the "sit down" soon.

Javid broke into her thoughts. "By the way, love, you do have the bait for our little fish, correct?"

"Right here." She patted her purse. She'd wanted to fill the envelope with strips of newsprint, but Javid insisted it contain real cash, three times the amount asked for. He wouldn't have the blackmailer arrested and chance his tale of lies being fed to the press. But he would use the cash plus the threat of arrest and prosecution as leverage to buy the man's eternal silence. "I'll be arriving at the gallery at noon."

"I'll already be there. You may or may not see me. If you do, ignore me."

"But what if something should go awry on my end and I need to speak to you? Should I call you on the cell phone?"

"No. I'll have it turned off. I can't risk it ringing at an inopportune time."

"Okay. But—"

"No buts, love." He grinned. "If you really have to tell me something, just remember to call me Zahir."

She gave his chest a playful smack.

He laughed and pulled her close. "Nothing is going to go wrong. You'll drop off the money as you usually do, then leave—all without incident. The difference will be that you won't be as alone as you'll appear."

Miah wanted to embrace his reassurances, but she couldn't shake the feeling that something neither of them expected or could control was going to happen. Something that scared her to her soul.

EVEN SEEING THE IMPROVEMENT in her mother didn't shake the disquiet, but at least Lina was no longer thinking about the blackmailer's note. Miah could think of nothing else.

"You're glowing," her mother said. "Like a woman in love with her new husband."

Miah laughed, brushing aside the suggestion. What she and Javid had was a wonderful fantasy, a love affair perhaps, but their lives were far too complicated for it to develop into something permanent or lasting. She forced the dispiriting thought aside and kept a smile pinned in place. Lina needn't know the facts at this point. Miah took her hand, urging her to rest, watching as she slept, hoping that her mother's dreams were sweet ones of a prince and princess living happily ever after.

Noon approached sooner than she'd anticipated. She kissed her mother, promised to return later in the day, then hurried from the hospital escorted by two bodyguards. Both men were large, menacing and armed, but she felt no safer with them dogging her every move, just more of a target—like, "Here I am, come and shoot me." Her distress beat louder with every second that took her closer to the Brinkmire Cavalli Gallery, as though a huge clock were ticking inside her, counting her life down to the end.

At the gallery, she exited the car alone and made her way inside, her legs shaky, her pulse heavy. She gathered a bracing breath. A hot new artist had drawn in a good number of patrons who milled about the main salon, admiring his work. Miah scanned the long room. Was Javid there? The blackmailer? Anyone she knew who might upset the plan Javid had laid out? She spied a shock of red hair and blanched. Was that Rory Finnigan?

The possibility sent her scurrying from the salon. If Rory *was* the blackmailer, she didn't want to know. Not until she had to. Javid would handle him. As she entered the next room, she felt the nerves in her neck tingle. She spun around, half expecting to find Rory following her, but though she felt eyes on her, none of those in the room seemed to be paying her the least bit of attention.

''You're losing it, Miah,'' she whispered to herself, recalling Javid's promise that she was not as alone as she appeared. *It's probably one of his men spying on me. Just drop off the money and leave.*

She hurried into the next room, then the next. A hand wrapped her arm, pulling her to a sudden stop. She gasped and wrenched around. Javid.

''Miah, it's me. Zahir.''

''Yes…Zahir.'' Her breath rushed from her and her heart lurched. ''Has something gone wrong?''

''Everything. But I'm going to make it all right.''

He led her into the weapons gallery—which was empty—and tugged her down onto the viewer's bench. ''You've been lied to. The man you married is not me, but my twin brother pretending to be me.''

He pulled off his glasses, revealing his eyes. There

was no warmth in their dark depths, just humorless intensity. He was Javid, and yet he was not, despite the fact that he wore a white T-shirt, blue jeans, Chicago Cubs cap and mirrored aviator glasses. His words boomeranged through her mind. *The man you married is not me, but my twin brother pretending to be me.* Zahir. The real Zahir. A chill stabbed from Miah's head to her toes. When had he escaped? How had he escaped?

Fear as she'd never known ripped her breath from her throat, slammed her heart against her chest and buzzed inside her head like a wasp on attack. "What…what are you doing here…dressed like that?"

"I have observed you and Javid today. Followed you here. It's all part of the same long story, too long of a story for now, but suffice it to say, I can't be seen as myself for a while. So Javid pretends to be me, I pretend to be him…until Javid is no longer in the equation."

"No longer…?"

"Your father is taking care of him. By tonight, he'll be dead…gone forever."

Miah's blood ran cold. Khalaf knew that Javid was not Zahir. Oh God, she had to warn him. She jerked up from the bench, not sure where to find him, his name climbing her throat. Zahir lurched to his feet and caught her by the hand.

"Where are you going?"

"No—nowhere."

He held her left hand in both of his, thumbed the ring he'd stolen from his grandmother, then gazed at her, his smile like Javid's without the warmth. "I'm glad to see you're still wearing my ring, but this one, the one *he* gave you, has to go. Take it off, now."

Miah tugged her hand from his, shrinking back, so scared that the last piece of composure she'd been clinging to collapsed. She saw him recognize the fear in her, and her throat swelled shut.

"You already knew, didn't you?" Fury twisted his handsome face.

"Kn-knew what?"

"That Javid is pretending to be me. Your father swore you didn't, but I can see you did. He's made you afraid of me. What lies did that jackal tell you?"

The images of heinous crimes in the papers she'd gotten from Bobby Redwing flashed into her mind, the photograph of this man standing over his victims, grinning at the camera like some big game hunter proud of his kill. Her stomach flopped. She shook her head. "Javid didn't—"

"Don't lie to me. I can see it in your eyes."

He caught her by the upper arms, his fingers digging in like claws, and yanked her hard against his body, his grip so tight she could feel the bruises forming, his breath hot on her face. All pretense of charm had left him.

"You're *my* wife. We are going to rule Nurul together."

"No, I'm not married to you." She wrestled against his hold but couldn't break free. "I'm married to Javid."

"As far as the world is concerned, you and I are husband and wife. By dusk tonight, Javid will be nothing more than an unpleasant memory, and you and I will be enjoying *our* honeymoon."

No! No! This couldn't be happening. She didn't want Javid to be nothing more than a wonderful memory. She had to warn him. Had to reach him. But how? As her mind scrambled for ideas, Zahir kept talking.

"And in case it bothers you that our union isn't official, or legal, it will only be so for another week or two. The royal wedding ceremony in Nurul will solve that problem.''

"No...I..."

His fingers dug deeper into her arms and she whined in pain.

"You *are* coming with me—willingly or otherwise. Which is it, Miah?''

"Take your hands off my wife, Zahir." Javid stood in the doorway.

"She's *my* wife, brother." Zahir growled, releasing Miah so abruptly that she dropped to the floor.

She scooted away from him, rubbing her aching arms, her gaze locked on the two men who looked so alike that one might have been peering into a mirror at the other.

Javid started toward her. "Miah, are you all right?''

"Yes." Behind Javid, she saw Zahir rip a sword from a display on the wall. "Javid, look out!''

Javid spun around to face his twin. "Up to your old tricks, I see.''

"We never did finish that sword fight, Javid. If you recall, we were interrupted before the proper outcome could be reached.''

Javid touched his chest at the spot the sword had sliced into his flesh. "You mean you want to kill me as you were prevented from doing sixteen years ago.''

Zahir's grin was evil. "That's right.''

"Have you become such a coward you would run me through without giving me a fair chance to defend myself, Zahir?''

Zahir's eyes narrowed as he bounced the hilt of the sword in both hands. Javid noted that the hilt was shaped like a serpent of some sort and seemed every bit as large and ornate as the cobra-headed hilt adorning Grandfather

Hayward's dagger, but better fit the hand of the man than the other had fit that of the boy. The keen-edged blade glinted in the overhead light.

Zahir said, "I had thought, if ever I were faced with the opportunity, I would bring you down like the dog you are, but here I am, opportunity presented, and I find *that* end for you offers me no satisfaction."

Zahir swung back to the wall and grabbed the matching sword, tossing it hilt-first to Javid.

Javid caught it with ease, with the confidence of his years of familiarity with such weapons. But the moment its cold heft hit his warm palm a sense of déjà vu swept him, a sense that he had always known this day would come, this fight would be fought.

"Besting you, one last time—" Zahir laughed and lunged "—will bring me years of pleasure."

Javid sidestepped the deadly blade, but not before he saw in those dark eyes so like his own that awful light he'd seen all those years ago, that window into his twin's soul. The monster who lived within Zahir had grown blacker, more hideous, more evil. "You seem to forget that the only reason you 'bested' me that day was that I accidentally wounded you and dropped my sword in dismay."

"Is that the way you recall it?" Zahir sneered and touched the spot behind his ear, then aimed his blade toward Javid's chest, his own chest heaving. "You cut me on purpose. You jackal. You wanted me dead. You wanted everything that was mine. And now you seem to have it all—but not for long. Make no mistake, Javid. This is no game between boys, this is a fight to the death."

He lunged again and the swords came together with

a jarring *clang* of blade against blade. The blow reverberated up Javid's arm into his shoulder.

Miah watched in horror, wanting to run for help, to call for help, but her body and tongue seemed cast in iron, horror-struck by the scene playing out before her.

"If I have what was once yours—" Javid's breath huffed out as he slashed his sword near Zahir's cheek, the blade missing by a hair "—it is only because you chose to throw it all away."

"I have always known that you and our sire lack the ambition it takes to be both great and powerful." His sword nicked Javid's arm, a stinging slice. And Zahir crowed. "A pair of milksops."

"And what does that make you and Khalaf? When we fought in Grandfather's attic, I played the role of our enemy, the very hyena you now align yourself with." Javid's adrenaline pumped hard and fast, masking all pain from his injury. He flung himself toward Zahir, the tip of his blade catching his twin's T-shirt, his chest.

Zahir howled in insult; blood sprouted red on the white fabric. He leaped at Javid, lashing the blade once, twice, ten times, his breathing coming heavier and heavier.

When they were boys, Javid had always been quicker than Zahir. He was still, and he had other advantages over his twin. Zahir had been imprisoned these past four months, locked in a small cell, while Javid had had access to the gym, had kept up his workout schedule, his weekly fencing matches. Zahir, on the other hand, had the advantage of rage. He might not be as quick, or as light on his feet, but he was fearless, insane, intent on killing.

He lunged and parried, the blades clashing together, loud in the high-ceilinged room. But no one came to see

the cause of the commotion. Javid had his men keeping
the curious at bay. He noted that Miah looked horrified,
standing frozen against the wall one second, then duck-
ing out of the way the next.

Javid leaped up to the bench, jabbed, caught the other
sword in another jarring collision. He aimed for the
sword over and over again. He didn't want to hurt Zahir,
just to disarm him. The weight of the weapon began to
sap the strength of his arms. He spun around and felt
the tip of his brother's steel slice into his shoulder blade,
heard Miah yelp.

Miah no longer knew who was who, so swift and
deadly were the twin's movements. One's upper arm and
back were bloodied, the front of the other's T-shirt had
a ragged, bloodied tear.

Again and again the swords cut the air, clanged together, came close, missed wide, missed short, threatened and harmed as the brothers leaped and lunged,
danced and parried, whirling, changing positions. Then
one of them gripped his sword in both hands and
rounded on the other with a fierce growl.

The startled twin whipped back and rammed into the
concrete bench, catching the back of his knees, stum-
bling, going down, hitting the floor hard. The wind left
his lungs in a whooshing breath, and the sword clattered
out of his reach.

Miah's hands went to her heaving breasts. Too
stunned to move, she watched in horror. The standing
twin, sweating, breathing hard, pressed his foot onto the
chest of the fallen one and brought the tip of his sword
against his Adam's apple. A thin line of blood appeared.
"Are you prepared to die?"

"No!" she screamed.

Chapter Seventeen

"Are you prepared to die?" Javid glared at his brother.

"No!" Miah screamed. "Don't."

"Do it, Javid!" Zahir taunted. "It is what you have wanted since birth."

Javid blew out an angry breath. Zahir was the one who had wanted his twin dead since birth, the one he thought had robbed him of half his natural skill, half his mental prowess, half his strength, the one whom he deemed responsible for keeping him from reaching his own unique destiny.

"Do it, Javid. Now."

"No, Zahir." He pulled up on the sword. "No. I have never wished your death, and I certainly don't want to kill you. What I wish is that that monster inside you had never been born."

"Know this, Javid. Were I the one with the dagger at your throat, your blood would now be soaking the tiles of this floor."

Javid stepped back, lifting the sword and setting it aside. His twin scrambled to his feet, his gaze darting to the doorways, but as per his instructions, Javid's men waited at each exit. They grabbed Zahir. Javid said, "Take him to my car. I'll be there shortly."

As the men escorted a furious Zahir from the room, Javid glanced at Miah, and the warmth issuing from him seemed to be the one thing that could thaw her frozen limbs. Her legs and arms began to tingle as though the circulation had been cut off and was returning. She ran into his open arms.

Javid caught her, pulling her close. "I'm sorry he scared you, love. That *I* scared you. I wasn't going to kill him. I just wanted to show him every conflict doesn't have to end in death. If Zahir dies, it won't be at my hand."

"Did you know he'd escaped?"

"Yes. Vincent called me." He set her away from him. "It seems the man in charge of guarding him had some ego problems. I overheard the agents discuss replacing him a few days ago. For reasons no one can figure out, he gave his underlings the morning off. Each thought the other was there with him. I suspect the guy got off on guarding him alone, like it was a spitting contest or something. His conceit cost him his life."

He took out his cell phone and dialed from memory. "I've gotta let Vincent know I've recaptured Zahir. He'll want him locked up again before he screws up the mission."

"He may have already done that. Khalaf knows you've been impersonating Zahir. Zahir said Khalaf was going to make sure you were dead by dusk."

Javid swore and put the phone to his ear. Vincent assured him he'd send some of his people immediately to take Zahir into custody again. Javid thanked him. "But he was out long enough to cause us real problems, to contact Khalaf."

Vincent was silent a moment, and Javid pictured his serious expression, all black eyes and thunderous frown.

"That means Khalaf knows Zahir was arrested by an agency outside the regular police, that his diplomatic immunity was ignored and that someone is trying to put a stop to whatever activities the two of them have been planning. But Zahir does not know who we are. So, that won't compromise us.''

"No, and as long as Khalaf doesn't discover Solutions, Inc., is anything other than the computer company it appears to be, then we've nothing to fear on that score.''

"Andy Dexter and Kathy Renk have that end covered.''

"Good." Javid kept his voice low, his gaze watchful for anyone coming into this room. "Then, the biggest worry is that Khalaf will likely expedite whatever his and Zahir's plans are.''

"Even as we speak. But we're on it. Meanwhile, you and the princess should find a safe house and lay low.''

Javid wasn't as concerned about Khalaf's threat to end his life by dusk as he was about Miah's safety. Zahir had meant to take her with him, willingly or otherwise. Khalaf would also come after Miah. She was important to his ultimate goal. Until the sheik occupied a cell next to Zahir, she was in jeopardy. "Absolutely. As soon as I take care of one more thing.''

He hung up and brought Miah up to speed, including the fact they needed to go to a safe house somewhere and stay out of sight until Khalaf was arrested.

"I can't go into hiding, Javid. Mom needs me.''

"Khalaf knows I'm not Zahir.''

"Yes, but Zahir said Khalaf thinks *I* think you are Zahir. He hasn't told Khalaf that he's spoken with me and found out otherwise.''

Javid didn't want to scare her more than necessary,

but she had to see he was right. "Khalaf won't hesitate to kidnap you."

"He won't get close enough to me to do that. Those two guys you have guarding me will make sure of that."

He could see that arguing with her was a waste of time. Her mother was the only family she had left. She couldn't abandon her anymore than he could have abandoned his mother if the situations were reversed. But it scared him more than he could put into words. *Dear God, help me keep her safe.* "Okay, but I'm only agreeing because your mom is so ill."

Mom. "Oh God, Javid, did you catch the blackmailer?"

"No. When you didn't show up, I came looking for you."

She checked her wristwatch, and blanched. "I've missed the drop-off time. What should we do?"

"First, don't panic. Go and leave the money." He reached up to touch his wounded arm, glancing at it, wiping the blood on his T-shirt. "I'll be right behind you, love."

As much as Miah needed to meet the blackmailer's deadline, she couldn't go without being sure Javid was okay. She spun him around, checked his back, a whole new worry tripping through her. "You need medical attention."

"I have a weasel to catch first. Stop frowning. My cuts aren't deep."

"Are you certain? When was your last tetanus shot?"

"All my shots are current." He laughed softly, stroked her cheek tenderly. "I appreciate your concern, love. After we finish our business here, we'll go somewhere private and play doctor, okay?"

"It's a deal." They sealed it with a quick kiss.

Then Javid hung back as she hurried to the rear of the building to the short hallway where the trash bin sat. As she neared, Miah heard cursing and the dull *thud* of a foot colliding with tin. Someone was there. Rummaging through the barrel. A bulky hulk of a man. He was the last person she had expected to find doing what he was doing.

He spotted her staring at him and gave the bin another kick. "Where's my money, bitch?"

"Your money? You're the one who's been black-mailing me?" Shock ran through Miah. Surely, *he* didn't need the money; surely that piece of crap newspaper he published brought in half a million or more every year. "But why?"

Big Tony De Luca's famous green eyes glared at her, hard and cold as broken bottle glass. "I'll take whatever I can from Zahir, just as he took Angie from me."

"But you aren't hurting Zahir." All the crippling fear she'd felt for the past half hour dissolved in a white hot fury. This was the man who had nearly caused her mother's death. Somehow, she restrained the urge to strangle him as she'd told Javid she wanted to do, finding herself as incapable of murder as he. But her hands tightened on her purse, clenched in a death grip. "You're hurting me."

"You're his wife. Whatever hurts you hurts him. Especially when *The Clarion* hits the streets next week with the truth about your beloved husband. Then Homefront Security will toss his sorry hide in jail and throw away the key."

This creep had put her through hell, put her mother through worse—all because he was jealous of Zahir. Damn Zahir. He did belong behind bars for his crimes. But so did this man. "Don't think I won't press charges against you, De Luca. Because I will. If one of your lies about Grant Mohairbi ever reaches my mother again, I'll have you hauled into jail so fast for extortion your head will spin, and then I'll sue you for every penny your crummy paper brings in. You'll rue the day you tangled with me.''

"You don't scare me, Princess.''

"You're a fool. No man has so much power that his enemies can't bring him down if they're so determined. And I'm one determined woman.''

Big Tony gave her a pitying look. "Zahir has you fooled with those movie-actor looks, that smooth talk. Just like he fooled my Angie. She thought he loved her. He tell you that? She was gonna leave me. For him. But he was about to get engaged to you. So, he dumped her. She moped around for months, then just when she starts coming out of it, *bam,* she's dead. Police said suicide. Hell, she wasn't depressed anymore. She was going to make Zahir pay. But he stopped her. I know he did. She didn't commit suicide like the cops think. But they wouldn't listen to me.''

Miah knew Zahir hadn't killed Angie De Luca. He couldn't have. She'd died five or six weeks ago. Zahir had been imprisoned by the Confidential unit for the past four months. He couldn't have killed her. But Tony De Luca wouldn't believe that, even if she could tell him. And she couldn't tell him. Couldn't give away the secret agents and their mission.

"Didn't she leave a suicide note?'' Miah asked, glancing at the black armband still prominent on the sleeve of his suit coat.

"Yeah, there was a note, but *he* forced her to write it.'' There were tears in his eyes, softening the broken-glass effect to a crème de menthe. "I know he did.''

She shook her head, finding she actually pitied this man who made his living on the tragedies of others. He didn't seem to realize his own life was the biggest tragedy of all. He'd been a winner once, but now he was a loser.

"You know what—I don't think I want to kill you in print," he said. "I'd rather just kill you, you bastard."

Big Tony took out a switchblade. Miah jerked back, thinking he meant to use it on her, but then she realized he was gazing at something or someone behind her. She spun to see Javid coming down the hall toward them.

Or was it Javid?

For a moment she wasn't sure, then he gazed at her and there was no mistaking which twin she was looking at. "Don't, Tony. That's not Zahir. It's his twin brother, Javid."

"Twin? He hasn't got a twin." He flicked the knife open, its eight-inch blade snapping into place.

"Not again." Miah squatted, grabbed the trash bin lid and slammed it into his wrist. Big Tony yelped in surprise, and the switchblade clattered to the floor near her feet. Miah kicked the knife back toward Javid, then plowed her knee into Big Tony's groin. "That's for my mother."

Big Tony dropped to his knees, groaning. Miah bent over him, panting. She pulled the envelope from her purse and slapped it at him. "The only thing you're going to kill is next week's exposé, or I promise you, I will both sue you and have you prosecuted for extortion. Not to mention attempted murder."

Big Tony glared at her, his green eyes indecisive.

"Did you hear me?"

He nodded.

"Are you going to kill the story and stop your nasty blackmailing?"

He nodded again. She wasn't sure if she believed him or not, but for the moment, she was satisfied.

She found Javid smiling at her. "That's a pretty wicked knee kick."

"I wasn't raised as a privileged princess. I've had to defend myself a time or two." She had forgotten that for a while there—when Zahir had attacked Javid. It showed her how conflicted she was these days, how uncertain she was about who she was.

"Remind me never to cross you, love." Javid pocketed the closed switchblade. He reached for her arm and they strode away from Tony De Luca. "Are you ready to go?"

"Just as soon as I detour into the ladies' room."

"I'll be waiting right here." Javid leaned against the wall.

Miah ducked into a stall and was out again a minute later. As she washed her hands, she saw the door to the adjoining stall swing open. Without glancing at the other woman, she moved away from the mirror to the paper towel holder and dried her hands. She heard the other woman pass the row of sinks, coming at her.

She's not going to wash her hands, Miah thought, a second before her hair was yanked hard from behind. Cold metal pressed the front of her neck, and a man's voice sounded soft against her ear.

"It's a knife, Miah."

Her heart stopped. *Zahir.* Dear God, no.

"It will slice your lovely throat open as if it were tape on a package," he said. "So, don't fight me. We're leaving here together. Now."

How had he escaped? What had happened to the two

men who'd led him away? Had he used the weapon pressed to her throat on them? Miah couldn't swallow. Couldn't risk jamming her elbow into his ribs—her first instinct—for fear he'd jerk back with the knife and slice her neck.

She willed herself to calm down. To think. Javid was right outside the door. His men were all around. He wouldn't let Zahir leave with her. "You can't make it out of here, Zahir. Javid is waiting outside this lavatory."

"And I have something he doesn't have, something he won't risk losing that will get me out of here and on my way. You."

But as he said it, Javid hollered from the other side of the door. "Miah, Zahir's escaped! Stay in there until I come back for you!"

"Speak and you're dead." Zahir pulled her hair harder, pressed the sharp blade closer.

Miah's scalp burned and the flesh at her throat stung. She could smell the tinny, acrid odor of fresh blood and knew she was cut.

"Ah, that's a good girl," Zahir crooned, his voice rougher, colder than Javid's. "Keep being a good girl and everything will turn out okay. Cause any problems for me and your mother won't live to see tomorrow."

"A KNIFE?" Javid's amazement was only surpassed by his distress. Of the two men he'd had on Zahir, one was dead. The one he was questioning had a serious cut on his chest and arm and would be leaving in a moment in the ambulance that was pulling up now. Javid held a cloth pressed to the man's chest where the most serious cut was. "He got away, then?"

The wounded man's voice was weak. "No. Went... inside."

Alarm shot through Javid. "Back into the gallery?"

"Yes."

Miah! Javid shouted for his men to surround the building, handed the wounded man over to the EMT, and ran into the gallery, racing to the bathroom.

"Miah! Miah!" He banged into the ladies' room. She wasn't there. His heart dropped to his gut.

"Man coming in!" he yelled, slamming open each stall. All empty. Fear spun him toward the mirror. Miah's purse, the one he'd handed her that morning, rested on the counter near the sinks.

He had her. Zahir had her.

Javid felt as though he'd been flash-frozen.

He charged out of the lavatory and into the men's room. Not there either. He dashed out. Where were they? Panic shortened his breath, and he knew if he gave in to it, he'd be no help to Miah. He forced himself to stand still and think. They hadn't gone out the way he'd just come in, so what did that leave?

His eyes went to the short hallway, to the exit near the trash bin. Was the door ajar? Yes. He ran down the hall and through it. There was another, heavier door, one to the outside, and an open stairwell leading to the two floors above this one. Which way had they gone?

He noticed the door had an alarm that was still activated. Upstairs, then. He stood a moment, listened, but heard no sounds from above. He took the steps two at a time, reaching the third floor landing breathless. His lungs ached from fear. He had minutes, maybe seconds. Miah's life hung on his guesses.

This door led to an open floor that seemed to be a storage area. He moved through the temperature-controlled room with the speed and caution of a great cat stalking dinner, peering behind paintings of every shape and size, around statuary and other art forms. It seemed warm in here. Too warm. The hair on his nape stood on end. He should have borrowed a gun from someone. His only weapon was the switchblade De Luca had lost to Miah.

Then he saw it. A window opened on a fire escape. He crept to it, pinned himself against the wall. No sound disturbed the hot air coming in from outside. Had Zahir already dragged Miah down the fire escape? Had he gotten away with her?

Javid stuck his head out the window. The lower steps were still in the up position. One of Javid's men paced the alleyway. He gestured to the man, silently asking if Zahir and Miah had come that way. The man shook his head and pointed up.

Javid nodded, climbed through the window, then tore up the creaking metal steps, more concerned about Miah than whether or not Zahir heard him coming. But if Zahir was on the roof, he didn't come to investigate.

Javid didn't want to speculate on what that meant.

He leaped over the parapet, landing on sticky tar paper. Heat rose up like an oven, driving the harsh stench of creosote into his nostrils. The roof was flat, with several structures obstructing the view across it. Past the entrance from the inside stairwell, he heard his twin.

"It's not that far. We can make it. On three."

"No. I can't." Miah sobbed. "Don't make me. It's too dangerous."

"I said we're going to jump and we are."

Javid ran to where the voices were, stopping only at the sight of Miah and Zahir balanced on the parapet, his brother's hand tightly grasping his wife's wrist. His twin was urging her to jump from this building to the next. Even from where he stood, he could see the distance was too great. "She's not going with you, Zahir."

Zahir started. He held Miah tighter and pivoted with care.

"The hell she's not."

"It's too far to jump. She won't make it. Neither will you."

"Then, we'll die together. She's mine. She always was. She's going with me…even if it's to hell."

Javid's throat thickened with fear for the woman he loved. Miah looked terrified, struggling against Zahir's grasp. He could see her skin above and below his brother's fingers was red, bruised. He had no idea when the switchblade had found its way into his palm. But he was suddenly aware of its heft.

As his brother spun back to face the other building, he flicked the knife open.

Zahir leaned toward Miah. "Ready?"

"Nooo!" She pulled against his hold.

Javid ran toward them. He hurled the knife. It flew end over end. The blade sank into Zahir's forearm, inches above Miah's wrist. Zahir yelped in pained surprise, reflexively releasing Miah. They both wobbled, knocked off balance. Miah began to pitch toward the edge, her arms flailing. Javid caught her around the waist and pulled her to safety.

Zahir reached for her too, but the effort upended him. His feet slipped, sending him off the parapet with an alarmed cry. As he dropped four floors to his death, he wasted his last breath not in seeking forgiveness for his vile acts of inhumanity, but in cursing Javid.

Chapter Eighteen

The screams, the sirens, the horror on the street were nothing compared to that within Javid's heart. Less than an hour ago, he'd told Miah, "If Zahir dies, it won't be at *my* hand." But now, his brother lay sprawled and broken on the pavement. Dead. And though he had not been directly responsible for Zahir's death, he *had* had a hand in it.

Had gone to that roof with murder in his heart.

He swallowed past the bad taste he couldn't get out of his mouth, knowing, despite the consequences, that he would do again what he'd done, would do more, would do whatever it took to save Miah.

He held her still trembling body to him, too aware of how close he'd come to losing her, needing her as he'd never needed her. She was all that kept him grounded, kept him moving when he might collapse in grief for the twin whose loss he had thought he'd mourned sixteen years ago.

But the loss felt fresh. Surprisingly fresh.

And damn painful. More painful than his cuts and wounds from the sword fight—which he'd all but forgotten about until he'd sat down and pulled her to him.

He rested his chin on her head and gazed out the window of the unmarked sedan that sped them toward downtown to a safe location. Vincent had sent the car, the driver and a key to an apartment near Northwestern Hospital.

But they hadn't left the gallery before coming face to face with Bobby Redwing, who arrived on scene before the police, before the ambulances, as if he'd known the exact hour and minute, the exact spot where Zahir would plunge to his death. He'd snapped several gruesome photographs before Javid's men snatched his camera, destroyed his film and frightened him off.

Miah wriggled in his arms and gazed up at him. "There's no hope now that De Luca will kill his exposé of Zahir."

"No, love. None. And we can't demand it. Zahir's death will hit media news outlets across the world. All of my family's efforts to suppress his involvement in terrorist activities until we could catch him and stop him will have been for naught."

"Your family…"

After what one part of his family had put her through, he couldn't believe she would think of that—of the further shame the new revelations would bring on good people, on his parents and grandparents. He hugged her. "They will survive the negative attention, bad as it will be."

"Good, because it's not their doing. Not yours. Not mine. Zahir brought pain and humiliation on us all. He embraced evil, made it a way of life and was destroyed by it."

Javid knew she was right. His heart still felt grief-swollen, but the devastating sense that he was facing the future without some vital part of himself seemed to be lessening. "I've got to call my parents and grandparents before reporters contact them."

"Oh God, Javid, what am I going to tell my mother? There's no way to explain all of this without sending her into a tailspin."

He stroked the frown from between her eyebrows. "I'll call the hospital and Dr. Forbes first, warn them of the possibility of reporters showing up, caution them to keep staff from mentioning anything to her."

"Hopefully, the staff already knows better, since they've been alerted about her reaction to stress of any kind. She's not even allowed to watch television."

"Then, we will have done all we can for now." He touched her hand with care. The wrist above seemed swollen, the skin rubbed raw, the flesh red—perhaps with his brother's blood—and bruised in an odd pattern, as though Zahir's fingers had left an imprint. A lurid symbol of how close they'd come to being victims of the monster who'd lived within his twin. A brutal reminder that, even with Zahir dead, the danger was far from over. Khalaf still had to be dealt with, but first they needed to find him.

For now, however, for the hours ahead, he didn't want to dwell on that, didn't want her to dwell on it. "After I've made my phone calls and you've iced that wrist, I think we should take turns bathing one another."

THE WATER POURING OVER Miah felt wonderful, but not nearly as delicious as Javid's hands on her naked flesh, on her aroused nipples, on her waist, her bottom. The tension in her neck and shoulders and back began to spill from her like the shampoo suds swirling into the drain. She moved into him, stretching, reaching, accepting his petting as though she were a cat with a favorite human. Javid was her favorite human.

He seemed to know just where to touch her, just where she was most sensitive, just where she needed release. And she couldn't seem to get enough of the feel of him, of his broad shoulders, of his strong chest, his beautiful legs, his muscled belly. Every male inch of him.

She grazed her hands over his skin with gentle strokes, careful of the cut on his arm, the one near his shoulder blade, cleansing them, kissing them, loving him for his bravery, for his chivalry, for his tenderness, his integrity, for the way he made her feel.

He nuzzled her neck, his mouth finding the hollow at her throat, going gentle as he neared her wound from the knife, going hungry as he found her breasts, kissing, sucking, nipping, rejuvenating her spirit, her soul, making her feel alive, glad to be alive. With him.

The scent of melon cucumber sweetened the air as he spread bath gel over her body, sudsing, cleansing, moving her, turning her, bending her, entering her, the connection a shock of exquisite delight, the pleasure superseded only by the sense of completeness she felt at their joining, as if without him, she would never be whole.

She sighed his name, began moving to the beat of his dance, losing herself in the rhythm, in the tune his body sang only for her, the answering harmony of her body to his. Every sway of his hips against hers pumped the volume higher, jumped the meter faster, lifting her, spinning her, making her dizzy with joy, wild to reach the release they raced toward.

And then it came, the final notes like a perfect stroke on violin strings, vibrations racing through her like live wires reaching connection, humming loud and clear through the air, through her mind, through her body.

Breathless, Miah clung to him, and he to her. Their heartbeats slowly gentling, calming. They washed again, toweled each other dry, then ran into the bedroom laughing, falling on the queen-size bed, making love over and over as though this would be the last night they would spend together. For now, Miah felt safe in the unimaginatively decorated apartment that resembled an eighties-style motel with kitchenette, locked away from the dangers of the outside world, the threat that was her own father. And finally she slept, in Javid's arms.

THE JARRING RINGS of a phone stabbed into her consciousness, startling her from an exhausted dreamless sleep. She opened her eyes on the strange bedroom, spied the light of day peeking through the blinds, felt Javid struggling up—and the horrors of yesterday rushed back to her.

Javid pushed away from her, found his cell phone, checked the readout and tossed on a robe. "I'll take this in the other room."

He headed to the living room, leaving Miah alone. She sat up, hugging her knees, wondering whom he was talking to and what he didn't want her overhearing. She threw back the covers and went to the suitcase the Confidential agents, or someone at their bidding, had filled with changes of clothing, makeup and other essentials for their stay here.

She chose a sundress and sandals, showered and dressed, pulled her hair off her neck with a giant clip, and tied a scarf loosely around her bruised wrist like a large bracelet, hiding the ugly marks Zahir had inflicted. She found Javid still in his robe, sitting at the dinette table, drinking coffee. His gaze swept her with blatant approval.

"Nice."

She sniffed the air and smiled at him. "Coffee? *You* made coffee? I can't believe you know how."

"I haven't spent my whole life being a pampered prince." His grin was devilish. "Fact is, I have domestic skills you would never suspect. I can even toast bread."

Laughing, she brought her own mug to the table, sat next to him and tried the coffee. She was surprised at how good it was. "It's delicious."

"Thank you. But don't ask for my recipe. It's a family secret." His grin widened. "Toast?"

"Yes." She was ravenous. "Have you spoken to Vincent or Quint this morning?"

"Yeah." His smile fell away. "The story made all the wire services everywhere. It's on TV, in the papers. Headline news."

She groaned. "Oh, man. I need to phone Cailin. She'll be worried silly. I should have thought to call her last night."

"What are you going to tell her?"

"I have no idea."

"Well, you should also know that someone caught us leaving the gallery together yesterday. The photograph caption says, 'Princess Miah of Nurul was being escorted from the death scene of her husband by his twin brother, Prince Javid Haji Haleem of Anbar'."

She blew out a weighted breath. "Then, we've been 'outed.'"

"Yes and no. The papers haven't gotten the real story yet. Nor are any being crude enough to suggest you and I are together as more than grieving widow and equally stricken, consoling brother-in-law."

"'Both unreachable for comment,'" she added with sarcasm.

"Exactly."

"I guess I'll hint to Cailin that the truth lies somewhere between what The Buzzard told us in De Luca's office and the discovery that Zahir had a twin brother. She'll need to know everything soon, but it's not something I'm going to explain to her over the telephone. As long as she knows I'm safe, she won't kick up too much of a fuss."

The thought of Cailin holding in her temper made Miah smile. Her friend didn't have all that red hair for nothing. "I'm not as concerned about how Cailin is going to take what I have to tell her, as I am about what Khalaf is making of all this."

"Wondering what he's going to do next?"

"Yes." He'd made no effort to contact her since Zahir's escape. She took a gulp of coffee. "It's like waiting for that other shoe to drop."

"The agents have someone trying to track him down. Soon as we know where he is, we're moving in. No more waiting. We're meeting this morning."

She would be so relieved when Khalaf was in custody. She hated this constant hiding out, being watched by bodyguards, the lack of privacy and freedom. She'd never felt the loss of freedom so personally as she had these past few days.

Javid refilled her mug. "The police are anxious to take our statements, but so far I'm using diplomatic immunity to hold them at bay. They don't like it, but they're dealing with it."

She'd wondered how he had managed to whisk her away from the gallery yesterday without their having given the police a statement. There were some perks to being foreign royalty. She looked at Javid's robe, at the whiskers on his chin, at the lazy way he was devouring his toast. "So, we have a meeting with the agents. How soon must we be there?"

"Too soon, sadly."

"Sadly?"

"Yes, love, it leaves no time for what I'm really hungering after. You."

She laughed. "How soon?"

"Half hour or less."

"While you make haste, my prince, I'll phone Cailin."

As she was explaining to her best friend as little as she could, she heard Javid's phone ring in the other room. She'd just rung off when he appeared, wearing beige linen slacks and a short-sleeved shirt. His black hair was still damp from his shower.

"That was Quint. They've found a bomb in the Quantum Industries building."

"Oh my God." Miah's hand went to her heart.

"It's all right. The building's been evacuated and the bomb squad is on site. They expect they'll find several more bombs, though, and have even called in dogs to aid in the search."

Miah shivered. "Is this what Zahir and Khalaf were planning all along? To blow up Quantum?"

"Seems more spur of the moment. A last ditch effort on the sheik's part to avenge Zahir's death. But, destroying the company records, and killing most, if not all of their employees would pretty much put them out of business. At least for a while. So, that might have been part of their original plan.

"Dear God, how can we prove it?"

His grin was unexpected. "That's the good news.

Khalaf was caught on tape lurking inside the building. An arrest warrant has been issued.''

She blew out a taut breath. ''Then, they know where Khalaf is?''

''Yes. It's all over but the shouting.'' He grasped her hands and pulled her to him. ''I'm meeting with the agents now to wrap up the details.''

''*You* are meeting with the agents?'' Miah felt as if a huge weight had fallen from her shoulders. ''I thought *we* were meeting with them.''

''That *was* the plan, but...it was a selfish one.'' He hesitated. ''As much as I can't stand the thought of letting you out of my sight for a single moment, well, I'm not sure our being seen together in public today is such a great idea. Tomorrow when the real story can be told, it won't matter. But until we can blow the lid off this thing, we shouldn't take any chances.''

She caught her lower lip in her teeth, biting back the disappointment of missing out on the payoff for the hell they'd endured. But Javid had a valid point. The more the news speculated on the situation, the more likely it was that some zealous reporter—like Bobby The Buzzard—would try to get in to interview her mother.

''Okay, I'll sit tight until I hear from you, but then, I'm going to have to tell my mother before she hears the news from someone else.''

''We'll tell her together.''

JAVID HAD BEEN GONE less than ten minutes, when her cell phone rang. She didn't recognize the number in the readout and answered with a cautious ''Hello.''

''Mrs. Haleem? It's Dr. Forbes.'' His usually calm voice rang with anxiety.

Miah's heart climbed into her throat. Oh God, had her

mother somehow gotten wind of this mess and had a relapse? "Has something happened to my mom?"

"It's the best possible news."

"The best...?" She was so prepared for bad news, she was sure she'd heard him wrong.

He said, "I didn't want to call you until the lab got back to me on the tissue matches."

"Tissue matches?" Was he saying what she thought he was? Dare she let that seed of hope take root?

"We couldn't have *bought* a better match."

"Are you saying a donor heart has been found for my mother?"

"Exactly that."

"Oh, that's wonderful." *A donor heart had been found for her mother.* She repeated the phrase three times before it began sinking in. Tears of joy filled Miah's eyes and her knees went weak. She slumped into the kitchen chair. This was turning into one terrific day. Miah's gratitude for all that was good in her life felt like a balloon swelling inside her. *Thank you, God. Thank you.*

"I'm on my way to the hospital now," the doctor said. "May I pick you up?"

"Yes. That would be perfect." She gave him the address of the apartment.

"I'll be there in about five minutes."

"I'll be waiting downstairs for you."

She rang off and felt so overwhelmed by the miracle, so humbled by the generosity of—and so grateful to— the family who'd given the ultimate gift so that her mother could live, she bowed her head and prayed for them, prayed for her mother.

But she was also full of fear. She knew the dangers of the surgery, knew the things that could go wrong, knew her last words to her mother might be her very last. She wanted Cailin there. She dialed Finnigan's Rainbow. Cailin answered, and the sound of her voice calmed Miah.

"Guess what? I'm heading to the hospital. A donor has been found for Mom."

Cailin let out a whoop of joy. She hollered something with her hand over the receiver, and Miah heard a louder cheer from the patrons of the bar and grill. Cailin said, "This is so great."

"Could you come and keep me company?"

"Will Javid be there, too?"

The question surprised her. Did Cailin know, or suspect, more than Miah gave her credit for? Had her supernatural intuition shown her more than Miah had had to tell her? "No. He had already left for a meeting, which I can't disrupt, when the call came. Can you meet me at the hospital?"

"Yes. Rory's here. He'll cover for me."

"Great. I'll see you there. I've got to run. Dr. Forbes is picking me up any minute."

She was outside on the curb seconds later as a large dark sedan crept toward her. The windows had been blackened to the point that she could not even make out the driver. The license plate caught her attention. Petrol 2. Why did the name Petrol sound so familiar?

The back passenger's door swung open, and Dr. Forbes leaned out like a ghost in the night, a gray form amidst his black surrounds. "Hurry, Miah."

He slid over, and she scrambled inside, sinking onto the seat. The second she closed the door, it locked. She reached for her seat belt and was jerked back against the headrest by the force of the car tearing away from the curb. She gave the doctor an anxious glance. He smiled at her reassuringly.

But as she gazed forward, she felt the first stirring of a different kind of anxiety. Mehemet was behind the wheel. And someone was seated beside him on the front passenger seat. She couldn't see who it was until he turned toward her. She would not have known him from the three-piece suit and Indiana Jones-style hat, so different were these from his usual dress.

But the moment his black eyes burned into her, Miah's blood froze. "Good morning, Daughter."

Chapter Nineteen

The tension in the special ops room could be cut with a knife as the agents and Javid awaited confirmation of Khalaf's arrest. *The subpoena should have been served by now. Why hadn't they heard anything?* Javid's eyes cut to the clock and back to the computer screen.

Andy Dexter had them reviewing the newest film clips he'd picked up from the informant he'd had tailing Khalaf. The agents hoped to compile more evidence against the sheik, but so far, all they'd seen was Khalaf driving around in one of Petrol Corporation's company cars.

Lawson sighed in disgust. "Clearly, someone at Petrol is working hand in hand with this terrorist, but I'm hanged if I can pinpoint anyone."

Vincent's black eyes reflected the frustration of the group. "With Khalaf arrested and the Quantum bombing averted, it's likely the Petrol connection will go to ground and stay there. We won't stop looking, but we may never know who it is."

Javid prayed that wasn't going to be the outcome, but he supposed he should be happy they were nailing Khalaf, putting an end to his reign of terror once and for all. He glanced at the clock again. What was taking so long?

His cell phone rang, startling everyone. It was not the call they were expecting. That call would come in on Vincent's phone. Not his. "Hello?"

"Is this a bad time?"

"It's not the best." But the truth was, he'd rather have the distraction. "What's up, Rory?"

"Bobby The Buzzard. How he keeps his job with that mouth of his is beyond me. He was just in the bar bragging about an exclusive *The Clarion* is putting out in a special edition tomorrow."

As much as Javid appreciated what a loyal employee Rory had been to him these past few months—keeping an eye on Miah, as well as a few other tasks—he had little patience for listening to more of The Buzzard's antics at the moment. He tapped his foot. "What's the exclusive?"

"Normally, I wouldn't bother you with this, but I thought you'd like to know since he was claiming Big Tony received a letter by messenger today. From you."

Javid laughed at the absurdity. He'd had absolutely no contact with De Luca since yesterday, nor did he intend to, as long as the editor played ball. "Not."

Rory hesitated, then said, "It was a suicide note."

"What?" Shock shot through Javid.

"Yep. He was flashing it around. I got a good look at it. I can't remember it verbatim, but the gist was that you, not Zahir, committed the hijacking of a plane carrying one of Quantum Industries' vice presidents, a bombing of the Quantum satellite office in Iceland and the attack today on Quantum's corporate offices. What's that last mean? Is the sheik attacking the Quantum building?"

"He *thought* he was but it's been averted."

Rory whistled. "Whew."

"Yeah."

Vincent's phone rang, and Javid's attention jerked toward the dark-haired man with the serious face. He saw light come into those black eyes and knew the news was good. Vincent nodded toward Javid and told the agents, "Elvis is in the building."

Khalaf was in custody. Javid felt the knot in his stomach ease, and he gave Rory his full attention now. "Anything else?"

"The letter ended with an admission that you, not Zahir or Khalaf, was behind the acts against humanity that were blamed on Khalaf and that caused the U.S. to place sanctions against Imad."

"Does the letter say how I'm supposed to be committing suicide?" That brought all of the agents' eyes glancing his way.

"Oh yeah, you're 'going to Paradise' by blowing yourself up in something called Solutions, Inc., whatever that is."

"What?" Javid covered the receiver with his palm. His pulse jumped as he relayed to the agents what he'd just been told. "Evacuate the building and get the bomb squad over here, too."

The room came alive with chairs moving and agents scrambling. Javid spoke into the phone again. "I've got to go, Rory, but you've earned yourself a huge bonus, pal."

"Cool. Hey, tell Miah I'm totally psyched about her mom."

"Excuse me?" But Rory had already disconnected.

Andy Dexter shut down the computer systems. Law was on the phone with the 911 operator, and Quint was calling the Langston Building information desk to get the clerk to announce the evacuation over the intercom system. Kathy Renk was not at her receptionist desk in the outer office. But she would hear the announcement and leave if she was still in the building.

The agents and Javid hustled into the stairwell and started down as quickly as the sudden swell of building evacuees allowed. It reminded him of the night he and Miah had been forced from their honeymoon suite into a similar stairwell. What had Rory meant that he was "totally psyched" about Miah's mother? What had happened? He phoned the apartment. But she didn't answer. Where had she gone? The hospital?

He dialed her cell phone and got the voice mail. If Miah *was* at the hospital, she'd have the phone off; cell phones were prohibited in hospitals. He hung up, listening with half an ear to Vincent cursing behind him. He glanced up and saw the agent on his own cell phone. He was barking furiously into the speaker.

"Are you sure? Damn it to hell!"

He rang off, but they couldn't talk in here. Too many prying eyes and ears. Javid looked ahead, trying now to shake off a new disquiet, an anxiety that was about more than the bomb threat. It seemed forever before they were outside in the hot shimmering air. The heat aggravated Javid's disquiet like red pepper poured on an open wound. They strode away from the building individually, acting as if they didn't know one another.

The agents regrouped four blocks away in a deserted alley. The air between the two buildings held the heat of a broiler. Sweat beaded Javid's forehead. Vincent signaled them into a huddle, but before he could speak, Javid's phone rang again. The readout said it was Rory calling back, and he excused himself, then answered.

"Have you spoken to Miah?" Rory asked over what was obviously a loud lunch crowd.

"Not since this morning. What's going on with her mother?"

"A heart donor has been found."

Relief swept Javid, soothing his tender nerves like cream to sore hands. "That's wonderful. Thanks for letting me know. I'll get to the hospital as soon as I can."

"Hey, don't hang up." Rory's voice was edged with tension. "That's not why I'm calling."

The disquiet Javid had felt earlier—and dismissed a breath ago—attacked like a mugger, punching, swift and brutal. "Why don't I like the sound of that?"

"Miah called Cailin on her way to the hospital and asked her to meet her there. Cailin took right off, but Miah hasn't shown up yet."

He tried telling himself there could be a million reasons for her being delayed, but the distress was clawing him now. "Maybe Cailin beat her there."

"That might be, except it makes no sense, because Mrs. Mohairbi is already in surgery and it was the doctor who was picking Miah up to bring her to the hospital."

"Dr. Forbes was taking Miah to the hospital? Why?"

Law's green eyes opened as wide as if Javid had punched his shoulder. "Did you say Dr. Forbes? Elias Forbes?"

Javid put his hand over the receiver of his phone. "Yes. He's Miah's mother's cardiologist."

Law described the doctor. "Is that him?"

"Yes."

"*If* Mrs. Mohairbi is being operated on, it's not by Forbes. He's no cardiology surgeon. He's Petrol Corporation's company doctor."

"But Miah said he came highly recommended—"

Javid broke off, swearing as it occurred to him that he had never checked. He had just trusted that Miah had. *Oh God.*

"Recommended by Khalaf, no doubt." Whitney's pretty face was twisted in a scowl.

"There's your Petrol connection, Law. The skunk's been right under our noses all the time and we couldn't even smell him." Quint tugged the rim of his Stetson even with his blue eyes.

Javid gripped the cell phone so tightly that the plastic covering cracked. "Rory, how long ago did Miah call Cailin?"

"Half an hour or so."

Javid disconnected. He glanced from agent to agent. His mouth was so dry he couldn't swallow. "Forbes has Miah."

"He and Khalaf," Vincent said in a terse voice.

Javid froze, unable to breathe. "What?"

"I'm afraid the man in custody is not Khalaf, but one of his henchmen, a look-alike."

"It was a lie, then, about my mother getting a new heart?" Miah sputtered, some small part of her brain screaming that she ought to be more worried at the moment about her own safety than her mother's. But she couldn't grasp that, couldn't get past the fact that Khalaf was here instead of in custody, couldn't get past the cruelty involved in tricking her into believing her mother had another shot at life. "It was just a ruse to get me into this car, right?"

"Well, no, actually, she is getting a new heart this morning," the doctor said, dragging a pen from his pocket.

"Then, we *are* going to the hospital?" But that hope

died as she looked out the window and saw they were headed in the opposite direction. Did Javid know Khalaf had eluded arrest? Were there police following this car even now? Or had the sheik completely outfoxed the agents, as he had her?

"Elias isn't the kind of doctor who replaces hearts, daughter."

"But I have colleagues who do." Dr. Forbes tapped the pen against his palm as though to the beat of some internal metronome. "I assure you Lina is in very capable hands."

Her mother was getting a new heart. She was in the hands of skilled and expert surgeons. A tremor shuddered through Miah, the aftershocks knocking her back to the reality of her abduction. To thoughts of Javid. "Where are we going?"

"You'll find out soon enough," Khalaf said.

The steel in his voice brought home the enormity of the danger she was in, narrowed her focus. Petrol. Of course, Petrol was Quantum Industries's largest competitor. She squirmed, trying to figure out the connection. How had Khalaf and Mehemet gotten hold of one of Petrol's company cars? Then it hit her. This car wasn't the sheik's. She shifted toward the doctor.

"How are you connected with Petrol Corporation?"

"I'm their company doctor." The tapping pen stilled for a beat, then began again.

Miah mentally kicked herself. What a fool she'd been. How naive and trusting. Taking Khalaf's recommendation of this doctor. Never questioning that recommendation even after she knew the truth about the sheik. "So, you're not a heart specialist?"

"I was. Once. I don't take many patients these days. Just those I find worthwhile. Your father and I are old friends. He asked me to take on your mother as a favor, one which I was glad to do for him.''

Old friends? He'd taken an oath to save lives, yet he embraced someone in friendship who would bomb an entire building full of innocent people. Miah's skin crawled. She'd trusted this charlatan with her mother's life, and he was as vile as the man who'd fathered her.

The sedan slowed and Miah studied their surroundings. Mehemet was heading for the basement garage of the building ahead. She spied the Petrol logo—a small world globe inside the loop of a giant red *P*—on the side of the building, and glanced at her father. ''What are we doing here?''

Khalaf said, ''We're leaving from the helipad on the roof of this building.''

''Leaving for where?'' she demanded, outraged at herself for falling for their trickery and landing herself in this situation, furious that her father thought he could offer her a crown that was tarnished with manipulation and greed and his lust for power.

''Nurul, of course.'' Khalaf removed the hat that looked ludicrous on him. ''Your people are expecting their princess.''

What the people of Nurul needed and expected was a leader, but Miah realized now that her father had never meant for *her* to be that. She also knew that if being a princess meant abandoning her will to the manipulations of others, she wanted no part of it.

''I can't leave Chicago until I know Mom has come through the surgery and that her body is not going to reject the new heart.''

''You'll be allowed to call the hospital once we're airborne.'' The sheik stepped from the car, looking less intimidating in his suit than he had in his military garb or his robes.

He's just a small man with a huge ego, Miah thought, taking heart at the realization, finding courage in it, praying that Javid and company were tailing them somehow, would arrive soon. But what if they didn't? Right now, she was all she had. She gathered a bolstering breath. "No. That's not good enough. I want to be there when she wakes up from surgery."

"Get out of the car, Miah," Khalaf ordered.

She considered telling him "Make me." But she dismissed it as childish, especially given the fact that Mehemet was holding her door open and reaching for her hand. His beefy mitts could crush her skull if he were so inclined. *If Khalaf were so inclined.* Swallowing hard, she climbed from the car.

"Thank you. If you continue to cooperate, daughter, there will be no need to subdue you."

Subdue her? Goose bumps rose on Miah's arms and legs as she followed the men into the elevator. "Exactly what do you mean by 'cooperate'?"

"Javid has ruined my plan to get the U.S. to lift sanctions from Imad and place them on Anbar. He has stopped me for now, but not for good." Khalaf pressed the button for the roof. "I have what Americans call a backup plan that will be executed by you and me. Starting with your royal wedding in Nurul."

"Royal wedding?" The elevator began to rise. Miah's head pounded and her stomach ached. "I'm still married to Javid."

"That wedding was a sham. You thought you were marrying Zahir. The world thinks you did, thinks you are now a widow. After an appropriate mourning period, you shall marry again. This time the groom will be someone less headstrong. Zahir was never as malleable as I'd have liked.''

Nor am I. Malleable, that is. She would not be told who to marry. She'd gone along with it once for the sake of her mother, for the whole romantic idea of it. But her rose-tinted glasses had not only been stripped off, they'd been stomped to pieces. ''And why would I let you choose another husband for me?''

He looked at her as if she were a child who didn't understand. ''So that you may claim your royal status.''

''I know the truth, Khalaf.'' She stood to one side away from the three men, her fingers curled around the hand grip, her desperation climbing with every floor the ascending elevator passed. ''I don't need to marry to claim my true heritage. Or my inheritance. I don't need you and I won't help you. You're an inhumane monster, and I'm repulsed and ashamed that your blood flows through my veins.''

His face burned red, and she feared he'd strike her.

The elevator stopped and the door opened. Miah's fears escalated. A helicopter waited, the rotor blades chopping the air.

Miah dug her heels in. ''I'm not going with you.''

''Oh, but you are.'' Khalaf grabbed her arm and twisted it against her back, shoving her out of the elevator, shocking Miah with his strength. ''Javid has ruined my plans, but I'm going to pay him back by taking from him the one thing he cannot bear to lose. You.''

''But I'm not going to lose her, Khalaf.'' Javid appeared in the open helicopter door. He had a huge gun in one hand trained on the sheik's midsection. ''It's you who loses on every level.''

The helicopter motor cut off.

Mehemet raced for the stairs, but Whitney and Vincent emerged and quickly had him handcuffed to the metal hand railing. Dr. Forbes ran for the elevator. Law and Quint cut him off. Law said, "I'll see that they throw the book at you."

"Yep," Quint drawled. "From now on, Doc, you'll be practicin' your voodoo on jailbirds."

"Release her, Khalaf," Javid demanded, waving the gun. "It's over."

Khalaf growled, shoved Miah aside, and lunged at Javid, dragging him by the barrel of the gun from the helicopter onto the rooftop. They struggled, Khalaf trying to wrest the weapon from Javid's hands, a battle as absurd as a monkey trying to snatch leaves from a giraffe's mouth. But suddenly Khalaf found purchase and yanked hard enough to bring Javid colliding into him. The gun fired. The blast was startling. Loud. Deadly.

"Javid!" Terror gripped Miah.

Javid staggered back from Khalaf, his pale linen shirt and slacks dark with blood. He was panting. His face pale. His eyes pained. She started toward him and stopped as Khalaf dropped, pitching onto his back like a toppled statue. Blood pumped from a gaping hole in his chest. His black eyes were open and staring in death, as lifeless as the eyes of a shark, reflecting the soulless predator that he had been.

Miah stared down at the monster who had fathered her and could find no tears, no grief. He may have given her life, but she felt no connection to him. The only thing she felt was a numbing shock…and the relief that he was dead, stopped from ever inflicting another atrocity on anyone.

Javid caught her around the shoulders and pulled her to his side. He leaned down and whispered to her, "It's over, love, it's over."

A cell phone rang, piercing her distress. Was that her phone? The hospital calling? She glanced around for her purse, but couldn't find it and realized it was still in the car in the parking garage. *Mom! She had to get to the hospital.*

"It's mine," Vincent said, answering. He listened for a few minutes, his eyes rounding in horror. "What about our missing receptionist? Has anyone located her?"

He nodded, then hung up. His expression was as serious as usual as he turned to the group. "That was Andy. He stayed at the Langston Building to monitor the search. The bad news is the bomb squad missed one. It destroyed the foyer of Solutions, Inc."

Shocked murmurs spilled from everyone.

"I hope there's some good news," Whitney said, moving to stand by her husband.

"I guess you could call it that. Seems while we were having our meeting in the special ops room, Kathy, our pushing-forty receptionist, and, Liam, the barely-legal-drinking-age maintenance guy, were in the closet. They didn't hear the evacuation call. They stumbled out through the smoke, covered in soot and shaken up pretty badly, but are both fine physically."

"I'm afraid to ask what they were doing in the closet." Law shook his head.

"Let's just say—" Vincent had an uncharacteristic smirk on his face "—they've redefined the parameters for what constitutes 'safe sex.'"

NIGHT HAD FALLEN by the time the police cleared them to go. Javid went to the apartment to shower and change, and Miah headed straight to the hospital. Lina had come through surgery with flying colors and was in recovery, but not yet awake.

Cailin had had to get back to the pub for the dinner crowd, but would come back later. Miah settled down in the empty waiting room, numb from all that had happened in the past few days, the past few hours. When she'd learned she was a princess, she'd embraced a fantasy of wealth and privilege and happiness, not a nightmare of terrorists and violence and death. She'd been naive in many ways and had gone along with so much of what Khalaf had proposed in order for her mother to have the health care she so badly needed, the luxuries she'd never enjoyed.

But somewhere along the way, she'd grown up. Being a princess meant taking responsibility as an adult, meant putting her country's well-being before her own happiness. She'd been given the opportunity to help stop terrorism in a way she'd never imagined and never wanted to experience again. As glad as she was that she'd done it, the horror of it repelled her. And when she'd thought she'd lost Javid today, she'd realized a basic truth about herself.

She glanced down at her left hand. At the wedding band, at the engagement ring Zahir had stolen from his grandmother. This part of the fantasy was as much a lie as the rest. She hadn't married Javid. She'd exchanged vows with his evil twin.

It's over, love, it's over.

"How is your mother?" Javid stood in the doorway of the waiting room, so handsome she almost could not bear to look at him. *But some things were not over,* Miah thought, eyeing the two bodyguards that flanked him, knowing she would have to come to terms with such people being a constant part of her daily life.

"She's holding her own. Surgery was a success. The

next few days are crucial. But the doctor is optimistic about her future.''

''What about our future, Miah?'' He came toward her, and the bodyguards stayed put.

''Our future?'' They had no future together. Their situations and circumstances, but mainly his passion to save the world, made that an impossibility.

''Yes, *our* future. I love you, Miah. I think you love me.''

Oh God, how she loved him. But it was not enough.

He took her hands in his, touched the rings as she had been touching them. ''Will you marry *me*, Prince Javid of Anbar?''

Her breath snagged. ''I think I am married to you.''

''I want to marry you as myself. I want my parents and grandparents there, as well as your mother. I want them all to know that you're marrying *me*. I want the world to know.''

She pulled her hand from his and stood. ''I can't. I do care for you, Javid.'' *From the depths of my being, with every inch of my heart and soul.* ''But at the moment, I have too many questions about my own future as the reigning princess of Nurul. Do you realize I've never even visited my own country? But even that must be put off until my mother is well.''

''That's okay. I understand. I have to leave tonight for Anbar. My parents and I must present a united front when the story of Zahir and Khalaf hits the news. I'm not sure how long I'll be gone. But I'll phone you every day, and we can settle this once I return.''

''No. Don't you see it won't work, Javid? It's not like Nurul and Anbar are neighboring countries. The Saudi deserts separate them. One day you'll be ruling Anbar. I'll be ruling Nurul…with my husband. It's impossible.''

He wanted to protest, but she could see in his eyes that he knew she was right. Hurt stabbed her heart, sliced it into tiny aching pieces.

"But, love, I won't be ruling Anbar for years and years. Surely we can work that out."

"Perhaps we could. But in the meantime, will you continue to be their Goodwill Ambassador, continue ferreting out and breaking up terrorist cells?"

"Yes." His passion seemed to switch on some internal light, causing his whole face to glow, as she'd expected it would.

"It's a job of constant jeopardy."

"Sometimes…" His inner light flickered.

"Zahir and Khalaf forced me to experience firsthand just how quickly life can be lost. I think I'll have scars from that long after this heals." She touched her bruised wrist gingerly.

"So, you see, even if we could overcome the differences of the responsibilities we each have to our individual countries, I could not bear living with you knowing that you risked life and limb every time you left my side."

"But I won't be facing danger every day of my life," he said, touching her hair, stroking her cheek.

"And that's the worst of it." She inhaled and felt a slow pain starting in her chest, as though something were ripping apart. "I'll be lulled into a complacency, into thinking you'll always be there, then, *bam,* one day something will go wrong and I'll be alone, more devastated than if I'd walked away now."

He was shaking his head hard, his eyes pleading. "It won't be that way."

"But it will be. You don't know. I'm a firefighter's daughter. I watched my mother go through hell every time there was a big fire, lived that hell myself when my dad died doing what he *had* to do. You are as passionate a man as was Grant Mohairbi. It is one of the reasons why I love you. But also why I cannot marry you.''

''Then, I'll give it up.''

She could see he meant it. Knew he would try. But stripping a man of his passion could destroy him. It would permanently switch off that internal light and diminish him in some way that she couldn't bear to think about. ''No. You can't. It's an honorable thing you do, and I can't ask you to quit. I won't ask you to.''

She slipped the rings from her finger and put them into his palm, kissed him one last time on the cheek and stood. ''Goodbye, Javid.''

With her heart withering in her chest, Miah crossed the waiting room on wobbly legs.

Behind her, she heard him say, ''This is not goodbye, love.''

Epilogue

"So far, so good." Quint reported, coming in from out-side. His white tuxedo was damp from the snow falling in great large flakes. "If any of the press has caught wind of this shindig, they're takin' their sweet time get-tin' here."

"I'd say it means they're not coming." Javid grinned with relief and straightened the Christmas-red cummer-bund at his waist, repinned the rose at his lapel, then fingered his bow tie. "Is this thing straight?"

"Nervous?"

"Yeah. But in a good way."

They were interrupted by the opening of the church door. Natalie Van Buren, now Quint's wife, swept in, accompanied by Law Davies and his wife, Natalie's sis-ter Caroline. Quint beamed at his wife and hurried over to give her a kiss, then ushered her into the church, Law and Caroline trailing arm in arm behind, looking just as content and just as much in love.

Quint was back shortly, his grin still lighting his blue

eyes. "Don't you ever tell her, but that little filly has me hog-tied and branded."

Javid smirked. "Ah, blackmail material."

Andy Dexter came in on a blast of winter wind, followed by Kathy Renk and Liam Wallace.

"Hey, hey, hey, love is in the air, man." Andy grinned his loopy smile. "Check out the rock Liam gave Kathy."

Kathy Renk flushed red to the roots of her frosted hair, her eyes crinkling, causing her to look closer to her fiancé's age than her own. Liam beamed. Javid wasn't the only one whose life was going well. Liam had signed a contract with a famous agency—a pretty lucrative contract, judging from the size of that ring—and was getting his shot at a career in modeling. His handsome face would soon grace magazines and billboards. "I finally convinced her love is indifferent to age."

"Congratulations," Javid said, shaking his hand. "I'm all for love and marriage."

Another blast of icy air blew in with the arrival of Vincent and Whitney. Vincent extended his hand. "Javid, this is a great day."

"Thank you, Vincent."

Vincent stepped closer and lowered his voice. "How goes the war on terrorism?"

"Slow, but sure."

"A branch of the Confidential agency is starting up in Colorado and I've been asked to extend you an invitation to join as an agent. Will you consider it?"

"No, but thank whomever made the offer." Javid glanced at the door as it swung open again, noting that the weather was worsening by the minute. "The thing is, I'll take sand over snow every day of the week."

"It's time, Javid," Quint said, catching his elbow. "It's time."

"IT'S ALMOST TIME, Me-Oh-Miah. Almost time." Lina Mohairbi grinned with excitement.

Miah embraced the happiness on her mother's face, knowing she didn't have to worry about excitement being bad for her. These past months, she had recovered from her heart transplant surgery, regaining energy and stamina, getting better every day. She'd gotten so strong that she'd even been allowed to accompany Miah on her last trip to Nurul.

"These are the ones I wanted you to see." Miah turned to Cailin, handing her the latest batch of photographs taken on that recent trip. She loved the small country on the Red Sea, had felt an immediate connection when her shoes touched down on the airport tarmac. "Have you ever seen such blue water, such white sand? I'm telling you, Cailin, you're going to love it. I can't wait for you to visit."

"I'd like to be there now." Cailin groused, referring to the weather battering the church. "I'm just glad you don't have to live there full time. I'd miss you way too much."

"Yeah, me, too." Though she'd arrived in Nurul with every expectation of taking over and running the country if that was required of her, Miah had discovered a government, not unlike that in the United States, in place and functioning like a well-oiled machine. Her obligations and duties as Princess Miah were mostly social, and included presiding over state social affairs, entertaining visiting dignitaries when required and otherwise acting as liaison of Goodwill, much like Javid. She did not have to live full time in Nurul if she chose not to.

Miah was grateful not only because she'd miss Cailin and her mother too much, but because she'd quickly discovered that she could never completely leave America behind. She'd even applied for dual citizenship.

"Do I look okay?"

Miah had chosen a gown similar to the one she'd worn in July—white satin with gold-colored highlights, this one more formal than the other. Her bouquet was red baby roses with golden ribbons that matched the flowers in her hair.

Cailin's gaze swept over her. "Impossibly, you're more beautiful than last time."

"Perhaps because this time, I'm truly a happy bride."

"It shows." Lina clasped her hands together. She'd chosen a wine-red suit this time. For the holidays, she claimed. It suited her healthy coloring. "Marrying a man you love is the most wonderful thing in the world, darling."

Miah thought back to how much trouble she'd had grasping that concept. Javid had done his best to win her over. He'd kept his promise to call every day, had been vigilant in his attempts to break down her resistance to marrying him, but she could not get past the worry that she'd lose him to his passion of making the world a safer place. She'd been terrified she'd end up as lonely as her mother had been since Grant's death.

"It's a good thing your mother is such a wise woman." Cailin checked her own appearance in the beveled mirror. "And that you were wise enough to take her advice."

Miah smiled at the memory. In November, she'd come home from Nurul, feeling blue, missing Javid, a constant pang in her chest. Lina had immediately diagnosed the problem. "Miah, why are you denying yourself the one thing your heart aches for?"

Miah had admitted that none of the good things in her life felt as good without Javid to share them.

Lina's advice: "Then share them with him."

Miah had sighed, not wanting to tell her mother the

real reason, and given her instead the line about the duties required of her by her country being in conflict with his obligations to Anbar.

Lina had shaken her head. "It's not like you need to be in Nurul more than a few times a year. For this you're losing the love of your life?"

Miah had finally told her the truth, that she was too afraid to give her heart one-hundred percent to a man whose passion was something that put his life in jeopardy every time he left the house. At that, Lina had taken her hand and said, "Darling, there are no guarantees in this life. Everything is a risk. But love is the biggest risk, the biggest danger, you'll ever face. True love, the kind you share with Javid, is only granted to a few. To turn your back on it is a crime. Sharing love with a man of passion, no matter how short a time that love is shared, no matter what constrictions one must deal with, what compromises must be made, is the greatest gift any woman can receive."

"'Happy's the bride the sun shines on...'" Cailin sang, interrupting her thoughts.

Miah peered out the tiny window at the huge fluffy snowflakes falling like spilled feathers, blowing and swirling in the wind, and she smiled. She didn't need sunshine to be a happy bride. This time she wasn't marrying a stranger, but the man she loved and adored, the one whose smile sang to her heart.

She glanced down at the engagement ring he'd given her. It had been designed by Tevo, the jeweler who'd made her special necklace. When Javid had placed the five-carat yellow diamond on her finger, he'd said he had chosen that particular gem because it reminded him of her sparkling eyes and mirrored the golden glow of his love for her.

"Darling, it's time," Lina said, opening the door.

The "Wedding March" beckoned.

Cailin started down the aisle, dropping scarlet rose petals on the white carpet. Miah's gaze skimmed over the room full of guests, relatives, friends, the whole Finnigan family, the Confidential agents and their life partners, Javid's Nana and Grandfather Hayward, his parents, American playwright Anna Hayward, and Salim Rizk Haleem, Emir of Anbar.

The very air seemed to shimmer with the joy of this occasion, and as her gaze finally met *his,* she felt her heart leap, felt her blood move a little faster, her breath deepen in anticipation. Javid. A prince in every meaning of the word. *Her prince.* Was there ever a groom more handsome? A man more loved? More cherished?

His glorious dark eyes came alive with light, and she saw his truest passion in the golden reflection of his love for her, shining and pure, reaching out to her, into her. Did he know he made her feel like the luckiest woman alive? She mouthed, *I love you.*

Javid blew her a kiss.

"Ready or not." Lina gripped her arm. "Here we go, Me-Oh-Miah."

*   *   *   *   *

*In July 2003, come with Harlequin Intrigue
to Colorado where a new branch of the
undercover agency is setting up shop.
But remember—keep it Confidential....*